I0558845

Slain in the Spirit

a near future mystery

WALT ROSENFELD

Cover design by William H. Tucker

SLAIN IN THE SPIRIT, Copyright © 2012 by Walter William Rosenfeld. All rights reserved. No part of this book may be used or reproduced in any manner whatsoever without written permission except in the case of brief quotations embodied in critical articles or reviews.

This is a work of fiction. Names, characters, places, and incidents either are the product of the author's imagination or are used fictitiously. Any resemblance to actual persons, living or dead, events, or locales is entirely coincidental.

ISBN: 0988434318
ISBN-13: 978-0-9884343-0-1

for my children

But – I couldn't have done it without the help and love of many, so many great people who have been supportive in so many ways. But particular thanks go out to Will, whose brilliance and standards of excellence I can only hope to attain and would never want to disappoint. And to Dave, who is my brother and without whom I couldn't be who I am; I'll always remember that muddy field where you saved my life.

Slain
in the
Spirit

A curse on him who is lax in doing the Lord's work!
A curse on him who keeps his sword from bloodshed!
Jeremiah 48:10

Contents

FOREWORD: A NOTE ON SCIENCE

Thank you for purchasing Slain in the Spirit! One aspect of the book is to provide a possible glimpse into what our grandchildren won't be able to believe we ever lived without! With that in mind, much of the technology in this book is real, though mostly still in its infancy.

Terahertz communications:
http://www.darpa.mil/Our_Work/MTO/Programs/THz_Electronics.aspx

ViSAR:
http://www.darpa.mil/Our_Work/STO/Programs/Video_Synthetic_Aperture_Radar_(ViSAR).aspx

Cars that drive themselves:
http://www.cbsnews.com/news/just-around-the-bend-a-brave-new-driverless-world/

HUCOs:
http://www.technologyreview.com/news/515666/contact-lens-computer-like-google-glass-without-the-glasses/

Quantum computing:

http://www.ia.ucsb.edu/pa/display.aspx?pkey=2135

Entangled quantum communications:
http://science.dodlive.mil/2014/06/10/beaming-data-at-light-speed/?source=GovDelivery

BOLT:
http://www.wired.com/dangerroom/2011/04/militarys-newest-recruit-c-3p0/

BigDog:
http://www.popsci.com/article/technology/darpa-spends-10-million-make-bigdog-stronger-and-stealthier#UgZ1faYXMZvAS7AX.03

LMG-trac:
http://www.popsci.com/article/technology/watch-army-robot-fire-machine-gun#sGiUyXHHiCiOXEKu.03

Nanites are mentioned often enough that I won't include a reference to them here. However, some parts of my book are not as much fiction as they should be:

Deforestation: A modern-day plague
http://environment.nationalgeographic.com/environment/global-warming/deforestation-overview/

Invasion of non-indigenous insects:
http://www.continentalforestdialogue.org/events/dialogue/2010-10-05/presentations/Sandy_Liebhold1.pdf

Again, thank you for choosing my book. Lord only knows the decisions that led you here!

Enjoy!
Twitter - @WalterRosenfeld
Facebook - https://www.facebook.com/slaininthespirit.

SLAIN IN THE SPIRIT

CHAPTER 1 – MURDER

Mayor Frank Nelson of Naperville, IL sat in his car beside the Fox River. When the day started, Frank didn't know he was going to be murdered. And knew still less of the effort behind his murder. Even if he had known, Frank had lived his life with a sense of service to others, and the decisions that had brought him to his car at this time at this place are ones he wouldn't have regretted.

His headlights didn't reach the river but reflected brightly off the surrounding snow.

Frank slipped off the worn, duck-hunter hat with the fuzzy ear-flaps he liked so much. A patina of sweat covered the mayor's bald head. It beaded and ran down smooth, fleshy cheeks.

The wait was long enough for his windows to fog. The heater filled the vehicle with warm air but cleared only a thin strip at the bottom of the windshield.

He'd been told to wait here with the windows up.

"GPS can you–?" Frank tsked then cursed lightly under his breath; he hadn't driven manual in decades.

"Window open two inches."

A puff of early morning, cold air blew in and removed the stifling feeling inside the car. The mayor fussed with his coat collar and then drummed his fingers. Through the cracked-open window, Frank heard approaching footsteps crunching the snow.

"Window full open," Frank said, and cold air shot down his collar. "Heater off." The blowers stopped. Frank's breath hovered in the frozen, unmoving air before wafting upward.
In the sudden quiet, the measured footsteps filled the air until they stopped beside his window.

He had stopped far enough away so that Frank could see

the expression on his murderer's face without craning his neck, and now the dear man was scared. "You know I love you," Frank said with sad desperation in his voice.

"Your love is rejected," was the crisp, emphatic reply.

"It may not be what you think it should be, but it is love for the right reason!"

"Then you are rejected."

The body of the man outside transformed into a fire with no flames. Instead, the roiling flames were the figure's form. There was an ugly, bitter smell but no heat.

A small but constant electrical current tingled Frank's skin.

Frank's eyes didn't reflect the glow—they internalized it, ate it, until all that was Frank became the glow that wormed through his eyes, encased his thoughts, and swallowed his identity.

Frank Nelson was gone, replaced by a sensation.

Frank's hands moved in a herky-jerky way to put the car in motion. He stomped on the accelerator, and the car fishtailed in the snow down the embankment. With a sound like a gunshot, the middle of the swerving car smacked into and snapped the trunk of a NuTree before slamming nearly broadside into the turgid river.

Frank's head whacked the steering wheel then lolled to the side where his temple rested gently on the edge of the open window. Eyes open. Mouth agape.

The car drifted smoothly for a moment before the heavy batteries sucked it below the surface. Ice water flooded through the window. The river's black water gurgled as it filled Frank's lungs.

He didn't cough once.

The man on the river bank extinguished the glow.

CHAPTER 2 – MY LEFT NUT

The last card came out; an innocent-looking 5 hit the river, but I knew I was in trouble.

The set of 10s I'd hit on the flop didn't inspire as much confidence. I looked across at the other player in the hand—his image was a black cowboy in a white hat and sunglasses. Had this donk called all my bets—pre-flop, flop, turn for almost all his chips—just to chase and *hit* some runner-runner miracle river card?

C'mon, Bill, there's no fucking way. An underset he thought was good? An overpair?

"All in," the cowboy said.

That board is crap. He thinks I missed and he's slow-played a higher pocket pair, like Kings or even Aces. "Call."

Cowboy digitally rolled over an unsuited 63. He had hit one of the four cards needed to complete his gut shot straight. An eight percent chance to win, at best.

The blonde surfer to my left said, "I folded a 5."

The last player, a mobster, said, "Shit. Me too."

Meaning, if they weren't lying, that cowboy had had only a two percent chance of getting the right card on the river. I jumped to my feet as a message from cowboy flashed. "I knew it would it hit."

Dumbass.

I ripped the feed off my head. "I'm done."

As Box logged me out of the sit-n-go, I managed to merely open my hand and drop the unit and not hurl it into a wall. *Could I afford to replace it?* I'd been the bubble boy in that SNG, one player removed from making any money.

"Register for another tournament?"

I took a deep breath. "Fuck. No." I ran my hand through my dirty hair. It was nearly collar length, which meant overdue to have Box order a cut. I replayed the hand in my head.

I'd *seen* him hit that straight. It was the only move that made sense. After playing it through another five or six times, I rubbed my palms on my stubble then picked up my pipe full of Banana Kush.

The Kush had already given me that light-headed, plastic-faced feeling, but I needed this last hit to take the edge off my bad decision. I filled my lungs and let it hang out there for a bit.

Now that's what I'm talkin' about.

Ash spilled out of the pipe when I set it down. I reared my head back and blew out a column of thick smoke then flopped back onto the couch. My exhale haze was a near-motionless cloud that the orange-yellow light from the fireplace danced on.

My internal clock told me it was the wee hours.

I closed my eyes and said, "I will have uninterrupted sleep."

Maybe it was a lie, but I needed to believe it only enough to fall asleep.

My eyelids drooped, and the last thoughts of the bad beat fell behind me. I smiled. I would definitely sleep through the night.

For the first time, my consciousness snapped me into awareness in the middle of the dream.

The dream had always started at the beginning. Always. This time I joined my dream in-progress.

I felt untethered, thrown into familiar seas in an unfamiliar boat. Inside the dream, my body was still doing what it always did, but my mind, my thoughts, weren't attached to those actions.

I knew. I knew what was about to happen wasn't happening all over again, but it didn't help. Knowing did nothing to shield against reliving the desperate calm and suppressed fear of a firefight. And when I woke, it never prevented the loss, the regret, and the shame.

It was the very end of my dream.

I had already ducked down behind the embankment to clear the jam from my rifle when I heard a noise that didn't belong. Incoming rounds still found the grey granite behind me and spit sharp shards off my helmet, but there wasn't the angry *whizz-crack-twang* that had always been there.

All other sound faded away.

My jammed bullet forgotten, I looked around the greys, blacks, and whites of the ditch at my feet and the sky above, but I couldn't find where in my dream that noise was coming from.

With sudden clarity, my dream self—not the dreaming me but the me in that muddy, Ukrainian ditch—realized the noise was the doorbell to my home in Naperville.

This time I didn't hear my brothers as they died, didn't hear their bodies hitting the ground, but I still looked. I may never again know anything in life, but I knew this: I must look down at the end of my dream.

I knew what I would see. Already I felt the terror of it as my lungs squeezed my chest, and I felt with incredible precision my blood *tha-thump* through the tightness in my throat.

I looked past the bright gleam of the half-in and half-out round and then beneath my rifle.

I looked through the warm mist of black blood, looked up from the white viscera and into their grey eyes and the expected readout on my Heads-up Contact lenses displaying their names and the red KIA flashing across my HUCOs that would bolt me awake.

Instead, my HUCOs were gone, and Sullivan and Chandler didn't have the flat, dead eyes I always saw. Their eyes ignored the death of their exploded bodies; they looked at me, actually saw me with eyes as alive as the sun, smiled, and said, "Answer the door, shitbird."

I woke with a start.

I was covered in sweat and sucking in air.

But… I felt my face. There were no tears.

Where was I?

I sat up quickly and glanced left and right.

I'm home.

I wasn't anything. I was...awake.

The clock on the fireplace mantle said I'd had just about three hours of sleep.

I lay back down and closed my eyes.

This time the doorbell brought me all the way awake.

"Doorbell! Right, doorbell." I put my face into my hands, ran my palms over the stubble, and drew a steadying breath. Reluctantly, I blew out the breath and asked, "Box, who's at the door?"

Box's baritone said, "Unknown."

I groggily smacked my lips and cleared my throat. "Visual."

I had slept on the couch, so the CCTV feed came to life with the Dark Star Countdown clock, now almost nine months overdue, on the wall to the left of the fireplace filled with a clump of dull red and near-dead coals.

It was Marvin.

Aw, shit.

"Kill visual." The wall returned to being a wall.

Why was Marvin at my door? And was there an answer to that question that wouldn't be a pain in my ass?

Maybe he'll go away.

I was delighted when the doorbell rang again, followed by three sharp raps and two fist thumps.

Of course he wouldn't go away. Marvin didn't know the

meaning of go-the-fuck-away.

I rolled my feet onto my red oak floor. I loved that floor, the way it gathered the warmth from the sun. I'd loved it when I was a kid, but now that it could never be done again in my lifetime—I loved it all the more.

The doorbell, again. This time a double ring and a series of elaborate, two-handed drum-solo knocks.

Sullivan and Chandler's words came back to me. "Answer the door, shitbird."

Will you let me sleep if I do?

My right shoulder where I'd slept on it was sore, and my lower back stiff. I stood up and rubbed my eyes then put my hands over my head and stretched out last night's weed. I thought I'd smoked enough to sleep well into the morning.

I looked at my front door.

The doorbell rang four times.

Denial won't make it go away.

I shuffled across the house and opened the door. A blast of frigid air burst in and smacked into my warm skin, really waking me up. The bright light and the cold stung my eyes.

For a moment, I wished for HUCOs to auto-adjust it all.

I blinked back tears to see Marvin standing there with a pale face and red-rimmed eyes. "You look like shit."

"And I'm cold, stoner. Can I come in?" It was barely a question. His words came out in thick plumes of quickly-whipped-away steam.

I drifted aside. "Want some coffee?"

"No, but clearly you could use some, so go ahead."

I shut the door behind him. "Thanks," I said, leaving the sarcastic, "Gee, thanks," unspoken but on display.

He slipped off his poufy white snow boots on the tiled entryway; he knew better than to wear any type of shoe on my wood floor. I walked back toward the kitchen, my wool socks muffling my footsteps, and waited for Marvin to catch up.

Cousin Marvin was flamboyantly, In-the-Navy gay. Still, I liked him.

Well, mostly.

Sort of.

Some people hated fingernails on a chalkboard, but that didn't mean they hated fingernails. Marvin was the nails to my chalkboard.

I absently rubbed my eye as he carefully draped his below-the-knee, white, down overcoat onto my paint-scraped, metal coatrack. On the back of Marvin's coat was a shoulder-to-shoulder, old-fashioned, embroidered rainbow. Below the rainbow, running the length of the coat was a seamless, fabric screen that displayed an animated downpour of pink triangles. My little-used military surplus coat was wadded up around the rack's feet. I liked to think of it as a bedraggled dog, but I knew it was too unkempt to resemble anything that lived with even a shred of dignity.

Underneath his coat, Marvin wore a brilliant, aquamarine silk shirt that shimmered when he moved. It might've been cold-weather functional, but the color would've put a blind cat on to its next life. His pants were a midnight black, fine wool, and his socks matched his shirt.

To my marijuana-weary eyes, the intense color of the socks and shirt with the dark pants between them made it seem like Marvin's feet and torso were floating dream-like, apart from each other.

I tossed some more pellets onto the cast iron stove on my way into the kitchen.

"Not that I don't love the company." I got the coffee out and measured the beans. "But it isn't like you drop by every day." In fact, it had been years. "So what's up?"

"I love how you small talk a guy."

And there it was. This was the Marvin attitude I could live without.

"The small-talk shop opens in three hours. By all means, feel free to come back then."

"Mayor Nelson is dead."

I paused in my coffee preparations. "Really?" I wasn't sure what I was hearing. *Why would he wake me up to tell me that?* "How did that happen?"

"His body and car were found in the Fox River."

"I met the guy. A while ago. Seemed decent enough. Bald. Doughy looking. Maybe a little slow on the uptake."

"I loved him."

"Okay." It was a scoop of coffee before that sank in. "Wait. What? Really? The doughy mayor was *your* lover?"

"Yes, really. And yes, Uncle Bill."

We were nearly the same age; Marvin only called me Uncle to be a dick. When Marvin and I were young, he was more of a little brother to me than a cousin. That was a very long time ago. Before training, killing, and dying.

I finished adding the beans and flipped the grinder on. I filled a kettle with water, put it on the stove, and then stood there in my slept-in flannel pajamas and capitalized on the conversation-obstructing noises to process things.

The mayor was, or used to be, at least two—and probably closer to three—decades older than Marvin and had spent most of those three decades as Mayor of Naperville. Hell, he was a recent widower. And where the mayor was doughy, Marvin worked out daily at The Flame, Naperville's one gay gym.

If you put the two of them side-by-side: one lean and well-coiffured, the other well-marbled and bald… Marvin and the mayor went together like a kangaroo in a dinner jacket.

The blades came to a stop. "So. You're having a bad day, right?" I brushed the coffee into a French press.

Marvin sighed, a genuine sigh. "A man comes to tell you the person he loves is dead, and that's your response?"

Shit. Annoying or not, I didn't mean to be such an ass. Some things just came naturally. But this was Marvin. Yeah, I didn't like him as much now as I used to, but whose fault was that? I might not have been the Bill he once knew, but he was still Marvin. Maybe a bit more aquamarine-colored but still the sincere kid I spent a good chunk of my childhood with.

Throw him out, or stop being a douche. Pick.

"Yeah." I stopped fussing with the coffee and looked at Marvin directly. "I'm sorry. And sorry for your loss."

He knew I wouldn't just say something like that; he silently nodded his thanks.

I turned back to my preparations. "I think I'm still processing that the mayor was your lover."

Marvin laughed, slipping into the overly jovial mood that was his preferred emotional defense. I'd watched him perfect it when we were kids. He did it now even as he swiped a tear off his cheek. He *tsk*ed at me then flopped his hand in a peculiar way to make a snapping noise. "Oh, please. One in ten people are fucking gay!"

I laughed with Marvin. *Fuckin' ironical Marvin, he's always been funny.* Careful of my own strength, I very gently leaned on the plunger, watching worthless clear water swirl into a deep, dark, expensive coffee. "When did the mayor pass?"

"Yesterday."

"Yesterday? Why didn't I hear anything about it?"

"Gee, I wonder?" He waved a hand in front of his face. "What do you use for air freshener, Ye Olde Opium Den Breeze?"

And – Poof! – the joviality was gone. *Wakes me up and gives me shit about my lifestyle. Awesome.*

"Besides, it was late last night, early this morning." Marvin glared into my eyes and didn't look away. "There is no way Frank would do that."

So the mayor had killed himself? "Okay." Marvin seemed sure about that, and I had no interest in arguing the point. I grabbed Dad's Pittsburgh Pirates coffee mug, ignored yesterday's ring of dried coffee, and poured a fresh cup. "Did you come to invite me to the funeral?"

"Would you go?"

"No fucking way." I'd been to enough.

"Then, not so much."

I leaned my ass on the counter and held the hot cup between both hands. Our eyes met as I took a small, trial sip.

The only sound was the flame inside the warming cast iron stove and the occasional ping of expanding metal.

"So. What can I do for you?"

Marvin's eye shot open. "Oh." He put the nails of a half-closed hand to his mouth. "Thank you!" He said it so breathlessly he more mouthed it than spoke it.

"Huh?"

Marvin gave a little bunny hop in the air and shouted. "I knew it!"

I couldn't keep up with the mood swings. Talking to a sad Marvin was like riding in an emotional helicopter with no rear rotor. I rattled my head. "Whoa, whoa. Knew it? Knew what?"

"I knew I came to the right place! So, you should know the police swear it was suicide."

I did not like where this was going. "Why should I know that?"

"Because it wasn't suicide!"

Marvin, don't fucking say it.

Marvin looked at me with puppy-eyed expectancy.

I glared back at him with all the world weariness I could summon, which, I felt sure, ought to have been a considerable amount of said weariness!

Don't say it. Do not, do not *say it!*

The pause was pregnant enough to gestate an elephant.

"You want me to investigate Frank's suicide?"

"Oh, thank you!" He fanned his face with both hands to ward off tears.

"Gottdammit, don't *thank* me! Why are you *thanking* me? I didn't say I'd do anything."

"What does that mean? But you will, right?" his tears forgotten.

"Why would I do that?"

Marvin daintily put the fingers of his left hand to his chest, blinked rapidly, and looked about as if lost before turning to ask me, "Why not?" As if I had just asked the universe's stupidest question.

"I can see you're sad and all, but – yeah! Why?"

"Because you're a Public Detective, so you Gottdamm can!"

My jaw locked in place and my molars made impression

molds of each other. *Dad, love you, but your fucking, inheritable Public Detective fucking license can suck my left nut!*

CHAPTER 3 – PLASTIC

With Marvin close behind, I stalked into the living room, my socks hardly muffling my steps at all. Once there, I flipped closed the pizza box from last night's dinner, then scooped up the blanket I'd slept in and tossed it behind the couch.

Marvin wrinkled his nose and shot a disapproving look at the recently slept on couch then perched gingerly on the edge of the nearby leather recliner.

I plopped down onto the couch and forced myself to blow slowly over the rim of my cup. As I sipped, I felt the hot liquid work its way down into my empty stomach.

Be nice, or throw him out.

I allowed myself a mental boondoggle and imagined how throwing out Marvin and his amazing Technicolor coat might go. He'd cry and scream like a wet cat with a lisp. Then he'd be back. I knew that much about Marvin. He'd be back.

Shit.

Another sip of coffee worked its way down as I shot a glance at Marvin; he looked perfectly content, ready to drag this out for as long as it would take for him to get his way. Probably why he was so good at sales.

Clearly, he wasn't going to take a flat-out no for an answer. So, option two: hear him out and help him to see things more clearly, or, at a minimum, less dramatically. In short, see if I could put him off and get him the hell out of my house.

Resigned to the conversation, I said, "Okay, look, they say suicide. You say what exactly?"

"Well, duh, *not* suicide."

"Great, Marvin, but why? Why not suicide?"

"Because I was in love with Frank, and Frank was in love with me. People in love don't kill themselves!"

"You mean besides people like Romeo and Juliet? Or the people in countless other songs, plays, poetry, operas, books, and movies?"

Marvin threw his nose in the air and waved his hand, batting logic aside before going on. "All Frank could talk about was how happy he was right now. How fulfilled he felt. I think his wife's death was an awakening for him. Frank was free and living life with *zest*! Extending himself in new ways, looking into a whole new side of who he was. Can you imagine how liberating, how alive that must feel?"

Marvin paused his giddy monologue for an answer.

All I could do was look at him blankly and think, *Is it okay if I don't?*

Seeing he wasn't going to get a response, Marvin filled in his own. "Yes, that's right! It felt fantastic! To be trapped inside your own skin for so long and then to escape from that. Frank was living his life for the very first time." Marvin clenched his right fist, held it over his heart then cupped it with his left hand.

I bit back my anger.

Marvin's "loss" seemed trivial to me compared to the death of my brothers in a Ukrainian ditch. I knew Marvin was being sincere, but it was difficult for me to take him as sincere.

Yeah, I was being callused. But, Gottdamm, I'd earned my calluses. I took a long sip of coffee. "Maybe he was having regrets?"

Marvin *tsk*ed again and looked at me coquettishly. "Oh, I am one hundred percent certain he regretted not a thing."

Marvin did that snappy, poppy thing again. Twice.

"Okay, okay. Enough." I snapped my fingers back on each "okay."

Marvin gave a little giggle at me.

And it seemed the helicopter had done another loop-the-loop. *One-one-thousand, two-one-thousand...* "Let's just assume he wasn't predisposed to suicide. On what grounds do you think the police are wrong?"

"There were some oddities when they found..." he paused quickly to collect himself. "...dear Frank, of course."

"Of course. Where did they find him?"

"I already said. In the Fox. This would go faster if you were listening."

"Probably not. How did he get in the river?"

"The police *say* he drove his car off the embankment near the river walk downtown."

"And you don't think he did."

Marvin got a smug look on his face. "I think he had help, that's what I think."

Now that he thought I was the one stalling, he was ready to get to the point. "Why? What're these oddities?"

"Two things." Marvin toed the vid set I'd dropped the night before out of the way and looked over his shoulder at the chair. After a small but deliberate pause, he seemed to decide that the chair was, if not up to his standards, clean enough. He scooted himself all the way back and precisely crossed his legs at the knee. "First, there may have been footprints near where the car idled."

"Was there evidence of a second person found in the car?"

"No. Or at least the police didn't record anything like that. Anyway, it was dark when the first units arrived on scene. And the sterling Naperville Police say when they first got there, they didn't know what kind of crime it was. I'm sure they weren't expecting a body to be in the car. And the officers weren't careful..." Marvin lowered his head. When he looked up, the somber man who wouldn't stop ringing my doorbell had returned. "They trampled the crime scene."

"So some think there was a set of footprints when they got there and some think there wasn't, right?"

"Yes."

"Why aren't the police looking into this possible second person?"

"Police Chief Maidenhead is–"

"A power-trippy fuck-stick."

"Undoubtedly," he nodded. "Aaand he's leading the investigation, and *he* thinks there wasn't a set of prints."

"Really? So no prints just cuz Maidenhead sez so?"

Marvin cleared his throat and looked at a faraway ceiling corner. "It seems Frank snipped a tree on his way down the embankment."

"He 'snipped' a tree? A tree? Or a NuTree?"

Marvin paused. "A NuTree."

"Gottdamm."

He waved a hand in dismissal. "Yes, yes quite the sensation."

"What's a NuTree go for these days?"

He held the fingers of one hand to his mouth as if covering a faux-yawn. "Yawn, very expensive, I'm sure."

Besides the money, there was the considerable time and energy for all the paperwork. And Feddy investigators would be auditing past years' paperwork as well. And if it all didn't go just right, the city would be hit with a barrage of those hefty NuTree Protection Act fines. I bet the town council was scrambling to cover their asses and get this investigation closed.

Sure, the dead guy may have been mayor, but, hell, they can just elect a new one of those.

The coffee had cooled enough that I could take a decent swallow. Even if another person was there, unless he or she, what? Drugged Frank with something that could get through a toxicology exam? Then *made* him push on the gas? It was hard to imagine how that person could've been involved.

"Okay, Marvin, that's thing one. What's thing two?"

"Well," this time Marvin looked at the fireplace and used a pinky to dab delicately at the corner of an eyebrow. "He did have cum in his pants, dear cousin."

I shrugged. "So? What kind of gum?"

Marvin gave an eye roll that involved most of his upper body. "Oh, sweet Jesus. Cum! Not gum."

"Oh." What a wonderful conversation this was. "Did you have anything to do with that?"

He batted his eyes. "Not this time."

"But you think someone did?"

Marvin rattled his head and stared at me, unsure he had indeed heard such an asinine question. "Don't *you?*"

It wasn't dispositive to me. After all, masturbation accounted for ninety percent of my sex life. "How did you find that, or any of this, out?"

Marvin gave a quick, demonstrative wink. "A little twinky who has access told me."

I looked outside.

Shit, it looks cold.

"Of course," Marvin lazily tossed out, "I'll pay you."

While I was in mid-sip, my nose over the rim of my coffee cup, my eyes darted toward Marvin.

"The *new,* standard PD amount per day is okay, right?" Marvin continued, patently not noticing my sudden, keen interest.

I swallowed my coffee. The new regulated rate was set exorbitantly high to discourage the use of PDs.

Marvin pulled a pre-paid card out of his back pocket and delicately held it up between two fingers. "Here's enough for three weeks. When you're done, I'll pay you double the standard fee for those three weeks as a bonus."

Six weeks? Three of them at double?

Nine fucking weeks. Jesus, it'd been a long time since I'd had that kind of excess money.

I looked at the card.

I wasn't going to retire on it, but Marvin was offering…shit, enough to make me notice.

I'd started with a bigger trust fund than Marvin, but he'd never married, or divorced, so his trust fund was unpillaged by a wife and her attorneys.

Not that I'm bitter.

At our age, his Juice—his percentage on the fund—might be out-earning even his taxes. Of course, nine weeks of PD fees would sting anyone's coffers, so his offer was enough to show me he wasn't fucking around.

Two people at the crime scene. *Maybe.*

Evidence of a sexual encounter. *Maybe.*

One person dead. *For sure.*

A Police Chief and town council eager to put the deceased in the ground and sweep a NuTree under the rug. *Undoubtedly.*

Marvin sat motionless, holding the money out.

Dammit. I snatched the card. *This is going to mean leaving the fucking house.*

CHAPTER 4 – POKER

I fired off a few perfunctory questions as Marvin bum-rushed his way to his boots and coat.

"Did anyone hate the mayor enough to kill him?"

"Had he been threatened recently?"

"Was he acting strange recently?"

No, no, and no. All Marvin had to offer was that Frank had been excited about a new community outreach program he was working on through the mayor's office.

The part of me not being paid didn't blame the police for assuming suicide.

Marvin shed a tear or three as he dressed quickly and left all in a prance. As he walked away from my door in his puffy, animated coat, he turned and gave me the gayest two-handed goodbye wave I wished I'd never seen.

I closed the door and decided to play a little poker before getting started with my new investigation. On the way back to the living room, I poked through the weed selection in my humidor and decided on some Purple Haze with a mix of Black Envelope. Army enhancements swatted down the more popular, designer chems, but marijuana was a medicinal plant and got through no problem.

I packed and sparked a bowl then went into the kitchen to

retrieve a protein shake from the fridge, crack it open, and chug it down.

"Breakfast of champions!" I clapped my hands loudly. "Box, boot up the vid and fire up my poker sim!" After using Box's card reader to take a week's PD pay off Marvin's card, I settled the sim hoop over my head. "Log me into a sit-n-go."

"Your THz Toob is down to fifteen percent life expectancy."

"Shit." I slipped off the sim hoop and shuffled over to the hall utility closet. Beside my dusty, Feddy-mandated med unit was the THz Toob that made communication along the submillimeter wave spectrum possible and allowed connectivity at speeds 100 gigabits per second—orders of magnitude faster than earlier in the century. The Toob glowed steadily on top of the access point.

"Box, disconnect from ViSAR."

"Cause?"

"Gottdammit, Box. You're the one who just told me the damn thing was low."

"Disconnecting from the Video Synthetic Aperture Radar to replace micro-vacuum necessary for terahertz speed communication. Begin." The THz Toob was the engine, but without ViSAR I wouldn't be able to communicate through cloud cover, let alone a roof.

The glow from the vacuum-tube bulb went out. Three-and-a-half inches tall and half as wide, it looked like something my great-great-grandfather might've had in the back of an antique physical television as he sat in front of it, fascinated by the "talkies" or whatever they called TV then.

I wrapped my hand around the Toob, carefully. The trick was to hold it firmly enough to remove it without separating the glass from the base. The smaller the Toob, the less it took to crack it. But, even at this size, it would take a direct hit from a .45 to shatter it and let out an electronics-killing EMF. The explosion from breaking a Toob this size would take my arm off up to the elbow.

Most people didn't have the strength to get Toobs in or

out. They made a special wrench for the unenhanced, but I tightened my grip then twisted the Toob up and clear of its casing.

I snapped my fingers and spun the Toob like a top in the palm of my hand before snatching my hand closed around it.

I pulled a replacement Toob from the storage drawer and dropped the low Toob in its place to re-charge. The male connector of the new bulb slotted into the cavity on top of the access point. I took a breath. It took more force to put the bulb into the initial clamp.

Slowly the pressure on the bulb built until it slipped past the clamp's containing hook and there was a solid *thunk*. Then it was a simple matter of mere strength to torque it around and seat it.

I looked down at my hand and opened and closed it. I still had excellent muscle control.

Good to know.

I laughed. "This what you do for excitement? Box…" I stopped and looked at the non-functioning access point.

Seconds passed.

If I waited too long, Box would ask some community functionary to come over and make sure I was okay. After all, who would willingly unplug from ViSAR for longer than absolutely necessary? Everything most people owned of value, from gold to grocery lists, required a ViSAR connection. Even a damn car couldn't find its way without persistent ViSAR connectivity.

"Do you need assistance?"

Of course, it worked both ways. If ViSAR allowed me instant access to the network that contained all I owned, then the network could, potentially, if approved by a panel of judges, be used for the same level of surveillance. Good thing this country still had a copy of the Constitution lying around somewhere. I hoped.

"Do I need to call someone?"

"Oh, don't go gettin' all panicky. Shut the fuck up and reconnect."

The bulb flared brightly enough to make me wince and, for a moment, miss my auto-dimming HUCOs.

"Terahertz communications re-enabled. ViSAR connectivity re-established. All systems opti—"

When I shut the closet door, Box got the hint and stopped the audio on the diagnostics.

I sat back down and put the unit back in place. "Can we now fire up a sit-n-go?"

"Same stakes?"

"No, no. High stakes." I watched absently as Box flipped through the protocols then waited for an SNG at that level to fill up.

I sparked a second hit, sucked in a lung's worth, and held it. As I exhaled a plume of blue and grey smoke, the SNG materialized around me. The Louisbourg Moment of Silence began with a watermark over everyone's display of the Dark Star Countdown marking the time since the crew had blasted off into deep space to attempt tapping into dark energy.

The Purple Haze crept through the space between my brain and skull. The effect the weed had on me was always directly proportional to my stress levels. And Marvin stressed me the fuck out.

During the Moment, I realized it was because terrorists had nuked Louisbourg that I could take Marvin's money. Of course, they hadn't meant to nuke tiny Louisbourg. One of the Blight's early cold snaps, before they even called it the Blight, had trapped the small Canadian community. The Dawn Steel, a freighter originally destined for New York from Egypt, diverted as part of an All Ships distress call. It was U.S. retaliation for Louisbourg that compelled Pakistani scientists to give terrorists working on drill teams across the world a nanite to decimate the global oil supply. Before the Oil Crisis, almost two centuries of oil had been left on the globe. After the Crisis hit, global supply became fifteen to twenty years, and the panic was on. The Great Riots led to the deputizing of responsible citizens, like Dad, as Public Detectives. And Dad had paid for me to inherit his PD license.

I laughed lightly at myself. *That's right. A nuke, nanites, and global riots all happened just so you get yerself a PD and have an excuse to leave yer house.* I wrapped my lungs around another small drag. *Leaving the house is really going to suck ass.*

I stopped myself before I put too much thought into how I'd change the universe so I wouldn't have to go outside. I'd save the effort to be maudlin for later when I hadn't just put a cute bit of money into a nine player SNG.

The Moment ended and my first cards were Jack 10 off-suit in the small blind, and I folded them to a raise.

I picked up my pipe. "Pause sim." The rest of the players remained animated, but Box froze my picture so they wouldn't see me smoking.

I puffed down another hit, holding it in, letting myself enjoy the sensation as the Black Envelope worked through my muscles. The all-but-forgotten stiffness in my back and shoulder melted away.

"Resume."

Next hand I folded 83 off. I picked up the Pirates cup and finished my coffee. Dad had bought that cup before the Oil Crisis and The Great Riots that had killed Granma and Grampa. Now, with gas so scarce nobody was flying professional athletes around the country, and virtual gaming was everything the old sports had been. Elite virtual Shooters and Rolers dated the hottest opera divas and had their own, subscription-only social networks.

As the first player to act in the next hand, I folded 2s.

If it wasn't for poker, I might actually have to do something to augment my military pension. Like be a lawyer or a plumber. But that was skinflint living. Every town had more service people than they it could use.

Can't throw a stone without hitting five of them.

No margin in that work. Not anymore. The real money was in farming.

Dad had been in the service biz. That was how he could afford this house and adorn it with these fine, red oak floors. Dad was a dentist back when being a dentist meant something.

The SNG dragged on, and my eyes drooped. I looked at the lizard head playing on my right and remembered I hadn't checked my random avatar generator. I was a Baby New Year, which made me laugh. Then I laughed at what a prick I'd been to Marvin. He was part of who I wasn't. From outside my post-military world.

My mouth was dry. *Am I scared of Marvin?*

The thought made me laugh until my jaws ached. I couldn't remember who'd said nothing feels as good as a real hard laugh, but that fucker was right!

So much for not letting the other players see me high.

I folded my next hand then slipped into a THC-inspired time warp. Each hand lasted forever. I recognized how high I was and tightened my play. Good thing, because these higher stakes SNGs ran considerably longer than my usual buy-in. I played well, got lucky a time or two, and eventually won.

I played two more SNGs and won both of those as well. At this level, the wins were a very nice payday, and after my sloppy play last night, especially gratifying.

It was now almost 4PM. Had I eaten at all?

It's too late to start on Marvin's shit today.

I withdrew my recent winnings into my personal bank account then had Box ring up Suniti's Dating Service and ordered a new date from the top price range.

Not that any date would be Gladys. But Gladys never understood, nor wanted to understand, who training, killing, and dying had made me. Couldn't comprehend why the DCAPS inoculations—their fancy, fucking Detection and Computational Analysis of Psychological Signals—didn't and couldn't "cure" me.

Fuckin' scientists and their fuckin' computers. Think they can just wave their magic computational wand and cure anything!

Why I wouldn't let it go.

"Because I'm *not* a machine! That's cock-suckin' why. Th*at's my* pain, and I won't let you take it from me!" I laughed like I was wolf trying to make the moon hear me.

I sparked up a mega-hit.

I missed only the idea of Gladys.

My previous date lasted three weeks. Right up until I fell asleep next to her. That was months ago. It was past time for a new date. One that hadn't yet seen me wake up from the dream.

Yes, a new, high-priced date eager to be a steady.

Not that any date would be Gladys.

I reminded myself that I didn't miss Gladys and waited.

By the time Margot left that evening, I was high enough to sleep with no dreams.

CHAPTER 5 – CRIME SCENE

I stood looking blankly out a garage door window.

I'd taken the money, so, "Time to leave the house."

I didn't move.

Why had I taken Marvin's money?

Oh, right. Because it's money. I bit my lip. I knew that was a dodge. Cold, hard plastic wouldn't have been enough to get me out there.

Nowadays, because nobody used their PDs, the last time I used mine had really pissed off the local officials. And if the Army had taught me anything, it was a healthy disrespect for authority.

"I guess I needed a hobby." I laughed nervously at myself.

I pressed my forehead to the garage door's thin window—it stung a little—and looked up and down the street. My breath fogged the window before freezing into a crystal web.

I could tell myself whatever floated my boat, but I knew all of it—from joining the Army to using my PD—came back to Granma and Grampa. Their deaths at the hands of an anonymous mob. They had been trampled almost to the point of dismemberment. Even now, thinking of what their last moments must've been like, made me grimace.

If Marvin was right, as much of a bitch as it might be to get back into the world, I'd give Frank justice. And if not justice, then whatever it was they got when they fucked with me.

If Frank Nelson was murdered, whoever did it wouldn't get away with it. Not if I could do something about it. Granma and Grampa hadn't gotten either justice or vengeance. If Frank was due either, then I'd happily oblige, with the prodding of Marvin's money, and do my duty as a PD.

But Gottdamm I hate leaving the fucking house.

That prickly feeling when it's getting too warm ran over my skin. The garage was warm for me in my sky-blue flannel shirt and wide-ribbed, golden-brown cords. But the difference-maker was the durable, tissue-thin, expensive NuWool underneath. My one treat from my last big poker win. It pained me to think that was late last year, almost eight months ago.

My knee-length, black wool coat felt tight across my shoulders.

I hadn't shaved. I was going to shave because, well, that's what the Army said should be done.

I should go inside and shave.

I strolled around the car to look at my last-century, carbon-burning Harley. I ran a loving finger over the burnished, gun-metal grey gas tank and patted the vibrant, magenta helmet that sat on the seat. A piece of art was what they were.

Compared to the Feddy-subsidized insurance on the silent volt suckers, the insurance on an old fuel burner like this was crazy—and worth every damn penny. Like my wood floors, this bike was illegal to make now, so I'd never be able replace either.

I walked back to the garage door and looked through the same window, this time at the old-time thermometer stuck to the lamppost beside the garage door. The big red arm pointed near 20°F. Of course, that was without factoring in the wind chill. And it was early May. Maybe Buffalo always had snow on the ground in May, but I grew up with "April showers bring

May flowers," and I'd be damned if I let something like global climate change ruin my expectations of what the weather should be.

Oh, but the fucking wind…the wind was scrotum-shrinking cold.

I crossed both arms and leaned on the car roof.

So there I was.

Standing in my garage.

Looking out my window.

Stalling.

"C'mon, fucknuts. It's all good." My hands trembled. I closed my eyes and sucked in a full lung's worth of air. I opened my eyes. My hands were steady.

Gottdamm right they are. "Box, open the garage."

The door rumbled and rolled up.

Immediately a blast of bright light and cold air blew under the garage door's skirt and baffle to fill my previously warm garage. I winced and told myself not to think of my HUCOs.

A smattering of flakes whirlwinded their way in.

I clambered into the volt burner and thumbed the ignition switch. The crash bags unfolded from my seat and conformed comfortably across my hips.

"Fox River and South Ewing Road." According to the police report I'd received when I logged my PD investigation, this was the cross street nearest to where the mayor's car had gone into the river.

"That's by the river. Are you going fishing?" GPS asked in her cheery, early-twenties, full-of-sunshine voice.

"That's one way of looking at it."

"How faaantastic for you! I know you're going to do *great.*"

"Close the garage, please."

"Of course!" As the car silently backed out the drive and headed down the road, GPS asked. "Would you like me to display the Dark Star Countdown for you?"

I ignored the question. GPS might have a mandate to ask, but I owed it no reply.

Finally, GPS said, "We're off to see the wizard!"

When I was high, I thought that voice was hee-larious. At other times, the perkiness made me wanna take a hammer to the speakers.

In warmer weather, I could've easily pedaled my bicycle the few miles to the river. Thankfully, there were no other cars on the road, which meant I didn't have to fork over any of Naperville's wonderful congestion taxes. It was a mid-morning on a weekday: kids already in school, and service workers already out servicing.

The wind gusted and pushed against the car as it pulled up to the curb. Miniature snow-devils swept down Ewing Road.

"We're here!" cheered my GPS, loud enough to startle me.

A police car was parked in front of me. To my right, an officer was pulling up collapsible stakes and rolling into a ball the yellow and black barrier tape with scrolling and blinking "POLICE SCENE: DO NOT CROSS" text.

"Whose car is in front of me?"

"That's a great question! This is a municipal car and is currently under the control of Officer Stanley Maroney. Yay!"

I pulled on my lined, leather gloves. My weight shift in the stopped car told GPS to relax the crash bags and open the door for me. As I stepped out of the car, another strong gust of wind shoved me in the back drove hard, stinging flakes down my coat collar, and then went away. As my car door shut behind me, I stuffed my gloved hands into my coat pockets and trudged over to the officer.

The iced-over snow was slick, and my wilderness shoes extended traction spikes. The spikes popped through the skin of ice under the balls of my feet and gave me decent grip.

Without any wind, Stan could clearly hear the icy snow crackle under foot. He tilted the round brim of his hat to keep the sun out of his eyes and looked up.

"Officer Maroney," I said with a nod. The sun glared off the snow and made my eyes sting. I shoved the thought of

HUCOs out of my head.

He moved the wad of tape under his arm to get a better grip. "It *is* you. I didn't believe it when GPS said that was you pulling up. Out of the house? During the day even? How unlike you, Bill."

"What can I say? I love the outdoors."

Stan guffawed. "My ass." And went back to rolling up the blinking tape.

"So this is where the mayor drove into the river?"

Stan stopped rolling and this time a shade deployed from the brim of his hat so he could look at me directly. "That is an interesting question." I presumed his visor was scanning me for weapons.

I shrugged. I'd filed my PD papers just before leaving the house, so it was no surprise Maroney didn't know about it yet. Though if that visor was interactive, I'm sure he knew it now.

When I didn't say anything he went on. "If it was Joe Citizen gliding up to a crime scene, I might think he was idly curious, in a vulturey sort of way. But when I see you, I think, hey, maybe Bill's just come to say hi to an old acquaintance. I think, maybe this is a coincidence. Maybe this is where Bill always goes for walks. But when you ask me about the mayor, I got to wonder why the only guy I know who's ever used his PD is asking about the mayor's suicide."

"So it was a suicide."

Stan went back to rolling the tape. "Yep."

"That's a pretty quick conclusion."

Stan dropped the tape. "What are you doing here?"

"I've been asked to look into the late mayor's sudden and unexpected passing."

"Hold on. You're using your PD? Doesn't anybody tell me anything!?" He took off his hat and tapped the visor on his leg. "Gottdamm visor is glitchy again." He put his hat back on. "And didn't you get enough trouble from the first go round as a PD?"

"Apparently not."

"By who?"

"By whom," I corrected. "And you know I don't have to tell you. Only you payroll guys have to FOIA-up."

"I *know* you don't have to, but I would really, *really* like it if you did."

I let the moment sink in for Officer Maroney. The great, independent thinker of his age he was not. He wasn't dumb, but, like most cops, nobody was going to read a book by the light of his intellect. All the same, the first time I used my PD, Stan had helped me by staying out of the way. It seemed he did not recall that previous experience with overt fondness.

Finally, he relented. "It's nothing you wouldn't find in a FOIA disclosure."

The Freedom of Information Act, a PD's best friend.

He put his best poker face on. "Yes," Officer Maroney intoned. "This is where the mayor drove his car into the river."

"Was he on drugs?"

"Toxicology says no," he said in the same flat voice. "But his state was…one of high energy."

"High energy? What would high energy look like?"

"Uh, typical stuff. Elevated heart rate, glandular secretions."

"I'll bet the mayor was secreting."

"What's that?"

"He was alone?"

"No foreign DNA, fibers, or any other sort of suspect collateral material could be found on the mayor's car or on his person."

The officer had definitely gotten better at what to say.

I walked past Stan to the edge of embankment's slope and stopped next to the two, small divots that would pass for skid marks in the ice-covered snow. Officer Maroney trailed behind. I looked down, but the only prints were mine and Stan's. The blowing snow had filled or erased all others.

My eyes followed what remained of the tire tracks as they fish-tailed down the slight incline. The flat, smooth stump of the decapitated NuTree jutted from the ground between the rear tire tracks.

Stan looked like he was mentally slicing me in two with an old-time surgical laser. "It appears the mayor parked here before flooring it and going for a brisk drowning."

"Is that a question, citizen?" He said "citizen" the way people in the South once would have said "Yankee."

"Why didn't he drown himself in a nice, warm bath? I'd rather drown in a warm bath. Wouldn't you rather drown in a warm bath?"

Stan had the look of someone with a slimy goober at the back of his throat he couldn't wait to spit in my direction. Instead of expectorating, he said. "I'm not obliged to answer speculative questions, or otherwise supply non-factual data."

Ah, yes. If one lesson had stuck in his head from last time, it would've been that one.

My lip twitched, but I managed to otherwise contain my smirk. "No note, right?"

"We didn't find one. Either in the car or at his home."

"So our beloved mayor of thirty years turned off the auto-drive, drove off the road, parked out here—"

"For about nine minutes," the officer chimed in.

"Thank you." Stan acknowledged my thanks by ignoring them. "For about nine minutes, turned off his seat bags, jerked off in his pants," Maroney looked away, shaking his head, "then did a little burnout, murdering a NuTree on the way to his suicide, for which, oh by the way, he left no note. Is that right?"

"You shouldn't know about the oyster in his pants. Look, I know I'm not obliged to share, but…" Stan threw a look up to where the cars were parked and then over his shoulder. I humored him and gave a "what the hell are you looking for" look over my own shoulder—actually, I humored myself with that look. Then he leaned in and half-whispered, "Why are you looking into the mayor's death?"

I half-whispered back, "Someone doesn't think it was a suicide."

Stan rolled his eyes. "No shit!" he blurted before returning to his *sotto voce* delivery. "What I'm saying is, who gives a fuck about the mayor?"

"What do *you* mean?"

"There are plenty of people in this world. Maybe not as many as before, but plenty. What we lack are Blight-resistant trees." Officer Maroney gave a knowing nod in the direction of the stump. "If I were you, I'd be looking into what happened to our NuTree."

Right. Because who cares about a person when a very expensive NuTree's been killed.

CHAPTER 6 – WE MISSED YOU

The officer asked, "Anything else I can do for you, citizen?" then turned and left without waiting for a reply.

If what Marvin had said about Frank having some kind of rebirth was true, and there seemed no reason to doubt Marvin, yet, then maybe I should've known that the NuTree murder would be what the officials remaining in this town cared about.

Back in my car, I pulled my hands out of my gloves and held them to my cheeks and nose. The car's heater tried to live up to the function implied in that name with little success.

Of course the municipality cared more about the NuTree than the mayor. Beside the cost and the microscopic Feddy oversight of all things NuTree, nobody hurt a NuTree. Everyone was fully aware of what the NuTree program was.

Only replacing the world's devastated forests could restore the necessary organic balance and stop Global Cooling. NuTrees, with their distinctive array of both evergreen and deciduous foliage, lived among and supported other trees. They could more easily survive the Blight caused by the spread of non-indigenous insects across the globe in wooden shipping crates. NuTrees were *the* critical portion of all reforesting efforts. So in addition to being heinously expensive, their well-being was a matter of both national and global security.

I didn't catch much news, but I knew the US continued to lead the world in both internal NuTree production and international NuTree aid. And that the EPA protected NuTrees, and what was left of America's forests just as they would any other national security resource, like oil and gold.

Bad enough Naperville had lost a NuTree, but the fact that it was the mayor who took it out had to be making for anxious times downtown. The Feddy paperwork for something like this was a bureaucratic nightmare. If the loss couldn't be proven "unavoidable," the city would pay one of those hefty Feddy fines.

Stan's words came back to me: *What happened to our tree?*

Not just that a NuTree was dead, an event shocking in and of itself, but murdered.

The questions everyone but me was asking had to be: Did Frank take out the NuTree? Or was the NuTree already gone when he took his drive into the Fox?

Fuck the tree. I cared about Frank's death.

Did Frank drown himself in a frozen river to cover up the death of the NuTree?

Was there something special about this NuTree?

From the growers, to the shippers, all the way to the arborists tending the trees, there was no shortage of people who made money off of NuTrees, but that money would always be there. I didn't see the angle in killing this particular one.

So, sticking with the premise Frank didn't commit suicide, then why was he murdered?

What's the opposite? What if Frank had intended to kill the NuTree and his suicide had been the accident?

That made me pause. It made no sense, but none of this made any sense to me.

"GPS, connect to Box."

"Oooh! Fantastic! I am now connected." She said the last in a seductively playful purr.

Great, just what I needed, my GPS acting like one of Suniti's dates. I shook my head. I really should just get rid of

GPS and use Box. I guess using two devices was an old-fashioned idiosyncrasy. Of course, eliminating GPS would mean one less personality to deal with, but I'd had GPS in my ear for so long now, I just couldn't bring myself to do away with her. Besides, I never went anywhere.

"Box, in votes brought to the city council to provide funds for NuTrees, how did the mayor vote?"

"He voted to support funding."

"Relevant news results?"

"An article in the *Naperville Sun* after the most recent expansion of funds, which happened in the budgetary meetings at the end of last calendar year, cites the mayor as instrumental in pushing for funding that exceeded the Federal mandate. The article quotes the mayor at length." Frank's now-dead voice came from the car's speakers. "We have a surplus, and I can think of nothing, not one thing better suited for this money than the purchase of additional NuTrees." There was a hubbub of agreement.

"Discontinue playback. New search Mayor Frank Nelson must include both NuTree and protection. Total number of results."

"Twelve thousand."

Shit, he talked on that a lot. "In the last six months, any trend up or down on frequency of results?"

"None. Peak result occurrence coincides with approaching elections."

GPS chimed in. "I believe the mayor likes NuTrees. That's wonderful! We should all love—"

"Shut up!"

GPS blew me a raspberry but then stayed quiet.

But she was right. The Mayor was strongly in favor of NuTrees. In fact, given his position on NuTrees, would Frank choose this spot to kill himself if there was even a chance of taking out a NuTree?

I laughed. Maybe this particular NuTree had wronged him, or owed him money.

Okay, maybe not.

Nonetheless, a NuTree had been murdered, and it wasn't likely to have been done by the mayor. And I was willing to accept Marvin's position that the mayor hadn't killed himself. So then, what question should this investigation be answering?

How about: Who would kill the NuTree to cover up the murder of the mayor?

Now that is a Gottdamm good question.

I thumbed the ignition, and the seat settled around me. "Box, find Mayor Frank Nelson's home address and instruct GPS to go there. Most direct route."

My outburst forgiven, GPS cheerily confirmed, "We're off!" as the car glided away from the curb.

Despite the bright sun, I kept the windows clear and actually paid attention to the route taken. The mayor's house wasn't very far from the river, but it did take me through the middle of the city.

There was nothing obvious—like a neighborhood bar—to stop and investigate along the way. Outside of Naperville's small downtown area, it was almost entirely residential. I passed a quaint, last-century strip mall that had been converted into a service hall for plumbers, tailors, abortion doctors, dentists, and assorted craftsman, all ready to do whatever you might need done in your home. Not that anybody got abortions, not since NuBorns. A little closer to his home, there was also a butcher and a fresh fruit and veggie store.

Had Frank gone directly from his home to the river? If not, then where had the mayor come from before driving to the river?

A peek at the navigational black box from the mayor's car would've been great. Sadly, it was part of an ongoing investigation, so it, and all its contents, would be considered personal information—not available for PD review and in all ways exempt from FOIA until a charge had been brought. Too bad. Maybe Officer Maroney would unobligingly share black box data with me. Or maybe Marvin's twinky friend would be willing to tell a bit more.

My car rolled quietly to a stop in front of the house. I was wondering if I should contact Marvin when someone walked up to the mayor's door.

He was a middle-aged man of sixty or so with a dark blue Chicago Bears knit cap with an orange ball on top. He wore thick, green wool pants and a brown leather, down-filled, knee-length coat with black leather patches at the elbows and in the trim along the collar. Expensive coat, but, after all, this was Naperville, home of the pretentiously rich. He left one of a handful of hangers swinging from the mayor's door handle.

As he turned away and walked down to the sidewalk, I got out of my car.

He looked at me warily but smiled. "Hello."

I tried to smile back but it wasn't my most practiced expression. "Hey. Whatcha got there?"

"Are you from the EPA? I'm not littering, or—"

I held my hands up and patted the air. "Easy. I'm not a Feddy, or a cop. Just curious."

"Oh." Clearly relieved he wasn't going to have to plead off one of the many exorbitant littering fines, he debated just a moment before shrugging. "It's a We Missed You card."

"We what?"

"We Missed You," he repeated and held out one of the yellow cards. "When someone doesn't show up for church on Sunday, we let them know we noticed they weren't there."

"Here," he said and passed over one of the door hangers.

"Thanks."

"You're welcome. Come by the Fox Valley Christian Church sometime." He smiled and waved as he walked off then stopped several doors down at what must've been another of the flock who'd missed last Sunday's services.

I jumped back into the relative warmth of the car.

The mayor was religious? Well, shit. Of course he was. When you don't see many of them, it's easy to forget that most people were. NuBorns had had that effect. A nationwide religious revival had already been underway—an unanticipated effect of urban Americans migrating to rural areas for work—then NuBorns.

"Box. Search. Parameters: exact phrase, Mayor Nelson and plus church or religion."

Box's well-articulated but flat voice responded. "Three years ago, the mayor appeared—"

"Last six months only."

"Search failed. No results above ten percent relevance."

"Box. Call Marvin."

"Connecting."

In a moment, GPS popped Marvin's face up onto the windshield. "Hola, tovarisch!"

"Hello. Did the mayor go to church?"

"You are just the master of small talk, aren't you?"

"Hooray," I responded. "Just what my day was missing: gay attitude."

Marvin laughed, well, gaily. "I know! Aren't we fun? Everyone should keep a fag around to brighten their lives."

I remained calm and said, "The mayor, Marvin, the mayor."

"Did he go to church? Well," Marvin cocked his head, folded his arms, and put a thoughtful forefinger to his pursed lips. "If by 'go' you mean 'cum' and if by 'church' you mean 'my ass' then two claps hell yeah!" he said with a petite clapping of his hands beside his head.

Marvin. I knew this game of his. This was all he did the year his NuBorn brother died and his parents got divorced. Yesterday, early in the morning and with minimal sleep, I'd recognized it, but still he'd gotten me to play along. Today, I was ready and awarded him no reaction.

Marvin pushed out his lower lip and pouted for a moment, then said soberly. "No, Bill, no church for the mayor. But it's not like I would know what he did with his Sunday mornings." He looked thoughtful. "He'd been busy on Wednesday nights recently."

Frank had been killed on a Wednesday night. "You know where he went?"

"Are you kidding?"

"I didn't think I was."

"Wednesday is charades night!"

"Yes, of course it is. Why wouldn't it be?"

"Exactly!"

"Frank didn't play charades?"

"He tried, but the poor, dear man just didn't have the flair so necessary to play gay charades, or, as we call it, Sha-*gay*!" He sang the last syllable in a falsetto with a big smile and framed his beaming face with jazz hands. He looked at me expectantly.

I had no idea what he was waiting for. A laugh? Applause? "Sha-gay?"

Marvin blew me a raspberry. "Oh, never mind. Frank did his thing on Wednesday, and I did mine."

"And that's that?"

"Oh, I asked, but he just said it was part of that community outreach program of his. He called it a 'special operation.'"

"Really? He said that specifically?"

Marvin put his palms up and shrugged. "I think he always felt he'd missed out on not choosing the military for his service."

"Thirty years in public service is nothing to take lightly. Okay, Marvin. Thanks."

"Oh, you know me, always a giver. Give, give, give that's all I—"

"Discon," I said, and Box cut Marvin short.

Special operations. That wasn't a common phrase.

I looked more closely at the We Missed You card.

The card was thick, stiff. Like nearly all "paper" products in America, it was made from cotton instead of wood-pulp. I would've thought they'd use some kind of bamboo for an outdoor hanger. This much cotton, compressed to this rigidity, made it an expensive card. Like getting a letter on soft bamboo paper. It was a canary yellow with black, raised ink that felt slightly fuzzy when I ran my thumb over it. Another expensive touch: haptic ink. The content on the card was generic, in that none of it mentioned Frank.

WE MISSED YOU ON SUNDAY!
FVCC is a large church, but we care about each of our attendees. While we thank God for our success, we are not satisfied. We believe God is moving in the Fox River Valley. He is touching hearts and mending broken lives. Without you, we cannot continue to grow and succeed in the mission of spreading the gospel of Christ's life, death, and resurrection.

We hope all is well with you! And we see you at church again real soon! If you would like a prayer champion to pray on your behalf, call our church offices at 196-6698.

The church address was at the bottom of the card, along with "Senior Pastor: Mitchell Slade" and another phone number.

I was liking this investigation less and less. Never mind dragging my ass outside in the cold, now it looked like I was going to go to church to get warm.

CHAPTER 7 – THE YELLOW BOX

I instructed Box to call the information number at the bottom of the card.

"Pastor Mitchell here." His voice had a smile behind it. Not cheery. Pleased.

"Pastor Mitchell?"

"Hi. What can I do for you?"

"Yes, sorry. I wasn't expecting you. Do you answer all calls to the church?"

"You called my private number. But Box says your ID is blocked."

I wasn't sure what to say about that. Instead of my video feed, the pastor was seeing the Dark Star Countdown on his display. Some people thought it was rude not to have your ID on when you called, but people's opinions about my rudeness was a very low concern of mine. I was confident my rudeness was excellent. "So why did you answer?"

"I always answer my private number."

Pretty brazen to put a private number on a card left lying around in public. "Day or night?" Who gave out their private deets like that?

"As long as I'm conscious." The preacher chuckled. "I don't recognize your voice. Have you been to our church before?"

"No, not yet." Was he running a voice recog?

"Well, I hope you do come. And please, introduce yourself to me when you do. Okay?"

"Okay."

"Can I have your first name?"

I wasn't sure why, but I felt hesitant to lie. What was the harm? "Bill."

"Bill. Thank you, Bill. See you Sunday then?"

"Sure. See you Sunday. Discon."

So the suddenly gay mayor was also unexpectedly, according to Marvin, religious, or at a minimum attending church enough to get a We Missed You card.

"Box, google, exact phrase: Fox Valley Christian Church, and must have NuTrees in the content. Sort by relevancy."

"Nothing above sixty-six percent relevancy. Report results?"

"Sort most relevant hits chronologically. Report top result only."

"The city of Naperville held an open discussion of the NuTree budget at Fox Valley Christian Church—"

"Stop read back. How recent is that? Disregard." It didn't matter how recently they'd held the meeting. If FVCC had any opinion on NuTrees, it wasn't strong enough to be more than sixty-six percent relevant, which made it irrelevant.

"GPS."

"Hi! Are we done fishing? Oooh. Where to now?"

"Direct route to Fox Valley Christian Church."

"Spiritual growth is great! In which city?"

"There's more than one?"

"Silly goose. There are three within thirty miles of us, right now. Awesome!"

FVCC was a franchise? "Is one listed as the main office?"

"Yes. That's right here in Naperville!"

"Direct route to that location."

"Pleeeaaase?" came the coy response, but the car was already moving.

The wind had died down and the weather had warmed since I first opened my garage door. It still amazed me how quickly the weather could swing around this time of year. Seemed Spring was fighting to reclaim its rightful place.

I opened my coat and enjoyed the warmth through the window. The heating element under the roads had already generated a thin layer of grey slush that the automated sweepers telescoping out from curbs squeegeed into the side drainage.

The church was a few miles away, on the other side of downtown, closer to where Frank had driven into the river. On the drive over, I passed three other cars—my congestion meter *cha-ching*ed after the third.

Wonderful.

Now every moving car within a certain radius would cost me until I hit the maximum monthly fee. It wasn't that the fees were very expensive; it was just an ass ache that the government taxed *me* simply because someone else was driving at the same time.

I should feel lucky they haven't gotten around to a breathing tax yet.

The neighborhood around the church had once had several strip malls. As was typical for these concrete and asphalt eye-sores that had been so popular earlier this century, all but one had been plowed under and replaced by a forest of NuTrees. Now there was just one service mall with a TV and car factory next to an elementary school. Otherwise, the church was embedded in completely residential forest. The houses in this neighborhood had to be sought-after properties.

The homes, like most in an old town like Naperville, were pre-Blight affairs made of wood, not the pre-fabs made from liquid, natural gas-based synthetics anyone could buy online and have UP-Exed.

I did a double take. Some of these homes had NuTrees!

That was real fuckin' money.

My car pulled up to the light at the corner the church. Architecturally, I never would've pegged it for a church. It was too big to be any kind of service shop, but the building itself was a simple, concrete, two-story rectangle about the length of three houses. The first floor was painted the same bright, canary yellow as the We Missed You card. The second was unpainted, grey concrete. Not only was the second floor not painted, but the yellow paint on the first floor wasn't in a neat line. Random brush strokes crossed over a few feet onto the second floor or didn't quite make it all the way to the top of the first. Outside the front door, on one half of a bi-fold board were the words, "Free Coffee on Sunday!!"

They couldn't be serious. Who could afford free coffee? It was a garish, hand-rendered sign with blue letters painted onto that same canary yellow background. Maybe it was a joke or the name of the church band or something.

Well, shit, free coffee? Okay, Bill, let's get your Sunday-go-ta-meetin' outfit on and getcher ass to church.

The light changed, and my car moved towards the church. Before I could stop her, GPS had turned into the church parking lot. She parked near the entrance. It was Friday, and the lot was empty except for three cars in the back corner furthest from the church.

Well, I'm here now.

"Box."

"Online."

"Open document. Business card. Painting business."

"Name?"

"Be creative."

"Address?"

"Be creative but local."

"How many?"

"Five."

I pulled the cards from the dash. Willy's Painting was written in bright purple across the top. I swiped my thumb across the words, and they looked like they were printed in green grass. I swiped my thumb back the other way and the words returned to their bright purple. There was no last name, just "Bill" at the bottom.

The wind had stopped, and the sun outside the car felt

awesome. In the calm air, I turned my face to its light and stood for a moment, just soaking it in. When I opened my eyes, the glow blobs of retina burn swam in my vision. I missed the HUCOs that would've shielded my eyes.

I closed my eyes again, and, for a moment, a standard HUCO battle readout appeared in the retina burn. I gasped.

I felt long-dormant parts of my brain come alive again. My world tilted sharply left, then swirled right as a wave of vertigo swept over me.

My eyes stayed closed, and I stood firm.

HUCOs. I wanted HUCOs. I knew thinking about them would make me think about my dream, and I never willingly thought about that.

I rattled my head to clear it. Gone was the readout. It was just the world. I turned to the church entrance, and a cold wind shoved me in the back.

Immediately upon entering, the smell of fresh coffee grounds hit me.

Oh, I was so coming to this church. *Could I just get the coffee to go and skip the service?*

The floor was a nice, expensively patterned, non-petroleum-based linoleum—the preferred floor covering of the well-to-do. The well-to-do who didn't have gorgeous, red oak floors.

The concrete walls had a stucco texture, swirling line patterns, and paintings of nature scenery: beaches, mountains, and the like. The Dark Star Countdown display, required for all public access buildings, was on the wall above the entry: 8 years 252 days 3 hours.

Beneath the Countdown was a Bible verse: "The God that made the world and all things therein, He, being Lord of heaven and earth, dwelleth not in temples made with hands. ACTS 17:24."

Aside from that, there was a staircase to my left and another set of doors in front of me that presumably led into the podium and pews section.

"Hello." I turned in the direction of the voice and saw a

woman about my age walking down the stairs. "Are you looking for someone?"

I put as much smile into my voice as I could. "Hello. I'm here about the painting outside."

"What painting?" She was a scrawny lady with legs that had too much muscle and not enough meat. Add this to her large breasts, a nearly non-existent waist, and she was, to be nice, not what I called a looker. She wore an over-wide, patent-leather belt with an enormous buckle cinched around the waist of her blue and purple paisley-patterned, mid-thigh dress. The belt almost grotesquely emphasized both her thin waist and large breasts. Completing the ensemble was shoulder-blade-length, raven-black hair cut so straight at the bottom I thought I could shave with it. It looked like she was trying to be a movie star from late last century.

The look was so obviously put together and so amazingly anachronistic that it felt rude not to comment. "Nice dress. It's very–"

"Thank you!" She put her hands to her waist. "The belt is vintage, but I made the dress myself. I know, you think it should have shoulder pads."

"Uh."

"But not every dress of this period had shoulder pads. Sometimes they were in the coat. Mine is upstairs." As she approached, with heels she was nearly eye level. Without, she'd be three or four inches shorter than my slightly-above-average six-foot-one and change.

"Nicely done," I said. Her shoes looked to be made of the same black, patent leather as her belt. *I wonder what her underwear looks like.*

"I just love the 80s!" She smiled.

Nice smile. "That's cool. So. How come you guys never finished painting the outside of this building?"

"Oh! *That* 'painting'!" She laughed, and my world shifted.

I saw her differently after that laugh.

It was the laughter of a small child being tossed into the air and caught by a loving parent.

"When you said it, I pictured, y'know, a painting. In a frame."

"No, I meant–"

"Yes, of course you did. Just how my brain works. But the building's paint is as finished as we want it to be."

"Bright yellow and concrete grey? And the line of yellow isn't very straight."

"Yellow is the color of hope. The outside of this building shows how God is never done in our lives. That there is always an improvement He could make."

"So then you don't need a painter?"

"No, we don't need a painter. Not right now." She laughed again.

For the first time I saw her eyes. They were a pale sea-foam green. Her lips were full with a red, matte lipstick; I imagined feeling them on my skin.

"Uh," I looked around. "Those are nice paintings."

"Thank you again." When she stepped toward me, her movements were in slow motion. The rub of her dress as it shifted against her skin generated a steamy heat that rolled off her and lapped against me. My lips went dry. My throat tightened. "Well. I—I, uh, should go." I fast-stepped my way past her to the exit.

I think she said, "Uh. Okay?" to my back as I double-timed it out of the church.

As soon as I got into the car, GPS chimed in with, "Are you feeling spiritually revived?"

"GPS: voice off. Destination: home. Direct route."

The car began to back out.

"No, hold it."

The car stopped.

"Reroute. Box, call ahead to Cheng's for pork fried rice, chicken lo mein, and Peking duck. Then home."

"Proceed to Cheng's or have it delivered?"

"Go to Cheng's."

GPS piped in with, "Which Cheng's? There are—"

"Gott*damm*! The one I always fucking go to. *Box*."

"Online."

"Box, help GPS out. In fact…" I clenched my jaw and stopped myself from yelling. "Don't help GPS. And don't call Cheng's. GPS, just go to the fucking Cheng's that Box tells you to go to."

I slid my seat over to the passenger side and started fishing around in my glove compartment for my emergency one-hitter. I'd had only coffee for breakfast. Low blood sugar must be why I was grumpy.

It had nothing to do with the woman.

Just had to get some food.

"Hooray! Weeerrrre off!" said the cheery voice of an early-twenties girl.

I glared at my dashboard. "I don't remember turning your voice back on, GPS."

Silence.

"That's better." Somehow, the silence felt sullen. "Box, tell Mr. Cheng I'm on my way."

I hadn't eaten out in a very long time.

I sparked the one-hitter and held in the smoke.

But from behind my closed eyes, I heard her laugh.

CHAPTER 8 – NUBORNS

"He is here! Everyone!" Mr. Cheng barked and gave a quick clap-clap of his hands as I entered.

The weed in my car was old and dry, and the hit quick and so hot it had scorched my throat and made me cough. Still, by the time I rolled up on Cheng's, my mood had definitely improved, and my forehead threatened to float away from the rest of my body.

This was exactly why I liked marijuana. My anxiety was gone, but I still felt completely functional.

"Hello, Mr. Cheng. Hello," I warmly greeted Mr. Cheng and his staff, whom he had lined up behind him. "How are you?" I extended my hand and bowed slightly. Even with that small movement, the blood rushed to my head and made me giggly.

"Mr. Bill." He returned my bow, then gently shook my hand in both of his small, smooth hands. "It has been so very long, Mr. Bill."

As I shook off my outer coat, the second person in line scurried behind me to catch and then precisely fold my coat over his bent arm.

Mr. Cheng was that rarity of rarities: a first-generation immigrant brought over in the womb, earlier this century, before they'd locked down the borders to shut out nanite-carrying terrorists and forest-destroying bugs. He'd been raised in Chicago's Chinatown before his father moved them to the suburbs. Of course, now, immigrants were practically extinct in America. These days everyone emigrated from America and Europe for the green belt of Africa. Mr. Cheng was lucky his parents came when they did; the ecological catastrophe known as China didn't have enough population left that it would allow any to emigrate, not that any Chinese national could pass an international-travel bio-screen, of course.

"Oh, c'mon now, Mr. Cheng. It hasn't been that long."

"My Box stop counting at five hundred day, but I think it longer since you last eat here, Mr. Bill."

That brought me up short. *That means not since I'd last used my PD.* Had it really been that long since I'd left the house for anything but a weed run?

"Here. You table here." Walking sideways, almost backwards, with one hand extended, Mr. Cheng guided me to a table in the back. It was still over an hour from prime dinner time, so I had the place to myself. I thought about asking for a booth and decided against it. I wouldn't want to offend Mr. Cheng, who seemed certain this was the place for me to sit. One of the staff pulled out my chair, and I sat down at the real wood table with varnish so thick nothing short of a blow-torch was going to damage that wood.

Cheng's was a Naperville tradition. My father and I had come here before and after every baseball road trip back when the senior Cheng ran it. The current Mr. Cheng wasn't young, but he also wasn't a withered fossil with a wispy, white beard. I couldn't even say how many of his father's beard hairs I'd plucked from my meals.

"Mr. Cheng, I'll take your best Peking duck, sir."

"Oh, it very good today, Mr. Bill. You like white or fried rice?"

"Pork fried rice, please."

"Yes, yes. Very good. Of course. And today you get our special discount!"

"I do?"

"Of course, Mr. Bill!" He again reached for my hand, which I held out with curious uncertainty. "Armed Forces Day today." While holding my hand Mr. Cheng bowed very deeply, and the staff around my table did the same. "Thank you, Mr. Bill. Thank you for you service."

I gripped Mr. Cheng's hand a little tighter and inclined my head. It had been a long time since anyone thanked me. "It's just what they... I mean, of course. You're welcome, Mr. Cheng."

For the first time that afternoon, Mr. Cheng looked me in the eye. He lowered his gaze briefly before lifting it again, and this time his eyes were a little red. It occurred to me that Mr. Cheng had known me my entire life, had seen me as a young boy and as a man gone to and come home from war.

I'd gotten better at this, but I didn't know if I'd ever get one hundred percent used to it. I blinked. Kept my jaw relaxed. And generally did all I could not to hear the words I always thought whenever someone thanked me.

Quietly, he repeated. "Thank you, Bill." Then he quickly dropped my hand and turned to go back to his kitchen while snapping something out in Chinese. I didn't need a BOLT ear implant to recognize the universal ring of a boss telling people to get their asses back to work.

At some point, someone had filled my small, Chinese tea cup. I blew too hard across the lip of the cup. I thought the words I could no longer hold back. *"On behalf of a grateful nation..."* Looking back over my shoulder, Mr. Cheng was just scooting into the kitchen.

Yeah, Mr. Cheng got it. *On behalf of a grateful nation, Mr. Cheng.*

Quiet as communion, I sipped the too hot tea. *Hooah.* Then put that behind me.

I ruminated on events, hoping the THC would help shake free an insight. Smoking had begun as a prescription, anxiety-reducing sleep aid, but I soon found it let me free associate and see poker scenarios in new ways. A different perspective was just what I needed now.

Frank went to a well-to-do church, in a well-to-do part of town. Nothing immediately suspicious there. Gays in church were about as noteworthy as snow in May. I thought of how Marvin would've decorated FVCC and laughed.

The waiter who'd remained behind to attend my table looked at me to see if I had something to say; when I didn't acknowledge him, he went back to giving me my dining space.

So Frank hadn't told Marvin about church. Some gay men still harbored resentment for how churches had ostracized homosexuals back in the day. Maybe Frank just hadn't felt comfortable sharing. I could see it.

And there I sat with my one singularly salient observation: Gay Frank had been killed near the spot a NuTree had been killed.

"Gay Frank." I pictured a homosexual hotdog in a boa and sparkles. Squeezing my eyes shut, I barely fought off a laughing fit, but this time I was utterly ignored by the waiter.

Oh yes. I laughed. *Completely functional!* I enjoyed my laugh for a moment then straightened myself out.

Okay, so it didn't seem likely that Frank had killed the NuTree. And I felt certain Frank had not committed suicide. But the murder of both Frank and the NuTree on the same day at the same place was too coincidental to be ignored. So then…what question should this investigation be asking?

I was working under the auspices of: Who would murder the mayor to cover up the murder of a NuTree?

Shit.

I still only had: Frank was newly gay and unexpectedly religious.

No point in putting off the inevitable. I pulled Box out of a pants pocket and turned to the waiter. "Privacy please."

The waiter gave a short bow as he backed out of earshot. "Call Marvin." Because I was in a public space, Box blinked and vibrated slightly to let me know it had received the order.

"No response. Leave a message?" Box whispered. Amazing how the new Boxes had audio intelligence built into their environmental assessments.

"Yes. Begin. Marvin, it's Bill. Call me. When's your next workout at The Flame? I'd like to go. Discon."

Maybe 'like' was too strong a word for meeting with Marvin to talk more about his and Frank's social life.

I shrugged. Maybe it wouldn't be so bad. I'd never been uncomfortable with the gay men I'd served with, just the version of gay that seemed to dominate the civilian world.

As soon as I disconnected, the waiter motioned and my complimentary soup and egg rolls arrived.

"Outstanding."

I sprinkled some salt and pepper onto my egg drop soup, which was thick, hot, and clumpy with the gelatinous goo of egg-y goodness.

I was five sips into my soup when a stoner thought came to me. "Box: search." It vibrated on the table. "Anti-NuTree groups within a twenty-five mile radius." I didn't think such a thing existed, but I hadn't thought Naperville had any murderers in it either, and the body in the morgue said I was wrong about that. There was an inordinately long pause, at least two or three seconds. "Box?"

"No results for those criteria."

"What were you thinking about?"

"There is a once-prominent, anti-genetic engineering group within that radius."

"I didn't know that."

"The group is defunct and had no anti-NuTree activity associated with it. There is no direct match to your search criteria."

"Tag the anti-genetic group." I dipped the end of the eggroll into the sweet and sour sauce; the flakey wrap crunched satisfyingly between my teeth, and my THC-laced tongue luxuriated over the eggroll.

NuBorns. Humanity's great psychic wound.

Near-AI computer processing, coupled with stem cell manipulation, gave doctors the tools to cure mankind. ALS, cholera, Ebola, AIDS, most cancers, Parkinson's—nearly all of the tens of thousands of diseases known at the time. But post-natal miracle cures hadn't been enough. Congenital disease accounted for over ninety percent of the remaining incurables.

In-vitro, DNA doctoring started with eliminating health complications like Down syndrome and autism. But why just correct? Why not augment, pick and choose? Athlete? No problem. Scientist? At your request *and* with FDA, fractal super-computing approval.

I re-dipped my eggroll in just the sweet sauce this time.

With on-the-spot manufacturing, it took only months to spread the technology across the globe. The poorest villagers in China and India might not have had indoor plumbing, but they sure as shit had a DNA doctor.

The results were a nightmare.

I sipped some tea.

Bio-engineering had done much for humanity. Hell, I had a kidney grown to replace the one I lost. And bio-engineering had made NuTrees possible—but it simply couldn't be done to an entire human. We were still too complicated.

After NuBorns, they quickly outlawed prenatal and heavily regulated prepubescent DNA doctoring. Practicing it meant a one-way trip to Mogadishu, the international prison city completely closed off from the rest of the world and hell on earth.

I poured the last of the sweet sauce onto the end of the eggroll and popped it into my mouth. A waitress, plump and round in all the right places, brought me my Peking duck. Wearing a fashionably loose-fitting, black wool dress that went all the way to her ankles, she was the sexy antithesis to the woman in the church. I thanked her then ogled her jiggling ass all the way back to the kitchen.

I bit into the duck. Oh my God. The skin was crisp and *so* much better than the version delivered to my home!

Quite the fun and games for you.

Today was church, and tomorrow a visit to the gay gym. On the plus side, a trip to the coroner was in order for tomorrow as well, and it would be good to see Moe again.

Strange days, Bill. Good Chinese food, but strange days.

CHAPTER 9 – THE FLAME

Later that night, I was very high, and deep into a sit-n-go, when Marvin returned my call.

I muted my game when Box flashed his ID on my holo. "Display call."

Marvin's face displaced the tournament table on my HUD, and because it was my first phone call at home that day, the Dark Star Countdown displayed in the upper-left corner for a long second before fading out.

"Hey, Marvin."

"Guess who just had sex?"

"I want to check out The Flame."

"I know! I got your message. That," snap, "is," snap, "fanta*aaa*stic!" He sang the middle part of "fantastic" in that falsetto voice I could only presume others found oh-so-charming, then ended with a double clap.

It all seemed like so much effort to me. "When's the busy time there?"

"Same as everywhere."

I stared blankly.

Marvin rolled his eyes. "After work and before dinner."

"Great. Let's call it 6 PM. I'll meet you there."

"Aweso—"

"Discon."

Ugh. I have to stop being a dick to Marvin.

I resolved to be patient, or at least not as short, with Marvin tomorrow. The day was going to be trying enough without having to put forth the energy to be shitty to Marvin.

I played poker. Got high. Slept. Woke up, not crying. Got high. Ate. Played poker. Got high. Napped. Got high. Ate. Worked out. Got high. Played poker. Then it was 6 PM, and I was standing in the lobby of The Flame, feeling conspicuous. The gym had its Dark Star Countdown embedded into the face of the front counter: 8 years 253 days 10 hours.

Despite my surroundings and the anxiety I always felt around people, I was in a good mood. Since moving up in stakes, I was on an incredible winning streak. I was catching cards and hitting outs like I'd never done before.

Marvin was running late. I checked Boxer, the smaller, portable version of Box I had strapped to my forearm. The gelatinous material used my body's electricity for what little power it needed and felt like an old-fashioned Band-Aid.

The attendant behind the counter gave me an over-the-top obvious up-and-down. Where Marvin was prance-y, this guy had a thick, black mustache and an aura of "I wear the leather chaps in my relationships."

"Ya know," he said, "If you want to go and work out, it's not a problem."

"I'm a little early. I'll wait."

"Sure. Suit yourself."

"Oh, he will, bitch," Marvin said over my shoulder.

"Hey, Marvin! Is this *your* date?"

"He wishes." Marvin brushed past me and put his ass in the air as he leaned over the counter to kiss the attendant on both cheeks. Still in mid-lean, Marvin peered over his shoulder to see the look on my face. "Besides, Eugene, he's hopelessly non-homo."

"Well, that *is* a shame."

Marvin put his hand on my shoulder and led me into The Flame's one locker room.

In a generic sense, it looked like any locker room would with a hell of a lot more penises flappin' around. It really was The Flame's busiest time. It was one hundred percent, wall-to-wall shlong. And nobody believed in covering up. Who the hell needed to stand naked in front of a mirror to brush their teeth?

Lockers. Showers. And penises on parade. Yay.

"Don't worry. We'll spare you the sight of the orgy Jacuzzi we keep in the back," Marvin joked.

"Of course."

"Of course what?"

"Where else would the gay gym keep an orgy Jacuzzi except in the back?"

Marvin's eyes popped open, showing the whites around both irises. "Oh my God! Oh. My. God!"

Marvin seemed genuinely distressed. I stepped back and glanced side-to-side. But I felt no *danger-close* buzz. "What?"

"Did *Bill* just tell a joke?"

Shee-it.

"You see? You can't help but be happy when you hang out with gay men! We're gay!" Men near us turned and laughed lightly at Marvin's comment; as he walked by, one gave Marvin's butt a slight smack. Marvin swiveled around. "You just wait, Elmer. Your turn is coming."

"Promises, promises," Elmer sing-songed back over his shoulder.

I gave my best effort at a laugh. It sounded bad even to me. Marvin gave me a "What the hell was that?" look that resembled the expression I imagined he would have if someone had stuck smelling salts under his nose.

"I think you need to have your med unit squeeze you out a cough pill."

I ducked my head and ignored the look and the comment. The Feddy health plan mandated every home have a med unit to do initial diagnosis through non-invasive tissue and fluid sampling. I never used it. The Army had me inoculated for everything, from an *Acanthamoeba* infection, so I could eat or drink about anything, to a *Yersinia pestis* disease, so I didn't have to worry about infectious animal bites, and all points in between and back again. Because many, or even most, of my inoculations were experimental and not yet available to consumers, it was one of the many everyday JOSOC things that I could never talk about.

I'd worn baggy sweats with tighter workout gear on underneath. It took me all of twenty seconds to thumb imprint a locker and throw my sweats in.

Marvin, on the other hand, got naked, grabbed a towel, which, of course, he didn't put around himself, and headed further into the locker room.

"Uh, Marvin?"

"Whaaat?"

"Where are you going?"

"To shower." The "duh" might've been only vocally implied but was clearly stated in the upper-body eye roll.

"But we haven't worked out yet."

"Okay, darling."

Darling?

"Maybe we don't have an orgy Jacuzzi in the back, but this is the gay social hour in this town, so I must fresh*eeen*." He fanned his face with one hand as he spun on a heel and sashayed over to the showers.

Great. Fucking great.

I should have known 6 PM meant 6:30 to Marvin.

I love being left at The Flame.

By myself.

In a sausage-fest of a locker room.

A guy wearing workout clothes and a military haircut walked up to me. "Come on," he said, "Let me show you where the juice bar is so you can wait while your diva friend freshens up."

Relieved, I followed him out. As we walked to the juice bar, I thanked him, shook his hand, and introduced myself.

His name was Clyde, and he was definitely military. When we stopped in front of the bar, he gave me an up-and-down that was similar but completely different from the one Eugene at the front desk had given me. "Can I ask you where you served?" It was one fighter taking stock of another.

Yeah, I guess there was no hiding that. "Here and there, but primarily with Naval Supply and Weapons Systems Support."

Clyde pressed on. "I didn't realize NAVSUP-WSS had a need for combat personnel."

"I was more of a guard." It was a standard deflection.

"Guard?"

I shrugged at his question.

Clyde let it go. "No worries. I haven't been coming here long, but I know I would've remembered seeing you. You local?"

"Yeah, my whole life. Except for the military."

"Oh."

"What?"

"I thought this was the only gay gym in the area."

"I'm pretty sure it is," I said.

"Do you usually work out at home?"

"Until today, I only worked out at home." There was only so much getting high and playing poker a guy could do. Besides, I liked the tax benefit I got from working out at least twenty minutes a day. I did it twice on most days for twice the benefit. I wasn't as lean as Clyde, or as fit as I used to be. Still, they might've taken my HUCOs, but most of what the military had done to my body could not be undone.

"Are you visiting family?" I asked Clyde.

"No. In town for a few days on business."

The military had business in Naperville? No, that's ridiculous.

Oh, shit. Clyde was a Feddy, not military. FBI? Probably. Maybe EPA.

I reassessed him.

He might've been leaner than me, but I was pretty sure I could take him. That didn't mean I wanted to try. The fighter in me knew one or both of those were a lie.

Clyde, having *completely* misinterpreted my appraisal,

laughed in a light, flirty way. "Look, man, I'm here on business. It's not against regs, but casual sex with a citizen is highly frowned upon."

Oh. Fuck. Me.

"I didn't really think it'd be a problem because everyone here seems to be vying for queen for a day, but I like you."

All I could do was look at his nose. My brain was racing. If I could find out just a little data on Clyde, and if he was here about either the mayor or the NuTree, Clyde would be obligated to FOIA a PD all kinds of information. "Yeah, man. I, uh, y'know, dig your vibe. Believe me, I know what you're saying about the guys around here. If any of them picked the military for their Social Service, it was on a Navy cruiser." It was a tired joke. Still, it got another light laugh from Clyde.

"But…"

"Yeah, Clyde, look. I'm really not…ready. I'm getting over a thing." Which was a lie. I only missed the idea of a Gladys.

"Well, I didn't–"

"But, y'know," gotta keep the fish on the hook. "I heal quick. So. How long you in town for?"

He shrugged noncommittally. "Hard to say, but at least a couple of more days."

"You're staying at the Hilton Inn?"

He laughed. "Am I being stalked?"

"Shit, it's the only decent hotel around."

"You don't like the Days Sheraton?"

"Are you fucking kidding me? The Days Sheraton here is an enlisted man's piss hole. If you're at the Days, believe me, you'll be so much happier at the Hilton Inn."

"Cool, man. Thanks." He put his hand out, and we shook again. "If you feel like it, ask for Clyde Somers, S-O-M not S-U-M-M, at the Hilton Inn."

"With an O and one M. Got it."

Clyde gave a shoulder-high, faux salute—that I didn't return—and went into the gym.

I remained standing at the juice bar where I studiously

avoided all eye contact while trying to look at the faces around me. Would I recognize any of them when I went to church tomorrow? I checked out the sundry postings pinned to the bamboo corkboard in the hallway leading to the locker room. Nothing as convenient as a posting for a hit man of gay, local officials.

Gottdamm.

I began to feel like a fool.

Coming here had been a wild goose chase, which had already had a spectacular payoff when I stumbled across Somers. Finding a Feddy in town was a homerun. Wandering through the gym now felt like running out an infield popup.

I grabbed a seat at the juice bar to wait for Marvin. As I sat, I saw an old school, free weight bench press in the corner. Self-consciously, I looked around then walked over to the free weights. Everyone else used the other, newer machines. The small, sleek machines better targeted muscles groups and gave a more efficient work out, but I loved the clunky feel of real weight. I ran a finger over the bar and looked around again. Would anyone notice me pumping six or so hundred pounds? God, it would feel good to work up a real sweat.

Best not. Technically, if anybody should happen to notice, I would be in non-compliance of my NDA.

I walked back to my seat. Finally, Marvin arrived to over-power me with his cologne.

"Fuck, dude." I stood and desperately tried to fan his scent away from the front of my face.

"Don't hate me because I'm beautiful."

"Sure. Why pick one reason when there are so many."

"Ha. Oh. So droll. But never mind." He gave me a genuine smile. "Shall we?"

"Marv, you're gonna hate me, but I, uh," I put a hand to the back of my right leg. "I pulled a hammy while I was waiting for you."

"Yeah, I'll bet you got your hammy pulled, sailor."

I laughed. *Fuckin' Marvin, he's always been funny.* "Look, I think I'm going to check another angle."

Marvin puffed out his chest and looked ready to explode. "Of all the balls!"

"Come on, Marv. Don't go into a pout."

He crossed his arms, looked at me sternly, and I knew he was definitely going to go into a pout.

"Bill, I know I make you uncomfortable, but I can't help who I am. I thought that you coming here meant you were being more accepting. I am wounded that you are now leaving, Bill. Wounded!" Angry snap!

As Marvin delivered his diatribe, eyes, peeking out of barely turned heads, were echo-locating on the drama. And the legally-required red lights from temple-implanted video recorders popped to life around me like the small eyes of a horde of one-eyed, socially-voracious rats.

It went unnoticed by Marvin who was wrapping it up. "Haven't you ever met someone and, for no rhyme or reason, felt *something*?"

I thought of the woman at the church then shook that thought from my head. "Hold on!"

"What?"

"Marvin."

"*What?*"

"You think I care who you *fuck*?"

"Well." He put his nose up in the air. "Do you?"

"What kind of..." I was actually a little wounded. "Marvin."

Marvin's voice softened. "I know it's stupid. But then, I… Why aren't we still close?"

Around me I heard a gaggle of Box commands:

"Uplink."

"SN Simulcast."

"Audio sync."

"Send SN disclaimer."

"Tint the back light!"

"No, I don't have privacy agreements! Near Simulcast then."

"Link."

"Co-Proxy?"

"I'll co-proxy!"

"I want to proxy, too!"

"Shhhh!"

Best make it count.

"Hey, we aren't those same little boys," I walked toward Marvin. "But we are. You're always family. C'mon man, you know I love you." The area was now silent. "But do I also have to love the flair required to play Sha-*gay* charades?" When Marvin was in arm's reach, I stopped and put a hand on his neck, pulled him close, and spoke quietly into his ear. "Now tell me you couldn't have any man in this room?" I pushed him away. "Am I right?"

Marvin stumbled a step back and noticed the ring of hand-clasped-to-mouth faces, the red recording-on lights reflecting off wet cheeks. "Oooh, maybe. Hold on! About which?"

But Marvin knew. By this time five minutes ago, his Naperville social status had just gone zeit, and he'd become the city's most eligible gay man.

"All I do is give," I said with a smirk.

"Ha! Tell that to my trust fund. Do you really love me, Bill?"

"Don't be greedy. Besides," I said jovially, "I'm leaving because I already introduced myself to a guy."

He stomped a foot on the ground and held a quivering finger to the ceiling. "I will not be mocked!"

One of the guys closest to us said, "It's true, bitch. We saw it."

Marvin's jaw dropped and his arms flopped to his sides.

I gave him a shrug, my best "What can I say?" look, clapped him on the shoulder, and—pulled hammy forgotten—speed walked to the exit, just out of reach of a wave of "Oh my God! It's posted already? Marvin! Marvin? That was *so....!* Who was...?"

Of course, the first thing I did when I got out of earshot was tell Boxer to screen all calls from Marvin.

CHAPTER 10 – CORONER

The coroner's office was a white, square building slapped onto the back end of the larger, black, glass police department building. I was talking to a young, perky thing with a shoulder-length shower of red ringlets and a pert nose. Her name tag said "Vera."

"Public Detective?"

I flipped my PD license holder closed and put it back in my coat's vest pocket. "That's right, Vera." I'd planned on seeing Moe after leaving The Flame, so on the drive over I put the clothes I'd brought with—dark green corduroy pants and a white shirt with a Mandarin collar—over my tight workout gear. I'd forgotten a change of shoes, so I still had on my black, soft-soled workout shoes.

Vera opened and closed her mouth. "You want to see the report on the mayor?"

"Please and thank you. You have an hour to produce it. Would you like me to come back?"

"An hour? But we close in *way* less than that."

They didn't train these kids for shit. "I'm a PD," I explained slowly. "I'm a Citizen with the right to expedited and expanded FOIA information."

"Oh, you do?" she said with the air of precociousness she

clearly knew was absolutely annoying.

Fuckin' natural redheads. Just because they're nearly extinct, they all think their shit don't stink.

I looked at the blank white walls and the blank white ceiling and the black-and-white chessboard pattern in the linoleum and overall did everything I could to hold my tongue and treat Vera as an officer should. As I weighed my response, the double doors behind Vera and beneath the building's Dark Star Countdown swung open and Coroner Moe Coughlan walked through.

As the doors fluttered closed, Moe looked from me to Vera to the white clock with black arms and numbers and quickly figured it out. "Bill." He nodded. "You made it just before closing time. How convenient of you."

I nodded back. "Moe. Maybe Vera needs the overtime. Vera?" Her face was crimson. "Vera's look says not so much."

The last time I used my PD, I'd helped Moe out of a real problem, and it was only because of my discretion that he was still coroner.

"Vera, this is Bill. Naperville's pain in the ass." He jerked his head to indicate I should follow him through the double doors.

"He asked to see the mayor's report," Vera called concernedly to our backs.

Two steps into the hallway, Moe stopped and raised his thick, black caterpillar eyebrows so high they threatened to crawl over his small, bald head. "The mayor's report? I suppose I could make you wait an hour, but that would mean I would have to stay late. Besides, why would seeing you twice in one day ever be the right choice?" He smirked, presumably to show that he was kidding.

Smiling not being high on our practiced facial expressions was another thing we had in common, along with our open disdain for Naperville city politics.

"Officer Maroney told me he ran into you. I've got the report in an exam room." He turned and gestured that I should come with him.

In an exam room? Why not his office?

This near to closing for the weekend, the building was empty as Moe led me down a white corridor with the same black-and-white patterned floors, then left at the intersection and into a shorter hall. Because we both wore soft-soled shoes, we walked without making a sound except for the soft rustle of our clothes.

We passed his office then stopped at a set of white double-doors at the end of the hallway. "Examination Room: 1" was etched in white ink on a lacquer, black plaque on the left door. There Moe swiped his keycard, entered a code on the keypad, gave a retinal scan, and finally said, "Coroner Moe Coughlin and guest."

The door chimed and swung open.

I stopped as soon as we entered the exam room.

The room, like the reception area and the corridor, was all a gleaming sterile white punctuated by that chess pattern linoleum floor. The bright lights reflected off every shiny, exactly-in-place corner of the room. Even Moe conformed to the visual schema with his white, crisply-creased pants and lab coat, bald pate, pale complexion, and stark black eyebrows. The antiseptic smell and cool, dry air perfectly matched the sparse colors.

All this black and white made me feel like I'd walked into a colorless and eerily quiet dream.

The door snikt shut behind me.

And the world closed in around me.

Without meaning to, I rose up on the balls of my feet and shifted my right foot slightly behind my left. I kept my hands open and to my sides. I knew what I was feeling. This was the beginning tickle of *danger-close* kicking in.

I called to the coroner. "Moe…"

He held up one long, boney finger. "Exam Room 1." He'd walked past the exam table to the far side of the room. On light feet, I came into the room behind him and stood with the gleaming metal table between us. I looked over my shoulder at the doors behind me. Something was just outside them.

"Online," the room said in a somber baritone.

Moe pushed the examination lights an arm's length above his head. "Enable security protocols."

"Enabled."

"Moe, what the—"

He shook his head at me. "Sweep and confirm."

A listening devices sweep?

"Confirmed."

"Close and confirm all external networks."

"Go to confirm all external networks."

"Confirmation as follows: voice ID Moe Coughlin, Naperville coroner."

"Confirmed."

"Pass code whispering palm 91 asterisk Cubs win."

"Voice ID and pass code confirmed." There was a slight pause before the baritone continued. "Room isolation: Confirmed."

So this was why Moe wanted to talk here and not his office. To protect sensitive information in on-going investigations, an examination room had extraordinary security protocols that the coroner's office did not. We were now disconnected from ViSAR. We were NetFree and as detached from the rest of the world as a human could be.

I glanced at Boxer on my forearm and noted the blinking red light telling me communications were down. In this room, I could be dead or alive, or both—like that quantum guy's cat—and nobody would know until somebody opened that door and looked inside.

The room suddenly felt cavernous. This did nothing to alleviate my feeling of being threatened.

Moe let out a breath he didn't seem to realize he'd been holding, then extended his hand over the exam table. "Okay, now we can talk."

"Moe, what the hell?" I shook his hand, glad to feel this connection to the present.

"Good to see you again, Bill."

I smiled. "Yeah, same here." Moe and I didn't know each other well, but that didn't stop us from liking each other or, more than that, from having a deep and honest respect. Our previous experience had confirmed that Moe was someone Dad called good people. That wasn't to say he wasn't a tad ornery and irascible.

"Seen Gladys lately?" he asked.

"What's with the NetFree action?"

Moe took the change in subject in stride. "Fuckin' Feddys," he said with an aggravated swat at the air. "Seems like they were here even before the Gottdamm NuTree hit the fuckin' ground."

"Somers?"

"You know him?" Moe seemed genuinely surprised.

"Bumped into him the other day at the, uh…" I couldn't bring myself to say The Flame and then endure the ensuing conversation with Moe thinking I was another Naperville divorcee experiencing a reawakening of my sexuality. "…around town. You know his service designation?"

"No. He only shared his badge with me." Moe stopped himself and thought a moment before continuing. "Be careful." He looked at me steadily.

"I'm always careful."

"I doubt your meeting was an accident."

If Moe only knew where we'd met, he'd know it was as accidental as a meeting could be. "What can you tell me about the mayor?"

"The mayor?" The question brought Moe up short. "He's dead." He said it with the kind of finality that would've ended the discussion with a more easily intimidated audience.

I couldn't help but smile gently at the coroner. *Oh, Moe. You don't scare me.* "Yes. What have you heard around the inner workings of city hall? Had the mayor been threatened recently?"

"Frank Nelson?"

"I'm just asking. Don't ask, don't get, right?"

"You think someone killed Frank? Our beloved mayor of

almost thirty years?"

Moe blew air out his nose then stopped and stood quietly. Some internal debate was playing itself out, and my mother had raised me with good enough manners not to interrupt someone else's conversation.

I waited. *I could seriously hear a mouse fart in here.*

Moe grumbled under his breath. "The good lord must love damn fools." Then he glared at me and said, "Fine! Let's talk about the mayor, who—after 28 years as mayor—had this town wrapped around his pleasantly plump little finger."

"Anything new happening? I heard something about a community outreach program."

"What's the name of the program?"

"I'm not sure."

"Stop bein' so helpful, will ya. But, no, I hadn't heard a thing about any new city program, outreach or otherwise."

"Nothing?"

"Didst I stutter?"

"Well, if there was a new program, would you have heard of it?"

"Yeah. As an SCR, I think I would have."

I was getting tired of people shouting unspoken *Duh*s at me. "SCR?"

Moe put his head down and rubbed the bridge of his nose between his thumb and forefinger. "Yes, a Senior Civilian Representative." He cut off my next question before I could ask. "New community outreach programs require SCR Board approval."

"Oh." I hadn't known that. "How did Frank die?"

Moe, now resigned to the conversation, sighed. "Frank Nelson died from drowning after driving his car into the Fox River." Moe snorted. "Ejaculated shortly before his death. He died with an *in flagrante delicto* erection. And I gotta say, the mayor was one well hung old guy."

"That's certainly fascinating, but that's really not what I need to know—"

"No, I mean it. As a coroner, I've seen all shapes and

sizes—"

"Moe."

"What?"

"Anything unusual *besides* the mayor's large erection?"

"Not a thing. Unless you know something I don't." He guffawed at the ridiculousness of such an idea.

"Is ejaculation before death common?"

Moe's face softened. He gestured at his work desk behind him. "The literature says it's happened before."

"Anything at the crime scene, uh…" I almost said, 'arouse suspicion.' "Seem suspect?"

Moe crossed his arms and looked at me sternly. "Bill, you do know there's a dead NuTree out there, right?"

"I think I heard something about that."

"Then why, oh why, are you bothering me with the Gottdamm mayor?"

"Just covering all my bases. So you're telling me there is something about the NuTree?"

Moe smiled and waggled a baton-like finger in my direction. "Now yer on to something!" He opened a drawer under the exam table and pulled out a bamboo folding file, which he flipped open and spun toward me so I could look at its contents right-side up.

Inside the folder was a photo of the Fox River with what I presumed was the trunk of Frank's car jutting out of the water. In the foreground was the same sheared-off NuTree stump I'd seen earlier. Judging from the light, this photo was taken in the very early morning.

I looked up at Moe.

"Notice anything?" he asked with great anticipation.

I furrowed my brow and looked again, scanning for some small detail I must be missing.

"Oh, good Gawd." Moe snatched the photo from my hand and jabbed a finger at it. "The Gottdamm stump. Wouldja lookit the Gottdamm stump!" He shoved the picture back into my hand.

I put my fingers on the photo and scrolled down to the

tree stump then zoomed in on it. Finally, I had to admit, "Moe, you're going to have to spell it out for me."

Moe drew a long, whistling breath in through his nose then started again in a tone straining to be even and measured. "That's a twelve-year-old NuTree. There's no way the mayor's volt burner was heavy enough to break that trunk. Not at the speed he was going from a dead stop on the embankment. And besides that, lookit the stump!"

I looked at the photo again, then back at Moe.

"Look how smooth it is!" he yelled. "It looks like it was snapped in two like a piece of asparagus. Trees don't snap like asparagus. If you crack a tree in two, it snaps jagged."

"I thought someone had trimmed the stump down."

"I took this at first light. Not only was there no time to do that, there's no sawdust on the ground around the stump. Let me spell it out for you. First," Moe put both fists on the exam table and leaned toward me. "Forget the mayor. The mayor's death was a straight-up what I like to call an unassisted murder. What you laymen would call a suicide. And, when he died, the mayor killed a NuTree."

"But you said his car—"

"I know what I said."

Now I knew why the Feddys were in town looking into the NuTree.

"Are you sure it was the mayor who killed the NuTree?"

"Am I what?" Moe leaned hard enough on his knuckles to turn them white. "Haven't we already covered me knowing what I said?"

"What makes you certain?"

With an eye roll that would've impressed even Marvin, Moe said, "The material on the side of Frank's car makes it certain. Can I go on?" He didn't wait long enough for me to ignore what was for him a rhetorical question. "Second, in its death that NuTree exhibited some uncommon characteristics."

"And?"

"And now the Feddys are finger fucking all my work! They've classified everything about the NuTree." He straightened up and jabbed an accusatory finger toward the photo. "I'm not even supposed to have that!"

Which explains the exam room lockdown.

I turned my back to Moe and leaned against the exam table looking at the exit. Moe was sure there was something odd about the NuTree, but I'd been hired to look into the mayor's murder. And now Moe was telling me there was no murder, and I had no reason to doubt Moe. Still…

"Listen," Moe spoke in even tones as he walked around the table. "There's nothing here for you about Frank." He put a hand on my shoulder. "Let it go. Get your PD fees and leave the NuTree to the Feddys." He barked out his version of a laugh. "I don't know who's paying your fees, but I know it ain't the NuTree."

I couldn't shake it. Despite Moe's protests, not everything there added up to an unassisted murder. As someone who'd considered it often enough, I couldn't imagine Frank killing himself in such a premeditated way with no note. I just couldn't get past that.

And I also couldn't discount what Marvin had said. He was nobody's idiot. If he said Frank was happy, I was sure he was right about that. And I agreed with him when he said that happy people didn't kill themselves.

Yeah, that's what's keeping me alive. Happiness.

"Hello? Earth to Bill?"

"Do you think Frank tried to hit that NuTree?" I asked.

"Mayor Frank Nelson? Kill a NuTree? Don't you pay any attention to politics in this town? Never in a million years would Frank Nelson hurt a NuTree."

I was near to something vital. The icy cold of the table seeped through the seat of my pants and the cloying, antiseptic smell of the room invaded my nostrils.

Moe's hand on my shoulder felt like a boulder. Panic was pushing in, my dream creeping up on me. I reached for a deep breath.

Held it.

Blew it out.

The world slowed down. Something was telling me I was not safe.

Logic and a trusted advisor say there is no murder. This is your out!

I could walk away from this right now. Go to Marvin and say... What? Lie? Say I'd followed every lead?

I thought of Granma and Grampa.

Fuck. No.

I was not going to do that. Marvin and I had come at this from two different places, but our purposes were identical.

Instinct told me intellect was wrong. I knew there had been a murder. I didn't know how. I didn't know why. But I was not going to just fold up tent and be part of the bullshit.

I laughed and looked up at Moe and lied. "You're right, Moe."

"Was there any doubt?"

"Thanks for the info."

"Hey, I owed you one." He patted me on the shoulder.

I wasn't going to drop my investigation, but what Moe didn't know wouldn't hurt him.

CHAPTER 11 – MOE

Moe Coughlin watched the doors close behind Bill. He had always been an overly cautious man. The sort of risk he had just taken was something he had spent his life arduously avoiding. He swept the photo into the folder, slid the folder in the exam table drawer, and said, "Exam Room 1, security status set to business operations."

"Confirmed."

And the real risk, Moe knew, was about to walk into the room.

He wasn't kept waiting long. Moe was looking at the doors when they swung open and Clyde Somers strode in; black, hard-soled shoes echoed off the white walls as he crossed the room.

"Mr. Coughlin."

Of course Somers would come. "Mr. Somers."

"Coroner, you went NetFree." Somers wore a grey suit and black tie that matched his short hair.

Somers stood across the exam table from Moe with his hands idling in his pants pockets. Even motionless, Moe felt acutely threatened by Somers.

"He's not an idiot. It had to be authentic. All of it."

Somers frowned. "What is your report?"

"He won't be looking into your mayor problem."

"How do you know?"

Moe shrugged his narrow shoulders. "I shared the NuTree photo with him." He had to make it look effortless.

Federal Agent Somers locked eyes with Coroner Coughlin. "You play a risky game." After a moment, Somers turned to leave.

Moe's knees went weak; he leaned on the exam table before saying, "Your name came up."

Somers stopped.

"He said he bumped into you."

"Yes." When Moe didn't say any more, Somers demeanor shifted as he turned full around. A dark shroud had fallen over Somers' face; his eyes had the same hypnotic intensity of a cobra's.

Even as he lived the moment, Moe Coughlin knew he was seeing what few men would ever live to say they saw: Somers as the killer he truly was.

"What did he say?" Somers softly asked.

To Moe, the voice felt as if the cold steel of a gun muzzle had just been placed on his temple.

But he had been anticipating this and when his moment came, Moe Coughlin was up to the task; his resolve held. "He only noted that a Feddy was working in town. I told him I'd met you. He asked if I knew your service designation. I lied."

He paused. He couldn't afford to be eager. Somers had to ask...

"Anything else?"

And now. Moe Coughlin, a smart, calculating man, had seen this moment since finding out Bill had filed his PD papers. Moe had known, and it had come.

But even knowing, Moe had made what was for him a most curious decision: To take a risk.

He had rehearsed his taunt, knew it must be said in just the right, off-the-cuff way. "He joked that you might be the cause of the ejaculant found with the mayor's body."

Moe Coughlin saw through Clyde Somers in a way

nobody else in Naperville could. Moe had been raised by a mentally unstable uncle and could sniff crazy from a hundred meters. That was how Moe knew what Somers could hide from others: He was far from stable. And indeed Somers teetered towards madness.

Moe felt Somers's animosity for Bill roil the air; it took his breath and stood him up. It seemed to Moe that the agent's skin crackled with a barely contained rage.

Somers realized Moe was waiting for him and asked, "Anything else, Mr. Coughlin? Anything, at all?"

Moe kept his face bland and lied again. "Nothing."

Moe had done what he could for Bill. It wasn't much. Maybe it was nothing…but Moe knew that pebbles had slain giants before. And Moe Coughlin was no warrior. Instead, he had done all he could do: He'd made it personal to Somers. And experience had taught Moe that people who took their work emotionally made mistakes.

Somers turned and spoke, "Your country appreciates your service, Citizen."

Somers left the room.

Moe Coughlin stood up straight and smiled broadly. When he held his hands up, they trembled. He clenched them into fists and released his nervous energy with a loud, barking laugh.

He turned his face to the ceiling. *For you, Frank! You were a good man. You deserved better.*

Moe held Bill Slaughter in the highest regard. And Bill was now in mortal danger, of that Moe was certain. Still, Moe was old enough to know it wasn't often he got to feel this good about a decision.

Moe stopped. His good mood gone. He had felt that chill.

There were times when Moe Coughlin knew he'd soon get a call.He didn't know where it came from, or exactly when into his decades-long career it had started. (Which was a lie Moe told himself, he knew it had started with the death of Adam Appel, one of the other, few remaining Jews in Naperville.) But Moe Coughlin knew it was real.

He hoped it wouldn't be Bill.

CHAPTER 12 – THE BIGGEST HEART

When I'd pulled up to the Municipal building, I'd known I was running short on time, so I'd parked in an empty reserved space. As I left the building, I was pleasantly surprised to find myself both un-towed and ticket-free.

"Aren't you going to thank me?"

Whatever pleasantness I was feeling fled as I turned. "Chief Maidenhead."

"Now, Mr. Slaughter, who do you think has the reserved spot closest to the building?"

I gave him my toothiest smile. "The guy with the biggest heart?"

He laughed a jolly, trained politician's laugh. "God. I, and I'm not just saying this, I really, truly dislike you."

"Oh." I flopped a hand at him. "Puh-shaw. You say that to all the PDs with enough balls to tell you to fuck off."

"Look." The chief held his hands to the sky like I was robbing him. "No love lost, but, c'mon—ya' got lucky." He shook his head. "Still, lucky or not, you were righ—" The word caught in his throat, and he gave a twitchy-lipped smile that never touched his eyes.

For the second time today I was thankful for my mother's good manners as I stood and watched Maidenhead wrestle the words out.

"Ultimately, what can I say?" He smiled even bigger. "You were right."

And people say there is no God. Somehow, I kept the shit-eating grin off my face. The chief had information I could use. If he was being talkative, I was all for that. "And so were you. Right, that is." That brought his head up. "I did get lucky."

"Mr. Slau—If I may, Bill?"

"Whatever's easier for you."

"Bill, then. Bill, can we talk about the death of the mayor and your investigation?"

"What's the harm in a talk?"

"Exactly! Thank you. So. The mayor," he doffed his hat to show off his standard-issue salt-and-pepper hair, "was a friend, a fellow civil servant. We're all—all of his colleagues, the whole community—we are all beside ourselves at his sudden passing."

"He was a good man."

"The best! I'm glad he started coming to church recently."

"You went to the same church?"

"Yes. We were closer the last few months than we'd been in years. Which is why, despite our opinions of one another, I'm asking you to stop your investigation."

Hold on… "You don't know who hired me."

The chief winced. But he knew if I played my PD card, which I was willing not to play as long as we were being all nice to each other, he'd have to FOIA me that information. "I don't."

Of course they don't. If they did, they'd be shaking down Marvin in some parking lot, trying to get him to void the contract. Frank had done an outstanding job of keeping his secrets.

If the chief didn't know, then Frank couldn't have shared anything about his relationship with Marvin. And when I asked Marvin, he'd had no idea about Frank's religious activities.

The chief interrupted my thoughts. "Bill? Please?"

"My mom would be mad at me."

"And why's that?"

"Because I'm going to have to say no even though you used the magic word."

The chief's jaw tightened. "What evidence are you pursuing? What logical line of investigation is driving your actions?"

"I don't need to tell you that. The whole point behind PDs is that they work autonomously."

"Don't tell me then." The chief stepped closer. "I really don't care to know. But I doubt you can even answer the questions."

"Okay, I lied. I didn't get fucking lucky."

Maidenhead's face went flush. "The fuck you say!"

"I don't have to explain myself to you." Not when I couldn't explain *danger-close* to myself. "I knew. I was prepared…"

The anger dropped from the chief's shoulders and his face relaxed. "Oh! Yes. *Captain* Slaughter, the ever-prepared! Let me show you my new toy." He put his head down and the fingers of his free hand to his eyes. After a moment's massage, he raised his head. "You like?"

HUCOs!

God, I miss my fucking HUCOs.

Not having them was like seeing half of everything. It was one of the things I enjoyed most about wearing the poker sim, with its display of live action and real-time stats.

The chief blinked and eye-scrolled through data. "Ah yes, Captain William David Slaughter. Says here you used to have Heads-Up Contacts yourself. And…oooh. You did that?"

"Why should you know any of this?"

"Says here…" He paused as his eyes flipped through data.

Because he was actually moving his eyes, except for being retractable, I knew his interface was rudimentary. I coveted them all the same.

"…they did something experimental with your body."

During missions, of course, mine were always on. Off mission, the only way not to use them was to power them down.

"They applied Micro-Fracture Technology…"

But I never did.

"…to your complete skeletal structure." His eyes refocused and looked at me. "Ouchie. Says here that even with meds that'll hurt like a fucker. But the payoff is 'bones are a 'classified amount' lighter and stronger' leading to 'reduced injuries and more efficient muscle use, including an overall increase in speed, strength, and reflexes.' You are *special*, Captain Slaughter. And then, y'know, nothing specific, but it says you lost men."

An anger crept up my spine.

"That on your last mission, you were— Hold on. It says here you were *ill*-prepared."

He was trying to goad me. And it was working. "I don't know why they would tell—"

"Why would they tell a dumb, hick cop like me? How'd I get so lucky to have two of you high and mighty retirees in my town? Gee, *Mister* Slaughter, why would they tell the local law enforcement about a man with advanced martial training and strength, speed, and reflexes far exceeding an average man of your size?"

He wants me to hit him.

"Cuz they give you guys all those neuro-tech preventative treatments," he stepped towards me, "and shoot you up with PTSD inoculations, but sometimes it just won't take. Cuz y'know," another step closer, definitely inside my personal space, "vets," he said it with a sneer, "they *never* have problems adjusting."

You decide how this ends—not him.

"You got yerself any PTSD? You sleepin' okay?" Another step, and now he was nearly under my nose. "Anything you can't wake up from?" Then he said with a smile, as if he'd just had a surprisingly pleasant thought. "Hey! How's Gladys these days?"

Then it was on me; like an old tune suddenly remembered, it all snapped into place. I was humming the chorus from inside the eye of the *danger-close* storm, and I could see it all.

Time slowed, but I was unaffected. I was keenly aware of the minutest details. The flutter of the chief's clothes. His body heat. His heart and breath. The contraction of his muscles. Above and behind me at my 4 o'clock flew a brown and grey sparrow. Under my foot was a pebble I hadn't noticed before. Vera's eyes were on us from inside the building.

It wasn't that these sensations fell on me one after the other. From inside *danger-close*, in a moment of awareness I could move inside of, I knew it all.

In the sudden clarity, I knew, *I'm in no danger.*

I said, "What? Gun. Emergency? Backup. Who said help? Officer help? Backup. Fire? Hose. Deploy?" I didn't yell. I didn't say anything in a threatening way. And because each word or phrase was ambiguously stated, it kicked off a data stream and then a parade of various, urgent, but not emergency-response-required options. Trainers called this the chaos stream, and it was what caused most to wash out of the HUCO program. Users couldn't shut it down, tune it out, or otherwise filter through and keep up with everything; if left unchecked, it induced a type of petit mal seizure. I stopped short of that.

With each phrase, the chief's struggles escalated. Finally, he stumbled back as the HUCOs overwhelmed his senses.

I stepped in but this time spoke in a soft, comforting voice. "I'm not stopping this fucking investigation for you, or fucking anyone. And I hope to fucking God this lands me on your doorstep."

As I turned to go to my car, I heard the chief flail. "Dismiss. Dismiss! All clear! Clear all? Dismiss all! Slaughter! Gottdamm you!"

I waved with one finger without turning as I climbed into my car.

CHAPTER 13 – START SIMPLE

As soon as my ass hit the seat, before the door even shut, I said, "GPS, silent run. Full tint windows. Direct route home."

Focus.

It was there… Something was right there… I needed to ask the right question.

Start simple. Frank, Marvin, church.

Was there one thing Frank had in common with Marvin and church?

They were both out of character and… and…

They both started recently.

What else had started recently?

The community outreach program Moe should've known about but didn't.

Moe didn't know about the project but Marvin did. If Marvin knew about the program but nobody at work did, then–then… *Frank, Marvin…*

"The program must involve the church!"

Marvin didn't know about the church. Work didn't know about Marvin. One hand didn't know what the other was doing. It had a very unsettling familiarity. Keeping things compartmentalized was SOP for operational security, so no one person could tell everything.

Marvin, and I, had assumed Frank's recent loss was what had prompted the changes in his life. What if we were wrong? What if it was something else?

What was your community outreach program, Frank?

CHAPTER 14 – CHURCH

The music at FVCC was contemporary yeral—that byproduct of the border lockdown that had forced farmers to pay livable wages to people already in the country. Urban Americans desperate for a life away from gangs and drugs had flocked to the rural jobs, a reverse of the migration a century earlier. And just like that migration, they'd brought music with them. Yeral was urban beats mashed against rural melodies.

After leaving Maidenhead, I'd spent the day playing some winning poker. And was now in the center section of a sea of utilitarian chairs obviously set up just for this service. The ceiling was surprisingly low, just twenty-five feet, which made the space all the louder.

The musical show at the church was quite the production with a full band, backup singers, choreographed dancers, and lots of orange and yellow lighting effects. The singing was good, and the songs were not horrible—they were catchy, if a bit too much treacle for me.

Not that I could focus on the lyrics with everything else that was going on. The bass of the music was so deep and so loud it thumped against my skin.

I looked around the audience. The reflective costumes shot

rippling patterns of light over a wave of bare arms; the arms were bathed in orange and yellow lights from the stage. I couldn't help but think they looked like flickering candle flames and wondered if the effect was intentional.

Lots of upturned faces, but this branch of FVCC had two services each Sunday, so I was at best scanning only half the congregation.

I seemed to be the only one standing still, let alone not singing.

The coffee was definitely free. And, as Dad would say, I got what I'd paid for. FVCC's coffee tasted exactly how, using Dad's maxim, free coffee should: watered down and stingingly bitter. I drank my coffee strong, but even I had to yield to reality and add some milk product and sugar. I wondered who else in this crowd had been huckstered in by the "Free Coffee on Sunday" placard.

They stopped singing. There was a brief moment of silence, and then the guy at the piano says, "Let's pray. Dear God…"

Oh, crap. The gym full of heads around me bowed.

"Please be with us through our daily struggles. Guide us. Guide us to the abundant life you promised. Help our NuTree program to be a success…"

As soon as he said NuTree, one lone voice gave a quiet but distinct, "Boooo."

I prairie-dogged right and left but nobody stood out. Even odder, nobody else seemed to notice. I was the only one craning my neck to see who the crackpot was.

The guy at the piano gave a deliberate pause, before saying, "And we pray for Julie."

And the whole congregation replied, "And we pray for Julie." In unison. As if it were part of the shtick. The couple in front of me opened their eyes to exchange a knowing smile as they said it.

Then the guy at the piano went on with the rest of his prayer.

What the fuuuck?

With other heads bowed, I pulled up my sleeve and tapped

out a quick query to Boxer to check if there were podcasts of previous sermons.

Box sent back, "The library of podcasts is exhaustive."

The guy at the piano said, "Amen." I pulled my sleeve back over Boxer. "Now as you take your seats, turn to someone you don't know and say good morning."

The thin guy to my left gave me a pleasant smile beneath his accountant glasses and extended his hand out of his ill-fitting tweed coat.

"I'm Jeb."

"Hi, Jeb. I'm Bill."

"This is my wife, Deepa." An Indian women offered me a slight hand and a demure smile.

I shook her hand, feeling like the fingers would surely snap if I squeezed just a little. "Pleased to meet you," she said then leaned over to hug the woman in the row in front of her.

Jeb smiled at me. "I, uh, hope you don't mind, but I couldn't help but notice your reaction. During the prayer, I mean."

"Oh."

"That's just Julie."

"Yeah. That's what he said."

"She's the senior pastor's wife."

"Slade?"

"Yes, but Mitchell, not his brother, Peter. Peter's the assistant pastor."

"Okay. Is she serious?"

"I'm afraid so. It is a bit embarrassing, but y'know. Love the sinner, right?"

"Uh-huh. Sure." I grasped for questions, but I was stumped. The pastor's wife booed NuTrees. "Uh, why would—"

"Okay, everybody," said the guy at the piano. "I love to hear all those friendly conversations, but let's get Pastor Pete up here for some announcements. Pastor Pete?"

Chairs shuffled as people sat back down, and a slender man in his early thirties with a slim, unevenly grown mustache and receding hairline walked from the wings to take center stage. Pastor Pete basically read the same information that was on the cheap, cotton-paper program they'd handed me when I walked in.

Pastor Pete wore a genuine smile, but his reading was uninspired, bordering on the somnambulistic. If the rest of the service was like this, I wasn't going to be able to stay awake. It was bad enough that the service had started at 10 AM, which meant I'd had to be up at 9 AM to shit, shower, and shave.

"… and that's it. Let's pray."

Again?

"My God, please be in this place. Fill it with Your spirit. As Pastor Mitchell comes out to speak, let his words be Your words. You are the water, and he is the vessel. And be with our troops overseas."

Now there's something we agree on.

As he prayed, a man who looked like Pete but was one-and-a-half times his thickness both in body and hair quietly walked onto stage to stand behind Pete. I could see the family resemblance around the nose and eyes. Both Pete and Mitchell were dressed casually. No suit and tie. No robes. Just slacks and button-down shirts for both of them. Not sure what I'd been expecting, but I didn't think the pastor would be more dressed down than his congregation.

"Amen."

As soon as the one brother said amen, the other replaced him. Where Peter was a sleep-inducing speaker, Mitchell's presence filled the stage.

I'd seen this charisma before. There had been a few really good, competent officers and a lot of dumbasses who didn't know their asshole from their pie hole, but only one true leader: Rick Leonardi. The men had loved the colonel.

Pastor Mitchell had the same charismatic presence as Colonel Leonardi. I could see it in the upturned, intent faces of the people around me.

I wasn't moved.

If Colonel Leonardi had asked me to shoot bullets out my

ass, I woulda pushed my shit in with a full clip. But the colonel and I shared a common purpose.

Whatever Mitchell's purpose was, I did not share in it.

Mitchell worked the room, mostly ignoring the podium that had been wheeled out for him. He talked about the seven deadly sins. His voice was calm, confident, and convivial as he crossed from one side of the stage to the other. The people laughed easily and sometimes heartily at his jokes, jotted notes as he quoted a little from the Bible and more from politicians, philosophers, and contemporary song lyrics.

It felt unctuous to me, and I had the distinct feeling that I shouldn't be here.

To my father's disappointment, the only religion I'd ever known was combat religion, the kind invoked when shells were falling all around and an Anti-Personnel Microwave emitter silently boiled the blood of the men on either side of you until they exploded.

After I was done with war and combat, I'd never thought of God again. It was only mother nature out there.

Most of the time, I felt this coming. Sometimes I could even catch myself and stop it in its tracks. Other times, it happened like this: In a flash flood of stimuli, my dream was now my waking nightmare.

I flinched from the phantom pop of muzzle flash and the equally non-existent boom of artillery. The angry *zzzwip* of incoming rounds tunneling through the air. The chilling pop of Chandler's and Sullivan's exploded bodies. The wet flopping as they hit the ground.

Cold sweat ran down my back as I fought against my perceptions, my mind's effort to put me back in the Ukraine.

The room spun.

This is why I don't leave the Gottdamm house!

I mashed my eyes shut. But nothing could stop the sound and smell of Sullivan's and Chandler's entrails as they slopped over my boots.

Even behind closed eyes, I could feel the room circle the drain, and the force of the vertigo made my body tremble. I clutched my knees to stop from spilling out of my seat.

"You, uh, okay?" Jeb asked.

With my jaw set shut–

"Bill?"

I half-turned my head.

What Jeb saw made him flinch and snatch his hand back. He muttered, "Sorry. So sorry," and slid closer to Deepa.

Sweat beaded across my forehead. I fought my instinct to flee. Jump up. Bolt from that gym as fast as my pumping legs and heaving lungs could carry me. Fear and vertigo trapped me in my seat.

The burn and acrid taste of vomit seared the back of my throat, and I knew I couldn't stand. Standing would only mean, *I'd fall down in a room full of strangers who couldn't fucking understand!*

I was trapped! I smothered a yell for a medic.

A single tear rolled from my eye.

Fuck. Oh, fuck. Don't cry, man. Not here.

I didn't trust my hands, so I used a shoulder to swipe it away.

The air pushed out of my mouth, and I groaned at the punch-like sensation of being shot. Even as my psyche relived war and did all it could to convince me of it, I told my body to ignore the tickle of phantom blood running down my back and stomach and to do what the shrinks had told me to do: in through the nose, out through the mouth.

I forced myself to feel the seat under my ass, the pants under my hands. Compelled myself to smell the perfumes and colognes in the air around me.

"Amen. Let's have Harvey back up here for a final song."

I opened my eyes.

Reality snapped back into place so hard it rocked my head back.

In my mind's eye, the incident faded away to a point and then disappeared. Gone. Just as quickly as it had come. My piston-pumping pulse throttled down to an idle.

Hesitantly, I peeled my hands off my pants. The grooves of the corduroy held an imprint in sweat of each hand. With surprisingly sure knees, when Harvey asked people to stand, I got to my feet with everyone else.

As the song wrapped up, Harvey, the bald guy at the piano, said, "Thank you all for coming. Have a blessed week, and we'll see you next Sunday."

The congregation flooded into the aisle. I wasn't ready to be in that shoulder-to-shoulder throng. I stepped forward so the rest of the row could easily pass behind me.

Deepa and Jeb said nothing as they passed.

Stagehands bustled about breaking down set pieces and storing lights, monitors, and what-not. In the midst of it, Mitchell Slade stood at the foot of the stage, smiling and shaking hands. The four-deep crowd lined up to shake the pastor's hand seemed a trigger-squeeze too eager, too adoring. But Slade was clearly in his element, beaming at his flock as he sucked up their adoration.

I stepped into an empty aisle and walked with measured strides into the atrium.

CHAPTER 15 – A DISH TO PASS

In the restroom I splashed some cool water on my face. Then, after queuing up in a short line for some coffee as the rest of the congregation milled around in the main portion of the atrium, I stood at one of the floor-to-ceiling windows, taking a sip.

As was typical, now that the episode was done, physically, it was as if it had never happened.

I drank the coffee black. It tasted like ape piss.

I turned my thoughts to why I was here at church, to the mayor's murder.

Who is Julie?

"Are you Bill?"

Even though I'd "drifted off" during the sermon, there was no mistaking the voice. I turned to look at the broad, white smile of Pastor Mitchell Slade. I squared my shoulders and set my own smile into place.

"Hello, Mitchell." I extended my hand.

Mitchell was short at five foot ten, but he looked me in the eye, and when he shook my right hand, he put his left one over it ensuring I couldn't escape. "Hello, Bill. Glad to meet you. How did you like the service?"

He let go, and I fought the urge to wipe-off my hand. "It

was, uh…effective?"

He wrinkled his brow. "Effective?"

"Sure. Why not?"

"Well," he broke into his smile, "thanks, Bill. That's a great compliment. People will say good or bad things, but you're a rubber hits the road type of guy, right? I can tell these things." He gave me quick wink. "Effective," he repeated as if rediscovering the compliment. "Thank you very much indeed."

"You're very much welcome, and thanks for the coffee by the way." I hoisted my self-heating styrocup in his direction. "I know it isn't DunkinBucks in here, but it's not oh-so bad."

"No, not at all." *Not if you like ape piss.* "So, Mitchell, how did you know I was Bill?"

"I already introduced myself to the other new attendees."

"You know how many new people show up at each service?"

"Of course. Wendy McKing's knows how many times a day, week, month, or year you eat at their establishments, right?"

"They do?"

Slade laughed. I had to admit, it was an infectious laugh. But I wasn't here to be infected.

"Oh, absolutely they do."

"Good to know."

"Could I interest you in some after-service lunch?"

"Hm. Where?"

"My home, of course!" He pulled out a direction card and handed it to me. The code formed the letters FVCC.

"Will it be only you and me?"

"My wife, Julie, will be there also."

"That sounds just fine. When should I arrive?"

"Give me forty-five minutes to take care of a few things here, and I'll see you there."

"Sounds good. Thanks."

With a parting handshake, he was off.

On my way out, I tossed the brackish, black water they

called coffee into a steaming bin of styrocups; the cups from before the service had already begun to decompose into recyclable pucks and inert gases.

When I got in my car, I told GPS to tint the windows. "Box, search FVCC podcasts, audio only. Specific phrase, all words, begin value, and we pray for Julie, end value. Limit to the last six months and the first twenty-five minutes of each podcast."

Audio searches could take a few minutes, so while Box churned away, I contemplated the replenished one-hitter I had in my car. Lunch with Mitchell stoned? Or not stoned? Unsurprisingly, I decided a little stoned was going to be necessary and sparked the one-hitter.

I blew out smoke. "Box, save the results from the podcast search. Secondary search, is there a protocol for lunch at a pastor's house?" Maybe I'd get lucky and being high would be a prerequisite for lunch with a twenty-first century pastor.

"It is customary to bring something to pass."

"Pass? Seriously? Like a joint?" I laughed.

"Typically, it is a dish or a dessert to share."

"Zat so? GPS."

"Spring has sprung! What a beautiful day!"

And it really was. It was so nice out that I didn't even let GPS's enthusiasm make me snarky. "Direct route to nearest open market. If there's a bakery nearby, go there."

"We're off!"

GPS outdid herself. As it turned out, there was an excellent bakery nearby—though she had taken it upon herself to not choose the closest bakery, cheeky GPS. I bought a cherry pie to take to Mitchell's for lunch, and scooped up some creampuffs with a light, delicate crust.

Oooh. Gonna smoke up a good appetite and chow on these later.

I fed Mitchell's direction card into GPS, and the route popped onto the windshield. I gestured for the map to zoom-in and then follow the route. It was a short ride there, but from the bakery it would take me past the spot where the NuTree and Frank had been murdered. I gestured to pin the NuTree location.

"GPS follow route. Stop at pin."

In a few minutes, I stood where I had a few days earlier. The rest of the NuTree, roots and all, had been removed. Sure, the NuTree's demise was in the electronic print and web media, but city planners certainly weren't eager to have the stump on display.

There were still a good thirty minutes before I needed to be at the Slade residence.

On a whim, I started down the slope to the river; it was damp with runoff from the quickly-melting snow. After just a few days of reasonably good weather, green grass was already starting to coat the embankment. I'd worn a pair of standard street shoes to church, which made the walk down the slick grass to the edge of the Fox a little unsteady.

I looked into the hole where the NuTree once stood.

Even though the river was swollen with melted snow, there were still clear tire tracks in the soft mud and moss at the river's edge. I felt like I should smooth them out, like closing a dead man's eyes.

I left them as they lay.

I scanned the opposite river bank. Then to my right and left.

The murdered NuTree was the only thing within fifty yards in either direction. Other than the NuTree, there was nothing remarkable about this location. No walking paths, no businesses nearby. Across the river, there was no embankment. Instead there was a twenty-foot, centuries-old rock wall. Between it and the river was a paved walkway. On top of the wall were an apothecary, a yoga studio, an art store, and a few other shops. Just up the street from that was the historical Naper Settlement. Behind me, on Ewing Road where I'd parked, stood the old, un-used police station. About two hundred yards to my right was the municipal library and two hundred yards to my left were some homes that had kept the petrified, seven-foot stumps of lost trees.

I hadn't noticed it before when I was with Maroney, but

this was easily one of the most isolated spots in Naperville. Standing at the river's edge, I watched the water flow. The air was warm and quiet. With electric cars and almost no commercial airline industry, the world was much quieter now than when I was a kid.

The sound of the swollen river's smooth easy rhythm settled over me. A soft breeze tickled my ear and cheek. I closed my eyes as the sun warmed the back of my head and a cardinal across the river sang out to stake his territory.

Indoors, there was always noise, some soft buzz. Now… I'd forgotten how at rest mother nature could be. It was easy to imagine this was what John Naper might have heard when he established Naperville two hundred plus years ago.

The world smelled of waking up. It was truly Spring.

It was peaceful.

I lingered in the moment.

Surprisingly, but pleasantly, refreshed and relaxed, I began up the embankment. Two thirds of the way, the smooth tread of my dress shoes failed me.

At first, only a knee hit the squishy earth. But as I tried to get a foot under me, no amount of enhanced muscle could negate the effects of zero traction and gravity. I slipped again and then slid down the embankment like an otter, digging my heels in in time to stop me just short of the river's edge. The seat of my pants and the back of my jacket were slick with wet grass and mud.

And I was laughing. Free and simple, like a kid.

I laughed until I cried then did both until my ass got too cold. I wiped my eyes.

When was the last time I'd cried?

Of course, after the dream with my body wracked in sweat.

I sniffled and used the back of my muddy hand to wipe my nose. "I guess not all cries are made the same."

I turned and made a more careful and uneventful ascent to my car.

"GPS—"

"You're wet! And cold!"

"—new destination: home."

"Should I have the house draw you a bath?"

"That sounds nice, thanks."

"You just settle back and be comfy. We're off! It's hard being you, isn't it?"

"Gettin' easier all the time."

As my car pulled away, there were two gouges from my heels etched in the muddy riverbank near Frank's tread marks. Of course, my marks stopped at the river's edge.

"Box, call the Slades—Sorry, but must reschedule. Please send a time for dinner. Discon."

My   lunch   date   would   have   to   wait.

CHAPTER 16 – PLEASE, SIT DOWN

When I got home, I climbed into the bath and disconnected myself from the world, silencing even Box. When I got out, all warm, high, and full of creampuffs, there was a message from Mitchell waiting on my bathroom mirror.

"Play."

"Hope everything is okay. Dinner would be great." An evite was attached for six that evening.

"Confirm that RSVP." I walked from the bathroom and flopped onto the couch. Six o'clock was a few hours off, but I wasn't hungry, or interested in any poker games.

"TV on. Sports. Cubs game?"

"Live or recorded?"

"Is there live?"

The TV popped to life on the wall above my outstretched feet. "Disable Countdown." The clock faded from the upper-left corner of the display.

The players wore short-sleeved shirts in the bright sun.

Be nice if games could be local again.

But even if the weather cooperated, no team could afford the gas to travel anymore, so now all major league baseball teams lived and played in their highly secure, twenty-five mile circle in Baja, California.

I hadn't watched a baseball game in forever. The Cubs had all the markings of being a miserable team this year. Not that they'd won a thing for decades. Not since we took four out of five, including those three astonishing years in a row. Still, that fourth unexpected win was my favorite.

It was still the pre-game show with the monk-like umpires standing in their grim, black vestments around home plate, ceremonially accepting the manager's lineup cards. Behind them, the starting pitchers were warming up. It was amazing what micro-muscle development had done for pitchers, who now topped out at eye-popping hundred and ten miles per hour from sixty four feet six inches away. Batters with their Popeye-like forearms had made hitting a round ball with a round bat into the finest of sciences, shattering old, even steroid-era, records.

With the game in progress, I contemplated Mitchell reaching out to me, which reminded me. "Box. How's that query on the church's podcasts?"

"There is one more match from last week."

"No others?"

"At the edge of the search criteria, six months ago, there is another match. Beyond that match, outside the search criteria, there are three additional and consecutive podcasts with a match."

"Beyond that?"

"Looking at older podcasts requires registering to view archival data. Should I register and go back further?"

"No." Two weeks on after six months off and at least a month on.

"Box, make sure I'm awake by 5:15."

"PM?"

"Really? Yes, PM. Chirp confirm, smartass." Of course Box wasn't GPS, so he really hadn't meant anything by it.

Box gave a confirmation chirp.

Since I was watching a baseball game, it was guaranteed that I would fall asleep.

###

GPS pulled my car up to the curb in front of the Mitchell household at 5:50. The sun was just going down behind the homes to my left, filling the sky with majestic red and orange clouds. To my right was the Slade home with a nice array of rare natural trees and dark squares of earth that would probably be flowerbeds in a week or so. It was a nice home in a nice neighborhood not too far from the church.

As I sat in my car, I looked through the large windows that faced the road and were painted with the orange and red reflection of the sunset. Through the glare my HUCOs would have compensated for, I could just make out Pastor Slade talking animatedly to a round woman in a blue dress. Her dark hair was pulled up into a bun, and she sat, arms crossed, on the edge of a chaise lounge, turned away from the window.

"Box. Load Fly on the Wall app."

Chirp.

"Direct toward glass surface approximately fifteen meters to the West. Calibrate for optimal resonance off clear glass." Of course, apps like these were heavily regulated; they were for government law enforcement entities and pseudo-law enforcement entities like PDs on a case.

Box spoke. "Audio synced. Playing."

"Julie, this stubbornness is beyond frustrating." Mitchell's voice came out crisp and tinny. There was an occasional warble and squeal to it, but I'd used Fly before to get a voice off a cereal bowl. Compared to that, those big sheets of glass were giving off studio-quality resonance.

"I'm stubborn? Why am I stubborn? You're the one who won't take no for an answer."

"I ask for so little from you. I allow you to travel, at great expense, I might add—"

"You're kidding, right?"

"—to do anything you would like. I ask a small thing of you, a very, very small thing, and you refuse me!"

"Christ. I guess it is a small thing, isn't it?" She shook her head and sat up straighter. "And, you still haven't explained, to my satisfaction, what you mean by it."

With the sunset coming through the window, neither had seen me arrive. Any movement could draw an eye, but I slowly turned my head to look straight ahead and then sat perfectly still. There was no logic to it, but I knew from experience that people could feel when they were being watched.

"Get close. Get close means what get close means. Do I need a dictionary? Get to know him. What's he doing. Maybe why he's doing it?"

"Spy?"

"No. Not really." Pause. "Just be minimally observant and…get close. Be friendly. Can you do that? Can you be friendly?"

"Mitchell, please. You think he needs a friend?"

"Margot says he's virtually a recluse."

My date, Margot? Goes to church?

Just then a city bus drove by, and I missed an exchange.

By the time the bus passed and Fly re-synced the resonance, Mitchell was responding to something Julie had said. "Please. I don't want to know!"

"Isn't that fitting."

"I'm your spouse, not your master. That choice, should it be presented, would be yours. It's…it is…I mean, you know my position…At any rate, clearly it is not at all the same." I wondered what a flustered Mitchell Slade would look like and exactly what he was flustered about, but I didn't risk a look. "Julie, I reviewed the camera footage of him at the service. I know he was affected by my sermon."

My event. He thought it was about him.

"And I know he's going to want to be a part of what's going on at FVCC. And someone with his skills could be very helpful."

"What skills?"

"I'm certain he's former military."

"Huh. A little over six foot?"

"Yes. Why?"

There was a pause, when she went on her voice sounded less defensive and more curious. "What's so important about him having a PD? My father gave me his PD."

"Yes, but did you ever use your father's PD?"

"Of course not." Julie's annoyance was plain in her voice. "Who uses a PD?"

"Bill Slaughter did."

How did he know that? It had been in the papers at the time, yes. But the articles were about the novelty of a PD solving a crime, and I damn sure hadn't approved any photos. I was also absolutely certain I hadn't given Mitchell my full name.

Shit. The cameras in the church.

He must have googled my image and come across the public record with my PD license photo.

Julie gave another deliberate pause. "So?"

"So? Really? So? So a handful of days after the mayor murders a NuTree. Come on now. You, of all people, must be able to conjure up some reason why a PD suddenly popping into our congregation just might be cause for us, for *you*, to be concerned."

"What do you need me for? Why not just ask Margot?"

"Seriously? Have you talked to Margot? She's sweet, but not bright."

True enough, but I hadn't hired her to talk.

"Okay?" I could tell from his tone that he'd won the argument. "I think that's him at the curb…"

Quickly, I said, "Box, shut down Fly. Boot up Boxer for deployment."

A chirp, then, "Boxer ready."

I pulled Boxer from the instrument panel, slapped him onto my wrist, and scooped up my pie as I casually stepped out. I could see Mitchell through the glass as I strolled to the door. He gave me a congenial, "Fight with my wife? About you? What fight with my wife about you?" wave.

When he opened the door, Mitchell had his charismatic smile in place. "Bill! We missed you at lunch. Come in, please, come in."

"Yeah, sorry about that. I went for a walk by the river,

slipped, and got all muddy."

"Oh, I'm so sorry."

"Nothing a hot bath couldn't fix."

I turned to Julie as if noticing her sitting there for the first time.

Oh.

It was the 80's woman from the church lobby. My mouth went dry. Her blue dress was below the knee in a contemporary, loose-fitting cut that made her look several sizes bigger and negated the effect of her large breasts and small waist.

She stood and stepped to me with hand extended. "Hi, I'm Julie Mitchell."

I had to clear my throat. "Mrs. Slade. Pleased to see you."

"Mrs. Slade?" She laughed.

My heart literally skipped a beat. Her hand was impossibly soft. Physically, she was as unappealing as I remembered her, but there was no denying the attraction.

"Where did you find this fine gentleman, Mitchell?" she asked.

Mitchell laughed his convivial laugh. "He called on the We Missed You line."

Mentally, I shrugged. If the Slades chose to move on and ignore Bill, painter-at-large, I wasn't going to dissuade them. There was no reason to think Mitchell knew about it, or to assume Julie would remember me from that short encounter.

"Really? But you haven't been to a FVCC service before, have you?"

Had she emphasized *service*? "Not to a service, but I did bring a dish to pass. Cherry pie."

"How lovely! Let me put it in the kitchen." Julie accepted the pie and made her way past Mitchell to the kitchen.

I shot a glimpse at her ass as she walked away.

Okay, maybe her breasts are a bit too pendulous, and her waist far too tiny, but that *is a nice ass.*

Like Dad said, if women really knew what men were thinking, they'd walk around slapping us every five seconds.

I turned my attention to the pastor. "Mitchell, this is a fine home. Thank you for your evite."

"Well, isn't that refreshing?" The smile never wavered.

"Nobody's ever thanked you before?"

"Calling me Mitchell. Most people call me Pastor Slade." In my periphery, over Mitchell's left shoulder, I saw Julie's head half-in half-out of the kitchen entry.

"I'm nothing if not a breath of fresh air, Mitchell."

He laughed again. "Indeed you are."

I really did not like this fucker.

He motioned to the living room. "Please. Sit down."

CHAPTER 17 – SEEING

Dinner passed easily. I didn't try to shock them into revealing anything, or even ask how they felt about NuTrees, and dislike him though I did, there was no denying that Mitchell really was an excellent conversationalist.

We ate in the dining area just off the kitchen on a beautiful, darkly-stained hardwood table. I wondered if Mitchell felt about this table the way I felt about my floors.

Dinner was a hearty Irish stew: chunks of tender lamb, carrots, and peas, covered in a blanket of buttery mashed potatoes with a thin, baked-crisp crust. The stew was served with plenty of steaming, fresh sourdough bread to run through the gravy.

The Oil Crisis and the Blight might not have been good for the globe, but it had done wonders for diets. Nothing could justify the cost of transporting goods, so every community needed its own local farms. Which is how farmers and herders, the majority of whom were part of the Great Urban Migration out of cities and back to the country, earned the type of cash they did inside their hugely expensive geodesic domes.

As it turned out, Mitchell was a long-suffering Cubs fan. He listened with apparent enthusiasm as I retold some of my road stories with Dad that I hadn't told in a long time. He loved the one about the drunken fans in that hillbilly town Cincinnati.

Mitchell didn't fool me. I knew pornography when I saw it, and I knew Mitchell was… A douche? No. He really hadn't done or said anything inappropriate

Snake oil salesman? No. I never felt like he was trying to sell me.

Really, I should've liked him. We had a lot in common, and he seemed to like me. But none of that fazed me. For no good reason, I didn't like him. But what the hell? I might as well have a good time. And I'd been to enough officers' dinners to know how to bullshit my way through this meal to my own amusement.

I all but ignored Julie. And I never stopped thinking of her.

Truth was, she made my hands go sweaty. I couldn't look at her. Every time we made eye contact, I could only hold it a moment before I looked away like she'd caught me ogling her. Which she had.

There was no lying to myself—I was attracted. The question was what to do with it in the context of going to church on Marvin's dime to investigate the murder of his lover. Her being married might give me pause, but not after what Fly had heard.

So I babbled. Not at all how I would've usually handled this dinner.

"… that's how, at fourteen, I ended up driving my Dad's car like a bat outta hell through the badlands outside of Dallas, Texas."

Mitchell laughed. "That's insane. What a great story!"

I looked at Julie.

When I was telling my stories, I'd only glanced at her. I wasn't studiously ignoring her, still the monologues definitely were given in Mitchell's direction.

But I'd heard her voice.

As I told the stories, I relaxed into a pattern of telling *him* the story to hear *her* sigh, or gasp, or laugh—often, very often, laugh. I got into it.

How long had it been since I'd talked like this? And in this volume? Amazingly, I was genuinely enjoying myself.

But then I finished the story about Dallas, and when I looked at Julie, I knew exactly why I didn't like Mitchell. *He never sees me.* Not how I knew Julie was seeing me with those incredibly green eyes.

I could hear her pulse accelerate.

The slight flaring of her nostrils.

Her barely audible gasp.

It was the moment where we saw each other.

We held eye contact for a heartbeat longer.

Bill, fuck Fly. That woman is as into you as you are her.

And then I was back to talking to Mitchell with my own pulse thrumming in my ears.

I pushed the plate with the remnants of my cherry pie away. "Mitchell," I wiped phantom crumbs from the corners of my mouth and put my linen napkin on my plate. "This has been great. Thank you."

Now was the time. If there was a reason Mitchell had brought me here, now was the time for him to show his hand.

He put his own napkin down. "I had a great time. Thank you so much for the fantastic stories."

"It was cool to tell them again, so thank *you* for listening."

Julie laughed behind me. By its timbre, the edged implication, I knew she was laughing at Mitchell. We both knew that, just like he never really saw me, he hadn't really been listening. Yes, he'd heard, but he wasn't listening.

I smirked.

Mitchell's smile froze for an instant. "Of course!"

"I really should go. Julie." I turned to her and offered my hand. When she took it, like in the church, I was again struck by the urge to feel her lips on my skin. "Thank you for letting me ramble on like that."

She shook my hand, softly this time. "Bill," she said, and bless me if she didn't blush just a little. "It was a treat."

Mitchell put his hand on my shoulder. "Let me walk you out." I opened my hand and immediately missed the feel of Julie.

Mitchell opened the door for me. "Thanks again. We'll see you Sunday, right?"

"Yeah, could be."

"Great." He waved and joked, "Watch out for the congestion taxes." Everybody hated those damn taxes.

I walked down the drive to my car, expecting at any moment for Mitchell to call out my name. "*Oh, and Bill, just one more thing…*" It didn't happen.

Then I was in my car.

Nothing. That was weird.

"Oh my Gawd! That was a greeeaat dinner! You gained nearly a pound since you've been gone."

I laughed. Fuckin' GPS givin' me shit. "Take me home." I always ate too much when I was nervous.

Maybe I'd misread Mitchell?

Julie. I closed my eyes and wondered what kind of underwear she might have had on at dinner and how good it would look crumpled up on my bedroom floor.

My congestion meter *cha-ching*ed. "Really?" Congestion at this time was a highly improbable event. I reached for my one-hitter when it *cha-ching*ed again.

I put the one-hitter away.

Two blocks from home, it happened again.

There was no doubt; I was being tailed. I toggled my windshield to show the road behind me. Nothing there. They must be on an adjacent or parallel street.

What idiot tails someone so closely that their congestion meter goes off?

An idiot who didn't have a congestion meter. Or had it turned off, maybe because they didn't have to pay municipal congestion taxes. Like, say, a Federal employee.

Shit was piling up.

Mitchell knew Margot. I was infatuated with the pastor's wife, and she with me. And a Feddy was tailing me.

I pulled into the garage. My car's battery must've been low, because as soon as I got out, the car immediately jacked itself into the floor plug for a recharge.

I left the garage door open and waited. No car passed.

Tonight was a good night to stay in and say hi to Margot.

CHAPTER 18 – DATE NIGHT

Initially, my service said Margot wasn't available. Well, first they put me on hold for a full ten minutes to check her availability. *Then* they said she wasn't available.

At a lower price bracket, I could've seen it. But for what I paid for Margot, she had Gottdamm better be available when I called. I made this point to Suniti, along with a not-very-subtle hint concerning my long-term patronage and the ready availability of competitive services in the area.

Suniti did a jig around giving me a straight answer, then put me on hold again. Which, of course, I just loved.

I was working up a good head of steam that a full bowl of Purple Haze couldn't have knocked down when Suniti finally came back. "Well, uh, it seems all is arranged?"

"Are you asking me or telling me, Suniti?"

"All is fine. Please give…uh, someone will be there in forty-five minutes?"

"Someone? You mean Margot, right?"

There was a momentary pause before she responded. "Yes. Certainly. It will be Margot there."

"Forty-five minutes? You bringing her here on a slow boat from China?"

"Oh, Mr. Bill, you always make me laugh," she twittered

nervously.

"Discon."

All right, so I had some time to kill, which was convenient since it was past time Mr. Somers and I had a talk. "Box, call the Hilton Inn and ask for Clyde Somers. Vid off."

Chirp. "Connected."

"Hello?"

"Hey, Clyde. It's Bill, from The Flame."

"Oh, sure. I'd given up on you calling."

"Oh ye of little faith. How 'bout some lunch tomorrow?"

"I don't see why not."

"Great. I'll box my deets over to your room."

"How's 11:30 work for you?"

"Fine by me. See you tomorrow."

"See you."

Okay, so now I had forty-three minutes to kill. I probably should've been strategizing about what to do when I talked to Clyde, but I had nothing. I didn't know his service designation. Hell, I didn't even hundred percent know why he was in town, but it had to be about the NuTree and Frank.

What to ask Margot was simple, and, as her customer, I felt I had significant pull. Dates with bad ratings from customers didn't stay in the dating pool long.

For me, Margot, and other women like her, were never more than a service. Some made the pretense of calling it a more honest alternative to dating a stranger, and if both parties were willing—for a price—you could exclusively date, or even marry, a woman from a dating service. It wasn't that I had a bad time, but I wasn't some doll-eyed kid who'd fall for his service. I didn't love my plumber, or my doctor, and I didn't love my dates.

Especially dates who spy.

What could Margot say? No matter what it was, I intended this to be the last time Margot, Suniti, and I met.

I thought of smoking some more, but no. I was marginally stoned enough right now to be relaxed. Definitely not enough time for poker.

I walked past the now only-warm cast iron stove and into the kitchen. I fixed up a Dagwood-sized sandwich that, given my recent meal, I shouldn't have been hungry for.

Dinner at the Slade's had been fine, but I was fucking bored. I decided a small hit would go with the sandwich.

I filled a glass chillum I kept in the kitchen junk drawer and sparked it. Then, like any good bachelor, I stood at the kitchen counter to eat my sandwich.

"Box, news on fridge."

The fridge door blinked to life.

I had time to kill. "Click through, please."

Box flipped through the stations at two-and-a-half second intervals, including ten twenty-four-hour sports stations and seven of the twenty-four-hour news networks. Box knew to speed-flip all the theatre, cinema, shopping, pet, and social networks—featuring such hard-hitting stories as which scientist was dating which diva. All channels included a Dark Star Countdown in the top-left corner. It seemed silly to keep throwing that in our faces when nobody even knew if they were still alive.

Even with the heavy censoring, I was a quarter of the way through the sandwich before the fridge got to the Chicago NBS outlet showing the local news.

I mumble, "Stop," around a mouth full of sandwich. I swallowed some and squirreled the rest into a cheek. "Replay from beginning." Box presented the animated Dark Star Countdown screen while it found the NBS server and the link to this newscast.

I pulled a Coke from the fridge as the newscast began.

Local news wasn't my thing—way too much personal drama, and I had enough of that in my own life. Box would've pinged me if any news of high direct relevance had come up, but it would be good to catch up on the general state of things.

The lead was the big to-do about the approval and pending signing of the Fourth Data Pipeline, this one to America's great allies in the Africa Nations. America would've starved in the early Blight years if not for African food support. In return,

America repaid them with a technological Marshall Plan and brought them into the twenty-first century. All my military ops into Europe had started from some base in Africa. And now, trillions of dollars later, they were ready to be full technology partners.

I'd run my share of missions supporting AN allies. There were good people there. I was sure this was a big day for them.

Twenty minutes into the telecast, the NuTree death was the first story after the sports, the spot reserved for top suburban items. The NBS reporter who'd covered Naperville and Aurora since forever, Jake Westerburg, stood in front of the Naperville police building and said nothing of note.

The NuTree was paid for with monies from the city's disaster relief fund so as not to impact the existing NuTree budget, replacement was on its way, and blah. The only thing useful from the entire newscast was that the weather should be nice for the next week. The reporter didn't even give an honorary mention of the dear old mayor's death.

"Box, mute TV. Google two queries. First, all words, any order: Naperville NuTree death. Second, all words, any order: Naperville mayor suicide but exclude words from the first query."

Chirp.

"Sort values." I took a big swig of Coke. "Ahh. Eliminate all results with hits for both queries." I burped.

Chirp.

"Okay. Give me the rounded totals for both instructions."

"First query results: one hundred and twenty thousand. Second query results: two."

"Two?"

"Confirmed."

"How many stories contained results for both queries?"

"Fifteen thousand."

"For the two mayor only hits, were they eprint or media?"

"Eprint."

"Post results on fridge."

I supposed it made sense that the mayor's death was linked

to the NuTree's death. But only two stories directly about the mayor? And what? Only about one percent of all stories even mentioned the mayor's suicide.

The two articles turned out to be his obituary and a local story in the *Naperville Sun* about his publicly known life and times. Less than useless. *Is the news of the mayor being suppressed?*

My key question going into this was? Who killed the mayor? But I'd replaced that with: Who was using the mayor's death as cover for the NuTree murder?

And Moe had deflated that question when he assured me the NuTree was done in by Frank on his way out.

The NuTree had snapped in an unnatural way.

Dammit. I wish I knew where Frank had been coming from when he turned off his GPS and drove off the road.

The doorbell rang.

It was now almost an hour since I'd first called Suniti's, but I'd been too distracted to get impatient. At any rate, certainly this would be the last time I saw Margot. I'd been wanting to try that Markoe's Market anyway.

When I opened the door, of all the things I thought I could expect to see there, none of them was Julie.

CHAPTER 19 – PROTOCOL LEVEL

She stood there in an overcoat.

Oh my God. What was it with this woman? I didn't know, but it was electric. My heart was in overdrive—

She pushed against me while stepping in and shutting the door behind her.

—and my dick instantly erect. "Julie? What are y—?"

She kissed me. Her lips were as soft as advertised. My hands rested on her hips and tingled where they touched her.

"Margot's not coming."

"Margot who?"

We kissed again, and—because being with her was my only concern—I scooped her into my arms and carried her to my bedroom, keeping at bay awkward silence and leaving cock-blocking questions unspoken.

She shouldn't have been here.

I don't care.

She was married.

I do not fucking care.

Her mouth was warm and wet and enthusiastic, and she was light and firm in my arms.

That's all I care about.

I laid her down on my bed.

When I opened her coat, her perfume washed over me. She wore nothing but a bright yellow lace bra and panties. Lace panties helped immensely with pushing logic to the side.

I undid the front snap on her bra and lowered my mouth to her nipple.

And her voice.

I did everything to hear that voice. It was the same as telling stories to Mitchell, but my tongue on her breast and my fingers on her clitoris were talking.

Later, with her hips locked against mine, her breathless, "Oh my God. Oh my God!" cries made me shiver.

This was what it was meant to be. I'd forgotten.

Her voice. Her hips. I hadn't touched my heart in so long. Her eyes. Her.

I lay on my back, breathing more heavily than an enhanced man should. I smiled in the same effortless way I'd laughed earlier on that muddy river bank.

Julie rolled onto her side to look at me, then used a fingernail to trace a figure eight around the two bullet scars on my abdomen.

"What?" she asked.

Those green eyes. "I feel…" I smiled. "I'm not sure how to say this, but I feel silly. Like a kid."

"What's funny about that?"

"Nothing." I settled my arm under her so she could rest her head on my chest. "I lived through my time in the military because I listened to my instincts. And now—why should I stop listening to them now?"

"Ah, that bitch, logic. Where is she? I'll kick her ass."

We laughed. I thought about *danger-close* and shook my head.

"What?"

"Nothing."

She wrinkled her brow.

"I was just thinking about, well…" I laughed again. "If you really want to know, I was thinking about HUCOs."

"What's a hew-koh?"

"Heads-up Contacts."

"Oh. You mean contact readers?"

"Sort of, but much more advanced and interactive. With a direct…um, they gave me some extra wiring."

"Why would you think of HUCOs now? Don't you have better things to be thinking of?"

"It isn't easy to explain… Do you ever write? I mean with a writing instrument."

"Like an old-fashioned pen?

"Exactly."

"Not often. Special occasions."

"When you do write, do you have to constantly remind your fingers to grip the pen?"

"No."

"Now imagine that you had a stream of data as necessary to your survival as holding onto a pen is to writing, and as much a part of what you do to survive as your unconscious use of your muscles is to holding a pen."

"That's what HUCOs were like?"

"For me, yeah."

"Didn't anyone else have HUCOs?"

"Some did, but… I don't know how to explain this…"

"Start simple," she said with a quick shrug that did wonderfully bouncy things to other—.

"Bill! HUCOs?"

"I was getting to it. Did you ever know anyone, maybe a parent or grandparent, who was in a car accident?"

"My mom was in one when she was in college. She said she saw her life flash before her eyes."

"Exactly. Okay, so that sense of time compressing and slowing down, of being able to notice minute details… I could do that."

"During combat?"

"Yes, but even before the firefight. I…"

"You had an intuition?"

"Exactly! And HUCOs enhanced it."

"You knew things. With absolute certainty, you knew. Even

though you couldn't know. So you acted."

"That's right!"

"But then it got very intense during combat."

"You're freakin' me out a little."

She laughed, and sat up.

"No, seriously. How— ?"

"There's nothing new under the sun."

"There's nothing… What's that mean?"

"I could show you, but I left my Box at home."

"Use mine."

"Really?" She asked it quickly and quietly, like she was trying not to scare away the answer.

I sat up to kiss her. People cohabitated for years before they shared Boxes.

I knew it was impulsive. But it didn't feel impulsive.

It felt right.

"Box."

"Online."

"Recognize Julie."

"Recognized."

"Allow access."

"Protocol level?"

"Family."

Julie's eyes widened. "Bill?"

"Confirm?"

I reached for her hand.

"Confirmed."

Julie kissed me firmly—

"Did you—?"

—and pushed me back onto the bed.

"— but Box?"

"Later."

Gottdamm, she had world class lips.

CHAPTER 20 – GLAD

Later we sat on the bed and snacked on some apples and cheese. She wore my pajama top and sat cross-legged with the sheet over her legs. Julie laughed around a wedge of apple. "Are you saying you have faith?"

"In my instincts."

"Everything happens for a reason," she said hurriedly "Haven't you ever felt guided, or directed?" She moved the tray off the bed onto the night stand.

"Of course."

"Of course?"

"Sure. In the military..."

She laughed again with no apple in the way and this time my heart skipped a beat and my dick perked up. "No," she said, "Maybe it would be something you wouldn't even have realized until you looked back on it. How things just seemed to go a certain way that led to something you could never have predicted, or maybe wouldn't even have chosen for yourself, but you're glad in the long run, in hindsight, that things happened the way they did."

"You mean fate?"

"Something like that, yes. Have you felt guided by fate? Like what if there hadn't been that early arctic blast that diverted that ship to Louisbourg?"

"You saying the Blight saved New York City?"

She plucked a hair on my chest.

"You collecting souvenirs?"

"You know what I mean."

I thought of Sullivan and Chandler and all the odd shit that had led to us being at that place and time. "Maybe. Anyone who's seen combat has had close calls. But one time, we were on a series of missions, and it was one mess-up after the next. We got bad intel, really bad intel, messed up directions, down communications—you name it and it happened. On the last in this series of missions, my gun jammed. And this kind of gun, it was jam-proof. Some trillion rounds put through it in testing, in all kinds of conditions, and it never jammed." I stopped.

"What is it?"

"We were in the Ukraine. It was just my squad on the mission. We were supposed to be dropped, according to intel, in a very secluded area with just one road in and no way for the bad guys to be equipped with artillery. And my gun jammed, and I dropped down…"

In my mind, I was behind that slab of rock, crouched below the rim of the ditch we stood in. Sullivan looked at me and yelled over the gun fire, "Hey, sir fucknuts, what're you doing down there?"

"My fucking rifle jammed," I slapped the side of my XR and pulled back on the action to try to cycle rounds. This wasn't supposed to happen. They didn't even train on us on how to fix this.

Sullivan yelled over to Chandler, "His gun jammed!"

"Who else could jam the jam-proof gun?"

A bullet smacked into the rock just above my head. I heard the whizz of the shards before they ricocheted off my helmet. I could see the glint of the bullet casing in the breach, and then I heard two quick, almost simultaneous popping sounds on either side of me, I could smell fried flesh and boiled blood, I heard the wet squish as their limp bodies flopped into the mud. I looked past the bullet and around the rifle to Sullivan and

Chandler.

And because I was in *danger-close*, it all happened in a moment of acute clarity. I saw, heard, smelt it all. Every droplet of blood. All of it in exquisite detail.

Julie's hand was on mine, the cool sheets on my back.

I kept going. "In my brain, I knew that it was an Anti-Personnel Microwave because I could see that their guns were unaffected. And I knew it had to be cannon-sized to hit more than one soldier and that APM cannons had a significant recharge time." I jerked back on the action and the jammed bullet spun out of the breach. I stood, and half a klik down range I could see the cannon that intel said couldn't be there. "I snapped the rifle to my shoulder and synced the red dot sites to my HUCOs." I looked at Julie. "And I screamed." I looked away. "I loved those men. Like I could never feel towards another human being ever. Not in that way."

After a moment, Julie put her incredibly soft hand on my cheek and brushed it dry.

"And?"

"APM emitters are fragile, so I took that out, then…the operators."

"Why didn't your friends see the cannon?"

"They didn't have HUCOs to filter out the foliage."

"Why didn't they have them?"

"Not everyone had them because HUCOs aren't shielded. An EMP grenade could take out all non-shielded electronics for one to five minutes. So a few officers had HUCOs but most didn't."

We were quiet. I turned my head towards Julie. "But you did?" she asked.

I nodded.

"You ducked when they didn't?"

I nodded.

"Your jam-proof gun made you duck, and you lived and they didn't?"

I nodded. "I ducked when nobody else around me had any cause to."

"I'm glad you did. Aren't you?"

I closed my eyes and thought of my nightmare of the grotesque sight and smell of my brothers' bodies. Then I opened my eyes to see Julie, "At this moment, I definitely am."

"But it isn't always like that?"

"No. There are times. The docs call it all kinds of things." I laughed but there wasn't much mirth to it. "I never thought any of that shit would apply to me. Not to guys like me who trained so hard, were there with a purpose, with no regrets for our service selection. But, yeah. There are times …"

"But not now," and she kissed me with those soft lips. I was kissing a dream.

Sometime later, Julie collapsed onto her stomach as I flopped beside her, onto my back and off my knees. I gotta admit; I was ready for some sleep. We laid there quietly for a few.

"Bill."

"Hmmm?" My eyelids were heavy.

"Mitchell owns Suniti's."

That woke my brain up, but my body was still not going anywhere soon. I knew Slade knew Margot, but I thought it was as a congregant. "The pastor owns a dating parlor?" I asked lazily.

"Not directly. Not under his own name, that is. He knows I know, but he doesn't know that Suniti and I are friends from high school. He owns it through a corporation."

"Corporations have taxes they need to pay. There's always a paper trail."

"He's listed as one of many owners with a wide range of investments. He just takes a very discreet personal interest in this one business. He uses the girls to find out things about people he's interested in."

I didn't want to, but since I wasn't falling asleep now, my obligations compelled me to ask, "Why do you boo NuTrees?"

"I don't think God wants the world to have NuTrees."

That took me aback. "Why? You think God wants humanity to die?"

Quietly, she said, "NuBorns?"

"What?"

"6n10. Right?"

Six years and ten months. The amount of time it took to reject the changes made through DNA doctoring. "Right."

Was there some other yet-to-be-defined master blueprint? Or perhaps there was some not-yet-quantified response to environmental stimuli? The doctors and scientists and their super computers didn't know and couldn't fix it. Whatever it was, it was something all of humanity shared. And when it happened, when the NuBorn body had their 6n10 "birthday," the changes made were horrific.

Parent after grieving parent lined up at abortion clinics around the country. Lines out the doors. Devastating images of grief. Repeated around the world at the same time.

My parents were done with kids when NuBorns came along, but that was no immunity.

In the early days, before they knew about 6n10, before they legalized euthanasia, it was hell. Because of the surge in popularity, many, so many children hit 6n10 at nearly the same time. At any time, in any place, a change could and did strike. Parents who got abortions were the lucky ones. Suddenly every doctor in America performed free abortions. Better death now than a NuBorn death. But no euthanasia, at least not right away. Not until 6n10 was conclusive. Out of the womb: murder. In the womb: abortion. Such were the vagaries of law. Finally they approved Euthanasia Kits for use at 6n9. And that did help.

But early on... Nobody who lived through that extinction could ever forget it. The world was forced to watch its children endure a brutal metamorphosis into grotesque creatures with mounds of crippling muscle, swollen craniums with multiple sets of eyes, or worse. Far, far worse. The world grieved the promise lost in a generation of beautiful, incredibly bright, and talented children.

"What's the date on NuTrees?" Julie asked.

"There is no date."

"How do we know?" she asked softly.

"They tested."

"Like they did with the babies? Like they did with my sister."

I hugged her. Even after all this time… I could never forget. Nobody ever forgot. "I'm sorry."

She nodded.

"Being trees makes a difference, right? At a minimum, they don't go through puberty."

She sat up and wiped her eyes. "But they do evolve. What if, not now, but in a generation or even two, something changes? And suddenly NuTrees are extinct."

"I don't know. Global ice ball, maybe? But we know that if we don't have NuTrees, we'll freeze."

"Yes, but right now we can do something about it."

"Like?"

"Learn to live differently. If we use NuTrees and they die suddenly, there will be no warning. Life will end. We shouldn't be playing God just because our vanity tells us to think we know better, that it's safe."

"The cold from the Blight killed the insects that caused the deforestation. So even if NuTrees don't make it for forever, they only need to be around long enough for real trees to grow back."

She sighed lightly. "I know. You're right. But I know it's wrong to pretend to be God. And that the last time we tried to do it, well, it didn't turn out so good."

I was quiet a moment. "I respect your principled position. Is it okay if we agree to disagree?"

She flashed me a smile and gave me a soft kiss. "I'd like that."

"Do you know anything about that NuTree?"

"Of course not. I am too fragile to be sent to Mogadishu."

"The mayor was a big NuTree supporter. Do you know

anyone who may have resented him for that?"

"No. Not at all."

Shit. I stared up at the ceiling. Julie put her head back on my chest and draped a leg over me. She began slowly tracing patterns on my chest and stomach. Mitchell owns a house of prostitution. Call me old-fashioned, but—legal or not—that dooesn't seem very pastor-ish.

"There's something you should know about me and NuTrees."

Her tone told me that this was not just personal, but private. "Okay."

"I–I've never even told Mitchell this," she paused, then went on, "It was three years ago, about the same time Mitchell began withdrawing into his non-church businesses. It was one of those rare, hot summer days. I was lying in the back on the hammock. And—I'm not sure how to say this, but…I felt compelled. Spoken to. Convicted by God."

"God spoke to you?"

"Of course not literally, but I did feel it. I felt God tell me to protest NuTrees. Do you believe in God?"

"You're not going to try to save me are you?"

"No," she smiled, pure and genuine and full of knowing who I was, "that's your job."

"Julie, to me, it's just mother nature out there."

"Would mother nature guide you?"

"Are you asking if mother nature jammed my gun…"

"What I've found is something that is a truth, for me, and that is this: God is love. And God loves me. Is actively in love with me. Helping me through my life. Guiding me."

"I believe it is true for you, but I don't see it. Not in my life."

"That's okay. It's my truth. Not yours." She smiled. "My belief is that if you want to see your true religion, you have to live it. You won't find your truth in someone else's religion."

"I …"

"Are you going to ask me about us?"

"Yes."

"Bill," a tear escaped the sea of her eyes, "I—you and I..." I reached over and brushed the hair off her ear. "I know I only know a little about you. I don't care. I'm married. I don't care. Adultery is a sin. I don't care. Should Mitchell find out about this, our divorce would be certain, and I don't care."

I thought of how lonely she must have been these last three years. I thought of how life had carried us both to this bed at this time, and how from different paths we had arrived at the same place in life: a place where logic was not a factor and all we cared about was being here with this person.

I kissed her. When I tasted salty tears, I pulled away. I wasn't expecting the tears to be mine.

I held Julie close. We might never have anything else ever again, we might never have anything beyond this moment, but we had this moment. And we didn't care.

This was our time.

This was the living I had fought and killed for.

When I opened my eyes, it was daylight. Julie was gone.

I'd   slept   without   dreaming.

CHAPTER 21 – PITCHERS AND CATCHERS

Julie had left a note. All it said was, "Romans 8:28."

I asked Box to look it up. "And we know that in all things God works for the good of those who love him, who have been called according to his purpose."

Fate. God. Things any soldier always thought about, and avoided thinking about.

"...and that's when I told him, Hey, get yer own damn sheep!" Clyde Somers laughed at his mountain training story.

Lunch with Clyde at 11:30 AM the next day had come early. I'd slept until almost 11.

"Hey, did you hear? I told him, 'Getcher own damn sheep!'"

"Oh yeah, that's a good one."

The restaurant at the Hilton Inn didn't make much of an effort at being unique, conforming almost entirely to the hotel restaurant cookie cutter mold. Considering the prices for a room at this joint, I would've thought they could come up with something that didn't emanate kitsch. There wasn't a scrap of real wood, or even bamboo, in the entire place. All cheap non-oil-based polymers lit by equally tacky, too-bright lighting. And it was still much better than the Sheraton Days.

"Shit, buddy, where's your head?" He rubbed his hands together. "Let's order."

"Yeah, sure." The menu was a dull digital hand-held with no animations, haptics, or enhancements of any sort.

Clyde motioned, and the waiter appeared at our table. "May I take your order?"

Clyde gestured for me to go ahead.

An old high school buddy grew the beef served here. "I'll have the porterhouse."

"For lunch?" Somers asked. "Somebody's looking to work up an appetite. Or maybe you had some exercise last night?" Somers gave me a wink.

Was he dropping hairpins? Since I was at lunch with him, that didn't seem necessary. Was this Somers's way of telling me he knew about last night?

My congestion meter had pinged twice on the way here. The dumbass tail with his meter turned off was good enough to avoid being spotted and was starting to get expensive. If it was Somers last night, then who had followed me here today? It wouldn't have been Somers. It made no sense for him to follow me to where he knew I was going.

I'd almost canceled the lunch, and not just because it was a rush to be here on time. Talking to Somers felt like a dead end. I didn't give a shit about the NuTree, and I was sure that was why this Feddy was in town.

Still—there was a murderer out there, and I had zero idea where to go for my next clue. When in doubt, leave no stone unturned.

"So I never asked, but what brings you to Naperville?" I was here now. *So just eat and get the fuck outta here.*

"Oh, you know, shit I shouldn't say."

"Pretty dull shit, I'm sure."

"If it's work-related, Congress legally requires it to be dull shit."

"Oh really?" I was no socialite, but I've got a gay cousin, and I'd known gay men in the military. Outside the context of The Flame, absolutely nothing about Somers felt gay.

"Yeah. Typical Federal interest, Homeland Security stuff but it's still nice to be here."

If he wasn't gay, what had he been doing at The Flame? I had a fuzzy-germ-in-a-petri-dish sized thought. "In what way nice?"

Hi lips curled into a smile when he said, "Great scenery."

Was he at The Flame because *I* was at The Flame? "Scenery?"

"Yeah. You know what I mean, right?" He winked at me, again.

The wink was... Okay. I couldn't act, but that didn't mean I didn't recognize bad acting when I saw it. Somers was as straight as the equator.

If he wasn't here for an assignation, why *was* he here? Holy shit. Who was pumping whom for information?

"I thought fun with the locals was discouraged?" What information was he looking to get from me? I didn't know shit about shinola.

"But not verboten."

Our drinks arrived. Coke for me, beer for him.

Let's try something different with Somers. "So you've met someone here?"

"I met you," he said in, what I could only assume, was his best effort to be charming. It was as seductive as cork board.

"Ooh, Clyde. Where do Feddys go for training to be this gay? I mean, you're so obviously gay. Do they make you wear butt plugs before coming to the gay paradise of Naperville?"

Somers adjusted, and his leather seat creaked. "Ha. Good one, Bill, but—uh, no. Butt plugs are for the weak." Somers picked up his beer.

"You mean you like to have your asshole torn up?"

"What?"

"What do you mean 'what'?"

"Hold on." A bit of beer slopped over the rim of Somers's glass as he hastily put it back on the table. "If anything's happening here, I'm pitching. Let's get that clear."

"That isn't very gay of you."

"Gay? I'm as gay as, uh…"

"Oh, Clyde," I said with my best imitation of Marvin's

voice and coy smile. "You're not just gay. *You* are definitely queer."

Somers's face turned red.

Why, I do believe Mr. Somers really wasn't ready for someone to think he's so convincing in his role.

Our waiter brought our salads. Clyde put his head down and dug into his, obviously welcoming the break from the conversation.

I fished around for some anchovies in my Caesar salad. Clyde wasn't gay. So he wasn't at The Flame by chance. He had either followed me there or knew I was going to be there.

Why would the Feddys care about lil' ol' me? Certainly not because I was investigating the mayor.

It had to be because of the NuTree angle. Right?

Maybe Somers hadn't intended on approaching me at The Flame. Maybe, not being a local, he hadn't known how "queen for the day" gay The Flame was. Then he realized how much he stuck out and that the only way for him to blend in was to introduce himself.

"Good salad, Clyde?"

Clyde stopped spearing salad with his fork and looked up. "What's that?"

"You seem really into that salad. I can only hope you suck cock the way you chow salad."

"Uh..."

I put my fork down and pushed my plate to the side. "You don't suck cock, do you?"

He gave a wan smile. "That's right. Not my thing, man. I'm a hundred percent pitching only type of guy."

"You're not gay, are you, Clyde?"

Deliberately, he swallowed the food in his mouth, put his fork on his plate, and pushed it to the side. Our waiter swooped in and picked up both our salad plates.

Somers's whole demeanor changed. The faux-mirth was gone. His eyes focused, and his face was now a jaw-clenched scowl. Gone was the awkward attempt at being a flibbertigibbet. He put one hand on top of the other on the table and sat rock still.

I continued. "Did you really think going to The Flame made me gay? Didn't you have any background on me?"

"I had plenty of background." Somers clearly didn't like being outted from his cover. He rattled off some quick biographical facts about my life. Then he gave a complete listing of my military deployments. My *classified* military deployments.

First Maidenhead and now Somers. Was my military record this Spring's required reading?

His reaction told me a lot about Somers. He cared more about his ego and personal success, or indignation, than about his mission's success.

"But you're not here to see me, are you? So, sweetie, why don't you tell me something I *don't* know? Like, why are you here in Naperville?"

"I'm not obligated to answer that. But, of course, the government wouldn't waste my valuable time with you. Why the fuck would anyone anywhere care about some washed-up, pot-soaked ex-GI."

"You trying to hurt my feelings, Somers?" I didn't care what Somers thought of me. I cared that I had him talking. *Now give me something I can use.* "All I know is that you showed up right after the mayor's suicide and the NuTree's murder. So if you're not here for the mayor, it has to be the NuTree."

No answer.

He dabbed at the corners of his mouth with the napkin from his lap, then dropped the napkin onto the table.

Cleaning yourself was one of the most obvious tells in poker. Players generally didn't have a napkin, but they would still put a hand to their mouth or nose, trying to hide discomfort or control the environment. I was zeroing in on something here.

"I've read the mayor's obit," I continued, "and I've known about him for a long time. There isn't anything of note there."

The waiter brought my steak and his rotisserie chicken. My food smelled divine. My stomach rumbled but my gaze never left Clyde's and his never left mine. Locking eyes like this was another effort toward control—by focusing on one point he could be less distracted and get his mental processes back in order.

After the waiter left, Clyde stood up.

"So soon?" As in *before you've had a chance to tell me something that will help find Frank's killer.*

"As a reward, I'll say this. You wouldn't find anything interesting about the mayor until recently." He about-faced and started to walk away.

"Why are you tailing me?"

He stopped. "Bill, you dumb fucker. We have ViSAR to do that shit." And he was gone.

Now that was smartly played. Well, not as smart as not saying anything, but that ship had sailed. At the end, Somers wasn't looking for smart. He was looking for the psychological upper-hand, to turn his fuck-up to his advantage. Trying to throw me off my game, to put me in my place.

I didn't like that the Feddy had such an interest in me, but it wasn't personal. It was for the same reason the chief knew; I was a now active asset in his field of operations. Of course he'd want to assess my involvement. Seems my line of questioning had confirmed for Somers that I wasn't there for the NuTree and, as soon as he knew that, he left. And on the way out, he had thrown me a mayoral crumb to keep me off the NuTree. *Nothing until recently…*

It seemed to confirm my thoughts about the mayor's community outreach program, but why would the Feddys be interested in Frank's program?

Whatever. I didn't care. As long as he stayed on his NuTree side of town and I stayed on my Frank Nelson side of town, all would be well between us.

Until recently… Of course! I laughed, pleased with my new clarity. Somers hadn't meant to be so literal, but he had given my investigation a direction. When in doubt, start at the beginning.

I had no idea how to find out, but the question I needed to

answer right now was, *Where did Frank come from before he drove to the river?*

CHAPTER 22 – CLYDE

If there was one thing Clyde Somers never doubted about himself, it was his patriotism. Whenever he spoke the word "patriot," he said it like an American. But in his head, Clyde Somers always pronounced with a short "a" like the British. And, undeniably, he was a patriot. If all gave some and some gave all, his decisions had led him to become the latter. A tab he was going to be forced to pay soon enough, but not before Bill lay dead at his feet.

The agent grimaced as he walked away and took the elevator back to his room.

He had been born in a small west Texas town and—the person he had been—took pride in being unflappably even-keeled. But Moe Coughlin was correct—this Somers had tripped over a most fragile precipice and was gripped by a madness that could remain hidden from people other than Moe only as long as it was tucked behind the mission: Terminate Bill Slaughter.

Somers had been revealed. And that was not supposed to have happened.

In his room, Somers sat stiffly on the edge of his bed.

It wasn't simply that failure was not acceptable for Clyde Somers. It was that his pathology could not tolerate it.

It was his insanity that had allowed Somers to succeed where so many others had failed, but of course Somers didn't see it as madness. No, it was simply this: control.

It was inconsequential that his actions wouldn't deter Bill from his investigation into the mayor. Or the NuTree. It didn't matter which. Though the white coat in town preferred it to be the mayor, Somers knew it only mattered that he continued to investigate.

No. The failure was personal.

Somers saw Bill as a smug asshole who had played him.

Clyde's body trembled, and the thing caged inside clamored for release. It made each fiber of every muscle quiver like a struck piano chord. Unseen by Somers, as his muscles vibrated, the faintest, foxfire of a sky-blue glow emanated from his exposed skin.

He gripped his wrist and glared at a spasmodic hand. "You are *my* tool." The spasms stopped, and the unnoticed glow disappeared.

Somers hadn't needed an excuse to murder Bill; it was simply the mission and nothing personal.

But not now.

Failure.

The word stung. Somers choked on the urge to smash his hotel window, drop the eight floors to the ground, run back to the restaurant, crush Bill's skull, and be mission complete. His leg muscles trembled and twitched.

No! They stopped. *Stay on mission.*

The white coats would fry him if he did that. While Somers did not know that the mission hid his insanity from most of the world, he was fully aware that being committed to eliminating Bill was the only thing stopping the white coats from vivisecting him to see why he had succeeded where others had not.

His birthday was coming and just before it did…it would be a time when scientists' threats would be meaningless.

Somers smiled.

If anyone else were to see that smile, they surely would run.

It was nothing less than the smile of a murderer. Should the old Clyde Somers from west Texas see that smile, he would have wept for what he had become, for the humanity he had lost.

Somers had volunteered for what the white coats had done, and his madness ignored that fact. He looked forward to giving the white coats some personal experiences to catalog with the animal they had given him.

Somers clenched his left fist and clicked his teeth shut to open the switch, then pushed his tongue against the toggle in the back of his front tooth to activate the micro-THz Toob there. His secure, personal ViSAR channel opened as retractable HUCOs slid from the top and bottom of his eyes to very faintly *snip* together.

Clyde made his report.

The response filled both HUCOs. "Beach" was all it said. The code word to remain on mission.

The HUCOs retracted. Clyde allowed himself a pleasant thought; he imagined Bill dead at his feet. *Maybe I'll dismember him first.*

A tremor he did nothing to stop ran through his muscles. He let his animal share in his maniacal obsession. With this report, Agent Clyde Somers knew the inevitability of Bill's death; he knew it as assuredly as he knew he was alive and not insane.

Somers's unflinching control of his body waivered. Without his say so, his jaw dropped slightly open and his breath came in quick, shallow pants. Sitting on the edge of his bed as he did, his madness now apparent for all to see, Agent Somers resembled a turn-of-century mental patient.

Clyde Somers was a patriot. He had given all. He intended to collect his dues. If he could recognize joy again, then he might say his anticipation was making him happy. But Somers clung to the real world by knowing only the mission. And that mission, to do what nobody before him could, was near completion. And then, then the white coats and he would talk without Somers living in fear of consequences.

Freedom was near.

Soon. Very soon.

Unseen, a faint, pale blue sheen emanated from his exposed skin.

He had decided; he was no longer just murdering Bill.

Clyde Somers was going to *enjoy* murdering Bill.

CHAPTER 23 – BLUFF

My steak had been delicious. Thick, bloody rare, and tender. I wished I'd had time to smoke a little before I ate it, but I'd gotten it into my head that delayed satisfaction would be a good thing, and had decided to be done with the second of my errands before smoking. I'd finished my steak at the hotel, but the steam from Clyde's chicken escaped the self-heating to-go bag next to me as I drove.

Hell, the bastard stuck me with the tab, so I wasn't going to let it go to waste.

The mayor had to be coming from somewhere. I couldn't imagine him bundling up to leave his house to drown in the freezing Fox River. There were easily a hundred more comfortable ways of checking out at home—I'd thought of seventy-eight.

And there had been no note. Now that I knew Frank had been murdered, a missing note was telling. If I wanted a murder to look like a suicide, I'd make damn sure the deceased left something pointing away from me. Especially when the suicide was so out of character. The murder couldn't have been premeditated.

A crime of passion? No. Marvin would have given me a heads-up on that front.

What's Julie doing now? I wondered how she had explained her night away from home.

"Box, can you find a ref for Julie Slade?"

Chirp. "Shall I request access to her social network?"

"No!" Not only did I not do all that bullshit myself, it would hardly be discreet for me to pop up on her grid.

Should I message? No. Julie already demonstrated that she wasn't shy about reaching out to me. *Let her make the next move.*

What would happen if I called Suniti for another visit from Margot? "Box, message Suniti and ask if Margot is available for another date. Like the *last* one, not the one before."

Chirp. Message sent.

I never was much for letting someone else take the lead.

What had I been thinking about before? "Black box! Right..."

I had to get the mayor's black box data. With the investigation ongoing, Officer Maroney wasn't going to fork that over unless I compelled him to do so. And I didn't have grounds for that.

I remembered that everyone except me only cared about the NuTree.

Of course! The NuTree was my in. Maroney didn't know what I did or didn't know.

I'd seen Army interrogators work like this. Assume knowledge that a detainee was worried the interrogator might know; a name, a place, something someone else had or hadn't said. I wasn't holding any cards, but an interrogation was like Texas Hold 'em: You play the player, not the cards.

"Box, look up the personal ref for Stan Maroney. Vid enabled. On windshield." The windshield showed the "ringing" Dark Star Countdown animation—8 years 254 days 4 hours—blocking my view of the road.

GPS piped up, "Whee. Look, ma, no hands!"

Fucking GPS.

Stan's face filled my windshield. "Citizen, why are you calling me on my personal reference?" He was in his squad car.

"Are you tailing me, Maroney?"

"What?"

"Never mind." That was a stupid question. While working as a PD, I was allowed to block all non-judicially approved access to my GPS data, so it wasn't impossible that the Naperville Police Department was following me. But no NPD squad car would register on my congestion meter.

"You called to ask a stupid question?"

"Box, please enable an official and secure PD record of this conversation. Officer Maroney, as an investigating Public Detective, I am requesting the mayor's black box data."

"On my personal ref? Request away! You know you have no right to personal information in an ongoing investigation."

"If either I or the NPD was investigating the mayor's death, you'd be right. However, I have evidence that the mayor is a material subject in my investigation into the murder of a NuTree."

"You're what?" The implications of that sunk in. Then more slowly, Stan said, "What evidence?"

"A statement from a Federal officer." If I amended my paperwork to include anything NuTree related, it would trigger a whole new level of Feddy scrutiny. How desperate is NPD be keep the NuTree out of my investigation? And I did have one other piece of solid information. "Was there anything unusual about the NuTree?" The expression on Stan's face froze. "Officer?"

"What's the Feddy's name?"

"Clyde Somers. With an O and one M." Would it be enough to carry the bluff?

Stan's face got Irish red. "Aw, fuck me." He said it quietly but sternly and, maybe, even a little sadly. "Don't you have someone else's job you can fuck with?"

"Fuck me? Is that proposition your official, on the record comment, Officer?"

Ah, if looks could arrest. "Turn it off, Bill."

"Box, discontinue and permanently delete."

Chirp.

"Okay, Stan. Recording off, and we're on our personal ref.

We're alone. Now, you can give me what I want, or I can file a formal PD request naming Clyde Somers and citing you as confirming the agent's involvement. You pick."

Stan buried his hands in his face. "Do you need all the data?"

I did feel a little sorry for him. "Don't be so crestfallen, Stan. I need just one thing." I paused. "What was the last destination on the mayor's GPS before he turned it off?"

Stan slapped his knee and looked away. With intense sincerity he said, "Oh, I am fucked."

I sat silently and let Stan apply his own pressure. I counted to a long twenty, then said, "Nobody will know. Where was he driving from?"

"Walk careful on this one."

"Where?"

"2520 South Central." He disconned.

"GPS, clear windshield." I winced as daylight flooded in.

GPS sang, "Here comes the sun!"

"GPS, twenty percent opaque on windows. Plot the course from 2520 South Central to where Frank Nelson's body was found. Display on windshield." The map grid sprung to life on the windshield with a pulsing trail from the address to the river. The two locations were just blocks away.

"Yaaay, Bill!" GPS cheered. Pom-poms rustled in the foreground as the car glided to the curb.

"Box, query: public records, 2520 South Central, Naperville, Illinois."

Chirp.

"Report."

"A private residence, owned by Stefan Maidenhead. Purchased—"

"Police Chief Maidenhead?"

"Confirmed."

"Box, new search: public records of municipal duty rosters. Any record of Police Chief Maidenhead's activities on the night of the mayor's suicide?"

Bloop. Failed search. "The police chief discontinued work at

5 PM." Whatever the chief had done with the mayor, it had been on his personal time.

"What's the next entry for the chief?"

"Next entry is 3:12 AM the following morning."

Probably when the chief had got the call about the mayor.

My   congestion   meter   *cha-ching*ed.

CHAPTER 24 – ALL THINGS GREEN

No car passed. Whoever they were, they were competent. If not for their oversight of the meter, I never would have made them.

2520 South Central. Maidenhead.

So this was why the chief had had a friendly chat with me at Moe's.

Now if I tried to play my PD card, the chief would fend off any question by claiming either that I needed a warrant to compel him to share Personally Identifiable Information, or that the information was now an ipso facto discovery and so not subject to a PD's request.

I didn't like him, but the chief was smarter and more capable than he let on behind that shtick of his, and he definitely did not like me. Never mind that I was actually trying to help people with my PD instead of using it as a status symbol.

"Gottdamm." I had a great piece of information and nothing I could do with it. I could bluff Maroney, but that shit wasn't going to fly with the chief.

"Continue previous route," I told GPS.

"Yea, shopping!"

For once, I agreed with her exuberance. It was time to give

Franco a visit.

The All Things Green Emporium hadn't always been *the* place to buy your marijuana. When I first started coming, it was nothing but a shed tacked onto the front of a greenhouse, but word had spread. A few High Times Golden Trophies, endorsements from the U.S. First-Person Shooter Champion and a couple of top-of-the-chart opera singers, and now Franco had himself a world class establishment. The corrugated metal shack had been replaced by a lushly-carpeted display room with real pine, shellacked a dark brown throughout.

I walked through the door and stopped a step in. I could feel all that wonderful THC wafting about next to me. The bouquet of it all.

Ah, *I love the smell of All Things Green!*

I hadn't started out to be a marijuana aficionado, but I'd smoked so many different flavors over the years, it had happened all on its own. *Now that I'm leaving the house, maybe I should go on one of those Weed Country tours.*

To my left was the Southwestern selection; it had a thicker smell to it and was heavy on the indica. The Northeast shit ran to my right and had a fruity bouquet. Out there they grew ninety percent sativa and blended it to be perfect for the recreational smoker. I wasn't sure what I wanted, but it wouldn't be anything from America's east coast.

"Bill!" Franco walked out from behind the display cases and came towards me.

Tall and broad, he had pale skin and black hair he kept pulled back into a thick ponytail that looked determined to burst free from whatever bound it. He was Swiss, but his English had just a trace of an Italian accent. I didn't know if I would call us friends, but I'd been a steady and loyal customer ever since I left the military and moved back to Naperville. We were certainly very friendly, confidants in the way Grampa might've been with a local bartende, or the way Mom was with that whackadoo hairdresser she had gone to once a week until she died.

He was also one of the only guys I greeted with a hug. "Franco!" Definitely the only one in Naperville. It was midday on a Tuesday, and the shop was empty. Later, there would be the usual string of customers oohing over the semi-circle of display cases.

"Oh my God. I was, like, literally just thinking of you."

"Do tell."

"You one lucky mother fucker!"

"I am?"

"Fucking A. Christmas came early!"

Christmas Kush, the height of Franco's craft. He only grew it in the late fall, and it was ready just as the holidays rolled in, hence the name. It was expensive, but I never passed it up.

"How? Why?" I stammered.

Franco smiled and put a hand on my shoulder as he guided me around the horseshoe. "As you know, is expensive to grow. But I keep one plant in a unique closet so I always have samples on hand. To keep the rep alive for new customers, and as a bone I throw to my special, or long-time customers—"

"Hey, I'm both of those."

"Of course you are!"

He opened a door and led me into the hallway that connected his show room to the geodesic growing dome that had replaced the old greenhouse. When we got to the dome's entrance, he parted the plastic screen and held it open for me to pass through. The white, high-ceilinged dome was partitioned into different areas for each type of plant. It was filled with fans, drip systems, hanging lights, and, of course, marijuana plants.

We walked through the grow room nearest us. The plants were all about chest high. "This year I had a special order from a fellow seller in Europe," he said.

"And the order fell through?" We spoke loudly as we walked to be heard above the fans.

"Like ten minutes ago, brother. But I got to warn you."

"About what?"

He opened a door in the back wall of the grow room.

Inside was his exclusive smoking room.

Oh, me and Franco are gonna get highdy highdy high!

I walked in, and when Franco closed the door behind me, it swooshed as it sealed the circular fifteen-foot room shut, blocking out the fan noise.

This smoking room was the shit! Old school, oil-based shag carpeting thick enough to trip on. Solid, real-wood paneling. Eight natural sun-light bulbs along the walls illuminated the room and fed the small bonsai trees that sat in cutouts under the lights.

In the middle of the room was a gnarled, real wood table with a crystal ashtray and two black leather, deeply-cushioned chairs on either side.

When Franco spoke, it was like listening to him through a set of headphones. "Because I put out some capital to grow this special order," he motioned for me to sit in the chair closest to the door, "it is more expensive."

I sat and felt the extravagant room settle in around my ass. "How much more?" Not that I gave a crap—if he had Christmas Kush, I was buying it—but the laws of the trade demanded that I at least act as if I was pained at the price.

"Three and a half as much, brother."

No acting required. "For how much?"

"Two ounces."

That was a lot of Christmas joy.

"But, for you Bill, three times as much. After all, local, so no shipping costs, right?"

"Three times?" Even with my recent winning streak and Marvin's cash, the price made me gulp, but I wasn't going to pass on come-early Christmas Kush, and Franco knew it.

"I know, but just so you do not think it is any less than what you are used to... let us smoke." Franco actually physically pushed an intercom button in the arm of his chair.

Was this room NetFree? I'd thought I was just running in and out, so I'd left Box in the car.

I recognized the voice of Irving, his assistant. "Yes?"

"You got the front. I am entertaining."

"It must be good to be the boss."

"Fucking A right it is, bitch." He laughed and released the button.

I'd smoked with Franco before, though never in this room, but I knew he was like me, old school. No contraption burners or tricky gadgets. I'd seen him use a spiral bong, but whenever we'd smoked before it was always a plain ol' pipe, or a joint.

He tapped on a drawer recessed into the wood table and pulled out a doobie as thick as my thumb and as long as the tip of my middle finger to the base of my palm.

"I just rolled this and was going to call you." He gently laid the unlit, Presidente-sized bone and a lighter in the thick, crystal ashtray and slid it my way for first hit dibs.

I could only hope that I wasn't literally drooling, but, figuratively, *hummada hummada!*

I picked up the expensive, silver lighter, sparked the end of that big fatty, and inhaled.

Smooth. Delicate. Tasty.

I laughed as I exhaled. "Motherfucking Christmas Kush, baby!"

Franco laughed, and I passed the joint to him.

He sucked down an impressively serious hit then, after exhaling an equally impressive plume of bluish-gray smoke, he reached back and shook out his ponytail. "I love my job! So, brother, what is up with you?"

Before Franco even handed the fatty back to me, I could feel it in my body.

Oh my God, I've been tense.

I rolled my neck and shoulders and shook out my hands.

"What's up with me?" I laughed and went for my own deep, deep drag. "I'm in love, bitch!" My words came out in puffs like an ancient smoke signal.

Was that right? Was I in *love* with Julie?

"Get the fuck out!"

"I just got here!"

Franco laughed. "In love? Really?"

"I think, I mean…" Why fight it? "Yeah, well kinda I guess,

mother fucker." I laughed.

"That is fucking awesome. I am so glad for you. It has been a long-ass time, right?"

"You know it."

"Who is she? Anybody I know?"

"No, no. You wouldn't know her."

"Where did you meet her?"

I was going to say church, but it would probably freak Franco out. "Dinner at a friend's house."

"Nice! How long you known her?"

Christmas Kush was no sneaker bud with a high that crept up on you. I was already high and laughed and laughed at that. "You wouldn't believe me."

When high, laughing was like yawning, and Franco caught a ride on my laughter. In between laughing, he asked, "What? Why?"

"Five days! And we'd only spoken *twice*. And not even that much before...oh, man, before some very intense time." There was something about being high with somebody, as a social thing. I'd forgotten how much more fun it was to share the experience.

Franco laughed and stomped his feet, then leaned over the table, hand extended. "True love, brother."

I reached over and slap-snapped shook his hand. "Fuckin' A, Franco. Why not?" I stopped short. I hadn't actually meant to do that. It was a thing we'd done amongst ourselves. "Hey, how'd you know how to do that?"

"Do what?"

"That slap-snap."

Franco laughed. "The what? Brother, I held my hand out, followed your lead, and did what felt natural."

I smiled. "That's kinda cool, bro." I sagged back into my chair. *True love, huh?* I let that thought sink in for two more hits. I was now singing the body electric. I floated up even as my body settled into the lush seat with the creaking of supple leather. Everything felt more.

"It's weird, right?"

"What?" Franco passed me back the nearly half-finished joint.

"She asked me if I ever felt guided by fate. And you know I don't believe in that shit, not really."

Franco looked at me sideways, nodded, and gave me a knowing smile. "So you tell me."

"Our lives are so different, but we're totally in sync. And I don't think we could've ever even met if I hadn't taken this PD job."

"How lucky for you this job came up. Or maybe it is fate?"

I shrugged. "It be what it be, and I'm glad to be in the right place at the right time, and that's as far as I care to think about it."

"Yeah, man, let it come to you. Do not over-think a good thing. Some guys have all the luck, right?" And because Franco knew my tale of romantic woe, we laughed our asses off at that.

Franco reached behind his chair and tapped the wall; a cleverly-hidden portion, recessed slightly and slid open. A slim, oblong fridge with a burnished silver shell rolled over and stopped next to his chair. The fridge door slid to the side, and a mist floated out as the cool air hit the warm pot smoke-filled room. Franco reached into the lighted compartment and withdrew a small tray with dark chocolate-covered strawberries. He placed the tray on the table and pushed it my way.

Franco smiled expansively. "It all comes around, right?" The fridge's door slid closed and it scooted back into its cubbie, which closed behind it. "I mean, give it time, have some faith that the circle of life will swing to your way."

"I suppose it must!" I picked a strawberry and bit into it. I hadn't realized how dry my mouth was. The mix of dark chocolate and cool, fresh, naturally sweet strawberry exploded on my tongue and soothed my throat. "That is fucking delicious." I used my hand to wipe chocolate and strawberry juice off my chin.

Franco hoisted a berry my way. "Not everyone can stay

lucky forever." He took a bite of a strawberry.

"You believe in fate, Franco?"

"Fucking A I do."

"Really?"

"Of course, man." Franco finished his strawberry then said, "Look, I am sitting on a big investment here and looking at a loss, and who comes walking through my door but my man, my main man." We laughed. "Fate, bitch, fate!"

"What about God? Huh? You believe in God?"

"Fucking A I do."

"C'mon. Really, Franco?"

"You got to be kidding me, brother."

"I didn't think I was."

Franco held the joint up at eye level. "Look at this sweet, sweet flower we are smoking. This is God's handiwork, brother."

There didn't seem to be any ventilation. The air around our heads now had a thick, murky layer of second-hand pot smoke that was hot-boxing my high along.

"I think you helped."

"Hells yeah I did!"

We laughed for, like, minutes.

"But," Franco composed himself, "I am a child of God." He flipped a toggle on the side of his chair. The opening of Bob Marley's Three Little Birds came through hidden speakers around the room.

Franco shouted over the deep bass, "The proof of a benevolent God is in the nature that is all around us, brother!" He smiled and, in an Italian-accented Rasta brogue, said, "God do not be making *no* mistakes, mahn!"

The deep bass thumped around me and through me; my skin tingled. In off-pitch warbles but at full volume, Franco and I sang along.

"Don't worry, about a thing!

Cuz every little thing gonna be aw'right!"

Laughing, I flopped back in my chair and stared at the bonsai tree across from me. The way the trunk bent. The meticulously trimmed branches, the slow growing branches made to look natural, hiding the hand of the gardener.

For the first time in a long time, I thought about Sullivan and Chandler outside my nightmare.

Franco dialed back the music. "What is in your head?"

"I had these two buddies. Guys I served with."

Franco killed the music.

CHAPTER 25 – WANTING TO REMEMBER

"You never talk about your service," Franco said.

"There was…this time. I did this thing like I'd never done it before."

"Before? You could always do this thing?"

"Yes. But this time…" I hadn't talked to Julie about this. For the first time since that day, I remembered without wanting to shit myself what happened after I saw Sullivan and Chandler's red KIA.

"I lost my brothers to something I couldn't have known about. A tank-sized Anti-Personnel Microwave Emitter."

"Why didn't you know?"

They shouldn't have been able to get a tank in there. "We weren't looking for it."

"Why didn't you just shoot the emitter?"

My gun jammed. "Something made me duck."

"You ducked? I don't—didn't you have a Toob and ViSAR connection?"

"The tank had a non-standard, extended range, beyond our battlefield sweep, and microwave was one attack that wouldn't be picked up by our passive sensors."

Franco snapped his fingers. "Because the microwaves wouldn't interfere with the THZ's submillimeter wavelengths!"

"After they died, I think—" I stopped to work my tongue around my suddenly dry mouth. "I think I went mad for a time."

In the silence, I thought I could hear the smoke swirl around my head and settle on my shoulders.

Finally, Franco asked, "Mad how?"

"It was one fuck up after another. All our tech had meltdowns. The BigDogs, our bio-suits, everything went sideways. Everything but these…special kinds of contacts I used—"

"HUCOs?"

"You know?"

"The police chief is a customer and loves to show off. They're not too different from contact readers, right?"

They were nothing like them.

"Yeah, sorta like those. My HUCOs—unlike all the other equipment—they never melted. And—" I looked at the bonsai again.

"What?"

"I don't want to sound all section eight, but—" I turned to look Franco square in the eye. "I always felt it was so someone could watch."

Franco looked suspended in time. He was leaned back in his chair, but judging by the hardness around his eyes, his shallow breathing, he was listening intently.

A thick tendril of smoke spiraled into the air off the lit-end of the joint in the ashtray.

"After they died, I moved like I was…the HUCOs and me…I lost sense of who I was. I wasn't just *me.* I was me and…and who I'd become with my HUCOs."

Very softly, Franco asked, "Was that a good thing?"

"I crossed the ground from the ditch to the tank faster than I'd ever moved." With a 360-degree awareness of where every man stood. I could see the angle of their guns, sense their intentions, hear their weapons, feel their muscles gathering to fire. I knew where the bullets were going better than they did, before the bullets even left their guns.

"I couldn't have done it without HUCOs. When I ran out of bullets a quarter of the way up their lines, I didn't bother picking up their guns."

The guns should have tempted me, but they didn't. That new me had no higher reasoning; I was purpose set to motion, and I *knew* there was a single path to survival and that was to kill them with only what I had carried with me. And kill them I did.

"At first, they were afraid to fire in case they hit their own. But then they saw what I could—what I'd become..." A whirling blur, moving at incredible speeds, stopping and starting at impossible angles, showered in blood, using my hands and the long, kukri-shaped knife I always carried to leave a swathe of dismembered, decapitated, and disemboweled bodies. "And they feared me more."

And it was effortless.

"My anger, my grief—all of who I was went away. It all came second to the absolute necessity of fulfilling a single purpose. I was going to kill all of them. I was going to survive."

"The...how do I say this? Intent? The intrinsic nature of this," I put my hand to my chest, "my enhanced body *and* my HUCOs—synchronized, merged." I closed my eyes. Phantom glimpses of HUCO data popped to life.

"Was this a good thing?"

"It was..." A thing. A new way of being. A horrible, peaceful thing. I opened my eyes. "Survival."

The leather groaned as Franco clutched the arm of his chair.

Behind closed eyes I saw me and my brothers. Alive and playing poker in a FOB somewhere outside the world. We were laughing and laughing.

I became oddly aware of the breath in my lungs. As I let it out, the pressure went away. The steady, in-the-background guilt that I ignored and couldn't ignore and was always there as a constant and incessant building pressure, a balloon *always*—just—*about*—to pop.

That pressure was gone.

With a surety as solid as anything I'd ever known with *danger-close*, my brothers were smiling and laughing at my sorry ass. Laughing that I was so happy and foolishly, recklessly in love.

I love you both.

They'd always been there, smiling and happy that I wasn't with them.

I opened my eyes. The room seemed brighter. The natural sun-lamps had a rainbow corona around them. I was in my body, but my body wasn't with me. I was lighter and thinner than air, lifted by the music and floating on beams of sunshine.

"Hey, the music's on."

For some reason, this seemed to strike Franco as very funny. He laughed until he almost rolled out of his chair.

I felt so good I laughed until my jaws ached. It was good to be alive. *Good not to feel guilty for my life.*

As I sat there, I knew something in that moment that I'd never known: *I am exactly where I should be.*

Life and, yes, death had led me here, and it was good. With no reservation, it was good to be alive.

I gasped. This was the person I'd been before. Before training and killing and dying. Before guilt.

My cheeks were wet, and I knew that the water had come from my eyes, but it wasn't tears. It was an unction of forgiveness for being alive.

I looked at Franco. He took another drag as he bopped his head. He smiled broadly, happy for his own reasons.

It was early evening and nearly dark when Franco escorted me and my not-quite-two ounces of Christmas Kush to my car. "Okay, GPS your way home, right? Do not even think of going manual."

"Manual? Who goes manual?"

"Cool." From behind magenta eyes, Franco put his arm

around my shoulders. "Bill."

I put my arm around his shoulder and said with mock seriousness, "Franco."

"I am really happy for you, bro. Truly, I am. Namaste."

For a yoga guy like Franco, that was a personal thing. I'd heard him say it to people he knew through yoga, but he'd never said it to me. "Thanks, man."

"Just..."

"What? Go ahead. You can say it."

"We have known each other a very long time. Remember this feeling. This happiness. We both know it will not last, cuz that is how life fucks with us."

"Fucking A it does."

"So enjoy it. Ruminate on your enjoyment, so when the ugly times come, you remember now and can say, yeah, but! I know there is love in God's universe."

"God is love?"

"Yes. You know it, brother." He closed the door behind me.

Brother.

I smiled. Mom hadn't gone to see that whackado lady once a week for her hair. I don't know about brother, but I did recognize my relationship with Franco was…special.

"GPS, home."

I didn't even notice if GPS replied.

When I got home, I immediately flopped onto my bed fully clothed and fell into a deep sleep.

In the middle of the night I woke with that nebulous, stretched feeling of just having had a dream I wanted to remember but couldn't.

I enjoyed the feeling of wanting to remember a dream. Then slept some more.

CHAPTER 26 – FRANCO

Franco watched Bill drive away. As a scientist, Franco took pride in not assuming data. This was what he told himself, but in truth, without intending to Franco routinely assumed knowledge. Today, he was particularly pleased with himself at how according to expectations it had all gone. He replayed Bill's words:

I was going to survive.

Survival.

Bill finally had come for an extended stay. And continued to greet him with a hug! They had smoked the accelerated weed, which he was certain—as Franco's data had shown would be the case, and he was confident the metrics from Bill's chair would validate—had been effective. Of course Franco had given Bill the non-accelerated variant to take home. It would retain most of the psychedelic effect, but none of the psychotropic.

As soon as he returned to the shop, Franco let out a loud cheer, "Yes!"

He couldn't control his exuberance and jumped in the air and yelled several more times before he acknowledged Somers. Which he did first by coming to a dead stop and noticing the stoic expression on his face, and then by falling into a knee-slapping laughing fit.

Behind him, the door to the shop swung itself shut with a gentle rattle.

Those who knew Franco from only his reputation, as a man of science, were always surprised at the joy he found in his job. He could not have "known" Bill would tell him things Clare would kill him to know. He could not have "known" Somers was in the shop waiting for him, but, as a man of science, of course he knew.

"Like a moth to a flame, Somers. Or, whatever animal you are to any compulsion it does not acknowledge but must yield to." Franco burst out laughing again knowing each raucous sound was a jibe at Somers, who continued to stand still and fill the room with the threat of violent death.

Franco did not know Somers had plans for white coats, so he was not intimidated. Not only was he a white coat, but he was now—after a very long exile—the white-coat-in-charge. After a moment, he wiped the tears off his cheeks and put his hands in his pockets. He giggled just once more then stood still.

Somers hadn't moved. "You terminated your ViSAR connection, sir. We haven't worked together long, but I'm sure you know establishing a NetFree area is not allowed without approval. Sir."

Franco walked the length of the show room.

Again, the sheer amazement of it occurred to him, *I know something about Bill that Clare does not.*

And then, the real mystery of what he knew dawned on him: it was something she could not ever have known, ever have measured. It validated his place, his long years in service to the project.

Franco almost wept.

"Sir?"

He cleared his throat. "Yes."

"Your ViSAR connection?"

"Is that what happens when that door closes? I wondered." Franco had used that Faraday Cage of a room for the first and last time. "I'll have Irving look into it." He'd built it with his own hands for just this reason: off-network time alone with Bill. Franco knew such a thing would never happen again. It was why Somers was here.

Bill could not escape Somers.

He had felt that way before—Franco smiled at the memory—and been wrong. His smile faltered. Being wrong about Bill was why he was in Naperville in the first place. But before was not like this. There had been no Somers before. Franco was sure that he, like only a few people on the planet, knew precisely how destructive both men could be, and so knew the outcome of the conflict.

Bill Slaughter was going to die.

Somers stepped towards Franco. "Anything noteworthy discussed?" When Franco said nothing else, Somers continued, "Is the mission still a go?"

Franco fervently wished he could be there. "Yes. I…"

"Sir?"

"Nothing, I repeat, nothing must get in the way of the mission."

Somers grinned. "Yes, sir. Terminate Captain Slaughter."

"Hold on, Somers." It was an intuitive flash of insight; Franco saw a way. Franco arrogantly assumed he understood the scenario, but he was right. Franco understood the scenario; the decision must be made now. No time for computations.

If he were an athlete, Franco would have said he was in the zone.

"Give the other team their shot at Bill." Franco was a man who did not surrender his calculations. And yet he just had.

Franco was superior at so much of what he could do; he would be amazed to learn he had terrible self-perception. Franco was suffused with a sense of confidence in his decision. Others would recognize that feeling as maybe joy. It was an abiding calm about a decision whose outcome they knew and yet could not know.

Somers entire body seemed to quiver slightly but there was no other reaction. "That's bullshit."

"They might succeed." As a white coat, lying was second nature.

Somers's features hardened and he now openly glared at Franco. "I will kill your pet." Somers's lip curled into a grim, tight-lipped smile. "I can wait."

"Not for too long."

"I'll show you. I will do what you could not."

Stiffly, Somers strode to the door and out.

Franco walked to the front display window and watched Somers leave. As a scientist, he envisioned the cold, impartial quantum calculations. Would it be enough?

Would Somers and the other forces gathered against Bill…would all of it finally be enough?

Franco didn't know the answer to that question, but he knew he would be there to see it answered.

CHAPTER 27 – POLICE

It was almost 11 AM when I woke up. Sprawled across my bed, I felt fantastic.

I yawned expansively on the way to the kitchen. Box whistled, indicating a new message. It was from Suniti. "Thanks for the call. Margot is available Wed. Call for a time." Today was Wednesday. Obviously this had come in yesterday when I was with Franco.

That sealed the deal. If Julie was coming over, I needed to do some domestic shit.

First was to start frying some sliced potatoes and sweet onions in virgin olive oil and lots of garlic. While that was cooking, I strolled into the garage to retrieve from the grocery slot the week's free bread and dairy delivery: rye bread, butter, eggs, milk. I made a mental note to order some special cheeses.

I was old enough to remember a pink slime MickeyD burger. What would kids today, so used to fresh food and produce, say if they ate that shit?

While eating over the kitchen counter, I mapped out my day. *Clean the house, do the laundry, get some additional food in here for a good meal-for-two.*

"Box, message Suniti. Excellent. I accept tonight's date proposal. Will call late afternoon with an early evening time."

I had Box pipe in some classic U2. Not the shit they did just before the end when they got weird and tried to do opera. Grampa had loved those guys, and Dad and I had played a lot of their music on our summer road trips. I sang along as I walked through my kitchen, with a shopping list following me from cabinet to pantry to fridge.

After Boxing in my order, I put the Christmas Kush in my living room humidor. The humidor was built into the wall and looked like a framed painting of a smoked glass door.

I smoked, but only a little from my old stash, some Monkey Bubble. A new Canadian herb with a nice balance of both indica and sativa. There was shit that needed doing; I'd smoke my Christmas Kush when I could relax and enjoy. People wouldn't chug a two-hundred-dollar glass of wine while they did house chores in their underwear, and I sure as hell wasn't going to smoke my Kush if I couldn't enjoy it.

With a load of laundry going in the washer, I policed my space, dusted, and mopped. *I love my floors.*

I'd just put some clean sheets on my bed and was about to steam-vacuum the couch when my washer buzzed as the doorbell rang with my grocery delivery.

The laundry room was through the kitchen. I shut off the washer's buzzer. Beside the dryer were my soft-soled, slip-on shoes. The gummy surfaces had excellent grip but were perfect for walking on my floors without worrying about scuffing.

Box used to let credentialed deliveries in. I ended that practice after the market kid dropped that bag of frozen goods. Luckily, it had hit the pizza box he'd tripped over, or it would've dinged my floor. So unlike most, I carried my own damn groceries.

While bending to pick up my shoes from between the dryer and the back door, I saw him.

He was dressed in police department regulation black assault gear complete with DuraFlex armor plating on his vest, shoulders, and legs. Rapid assault load-out so no helmet, only a police cap with a small bill. He held a pistol with both gloved hands. The gloves were padded at the knuckles but left the ends of each finger exposed. He was looking in my bedroom window to the left of the laundry room door and hadn't seen me.

I whispered quickly, "Box, silent running. Disable emergency alerts." I didn't want Box either giving me away or sending police.

I moved into the space beside the door and between the dryer and the wall. I quickly slipped my feet into my shoes, careful not to bang the side of the dryer.

The uniform might've been police regulation, but there was no bright white "POLICE" stenciled across the front, back, and shoulders.

Funny that they're worried about impersonating an officer while murdering someone.

His shadow appeared in the back door window.

Muffled by the glass, I heard, "He must be on his way up to you. Call him."

Another ring came from the front, accompanied this time by a series of loud knocks on the door. "Police! Open up!"

I heard the soft snick of a lock-hollower caving in my back door lock. The door swung silently toward me and the dryer. "I'm in. Moving to you."

More pounding on the front door answered.

As soon as he'd cleared the door, I swung it shut with a crash. As he turned, gun in hand, I moved to tuck the gun extended in his right arm under my left armpit.

His reaction time to the door told me he wasn't enhanced. I put my right hand to the back of his head and used his momentum to smash his head into the wall opposite the washer and dryer.

"Shit!"

His forehead had slammed into a two-by-four behind the drywall, and there had been an unmistakable crunch. I hadn't accounted for the wood.

When I let go, he fell to the floor convulsing. In addition to the general, blunt-force trauma from the two-by-four, a nail had punctured his skull and was now coated with a good chunk of brain.

Whoever was up front must've heard this through the open mic. The wood around the front door lock splintered. He would be on his way to the laundry room. I quickly and silently moved through the kitchen and crouched to the right of the kitchen entry.

"Police! Police get down!" he shouted in the living room.

Take him alive.

He moved into the kitchen wearing the same police rapid assault blacks. With his gun extended in a two-handed grip, he swung it my way to clear the room, but I was below the level of his gun.

I used my left hand to move the muzzle of the gun in a harmless direction then stepped into him, smashing my right elbow into his temple. I spun behind him, but he lunged awkwardly to where I wasn't and slammed the temple I'd already concussed into the edge of my kitchen counter. There was a splintering crunch and he dropped like a rock.

I twisted the gun from his limp hand—a .45. I didn't recognize the make. No fingerprint limiter, meaning anyone could fire it and there was no black box for police to review.

Very black market.

It was cocked with the safety off. I dropped the clip; in the side slot, I could see it was full. I slapped the clip in and racked the slide back. There was a round in the chamber. Max-damage, soft slugs.

It was my turn to move through the house with the gun in a two-handed grip. Out of the kitchen, past the cast iron, and into the living room. From there, I could see outside. A third guy, this one in NPD patrol blues with a badge on his chest, was standing on my lawn a few feet off my stoop, glancing nervously up and down the street while attempting to appear official.

When he checked the doorway for his friends, instead he saw me with his friend's gun pointed in his direction.

"Easy way, or hard way?" I asked.

His Adam's apple bobbed. "Easy."

"You're obviously not police. You the fuckers who've been running up my congestion meter?"

"Have we what?"

"Have you been tailing me?"

"Yes."

"Why?"

"It was the job."

Just that simple. America's ex-military were the world's mercenaries. I'd never heard of them working in the States, but it wasn't like I paid attention to that sort of thing.

"Where'd you get the unis?"

"They came with the instructions."

I put the pistol to my side. "I won't take this personal, so this is what I'm going to do. I'm *not* going to come out there and drag you inside just so I can shoot you. I know you don't know who sent you."

This time he gulped audibly. "That's right. It's all set through a handler."

It was standard OPSEC: never tell the grunts shit so they couldn't tell anyone anything.

"Aw'right. Go."

"My friends?"

"They stay." A hero look started creeping into his eyes. I refocused my gun in his direction. "You can come in and die next to them, if you like."

"Dead?"

"Undoubtedly."

"Fuck."

"Yeah, I didn't mean to do it, but I hope you don't mind if I'm not all broken up. Now go."

This time he went. I watched him walk off my lawn.

I walked back in. "9-1-1, 9-1-1." I wrapped the gun in a dishtowel, put it in a freezer-sized ziplock then stashed it in the toilet reservoir of my guest bathroom.

"Box, call a 24-hour emergency cleaning crew, locksmith, and handy man. Tell them I'll double their pay if they get here in an hour and leave in three." I wasn't going to let a little thing like an attempt on my life ruin dinner with Julie.

CHAPTER 28 – BOOTIES

I reached into my humidor and pulled out a cigarette-sized joint. As I sparked it, the siren came to a stop outside my home.

Officer Maroney came into the house, gun drawn, and did a quick—and not too terribly executed—left, right, up, down, clear until he saw me on my couch.

"What's the 9-1-1, Bill?"

"You my own personal officer, Officer?"

"Seems we keep similar hours. Your door is jizzed up. Someone break in?"

"They tried."

"Looks like they succeeded."

"I suppose they did, but they didn't make it back out. Check the kitchen and laundry room."

When Stan saw the body in the kitchen, he put the call out for a crime scene unit and the coroner. I expected Moe would be in general grateful for the business and not at all irritated.

Stan came back from the kitchen a little paler than his usual Irish self, which was pretty pale. "Damn, Bill."

"What? They broke in. I'm within my rights."

"Yeah, I'm sure, but—"

"What?"

"You've got two dead bodies in your house, and I find you sitting on your sofa smokin' a jay like nothing at all."

I shrugged. "We all have our own way of dealing with grief."

They sure as shit wouldn't have felt bad if it had been me.

The most disturbing thing was that, throughout it all, I'd never once felt a *danger-close* vibe. Then again, against two un-enhanced men, there really was no serious threat.

So then…

Whoever sent them didn't know that I'm enhanced.

"So, is this why you asked if I was following you?"

"Yeah, the one guy said they were following me."

"You talked to them?"

I blew out smoke. "There was a third guy outside. I let him go."

"Why?"

"Two reasons. He wasn't inside my house, so I couldn't shoot him." Inside your home: self-defense. Outside your home, unless they were pointing a gun at you: murder. Such were the vagaries of law.

"I'm not saying kill him! But you could've stopped him."

"Too much effort."

Maroney nodded in exasperated exaggeration. "Sure! Of course it was! Why would you actually *help* the police?" He threw his hands in the air. "And the second reason?"

"He couldn't tell me what I really need to know. And he was an ex-GI. I didn't take it personal."

"Oh, yeah." Stan pushed his hat up and rubbed his forehead. "Nothing is less personal than murder."

"If any of those fuckers had scratched my floor, I don't know if I would've been so charitable."

"It is a nice floor."

The distinctive sirens of EMT vehicles wailed in the distance.

"You like what they're wearing, Maroney?"

"Yeah, I saw that."

"How'd they get those BDUs?"

He avoided looking at me. "How would I know?"

"You didn't tell the chief about our conversation, did you?"

"Fuck *no* I didn't tell him."

"You got anything on what the mayor and the chief might've been doing a week ago?"

"At this point," Stan looked up, "off the record, I would if I could, but really, I don't know." Stan seemed unsettled.

I held the joint out to him. "You want some of this?"

"No. I'm on duty," his mouth said, but I could see his heart wasn't in it.

I stubbed it out then rolled my neck and bled off as much tension as I could. A little more smoke would've been nice, but there were questions to come and questions I needed to ask. Mainly revolving around finding out who was hiring mercenaries to kill me.

Color me surprised when Federal Agent Somers walked through my open door. Moe and the CSI units would be here any moment.

"Clyde."

He looked at me levelly. "Bill." He turned toward Maroney and blinked rapidly then looked quickly from Maroney to me and back again.

"You never send me flowers," I said.

Maroney, to his credit, remembered to forget our phone call and act surprised. "You guys know each other?"

"Sure. Somers likes it up the ass."

"Fuck you, Bill."

"If you're catching, I'm pitching, sailor. What're you doing here, Somers?"

"These mercs are out of state. That makes it a Federal issue."

"I bet they drove an out-of-state rental, right?"

Clyde didn't answer, but his blank look told me I was right.

That was why they didn't know I knew about them. Their car came from an area that didn't have Naperville's lovely congestion ordinances. They would've gotten the bill when they returned the car. *That's sloppy intel.*

"So," I crossed my arms and tapped a finger to my lips, "let's see. You're here because they crossed state lines."

Blank look.

"Some merc team is taking domestic hit orders, and the Feddy no likey."

Blank look.

"Did you know this team was in town when we talked at The Flame?"

Blank look.

I would've loved to play poker with Somers. He had tells you could see a mile away. "You knew mercs were here, but they hadn't done anything yet. So you laid low, did a little double duty looking into the NuTree, until they did something you could act on. That about sum it up?"

Nothing.

"Okay, good talk. Two mercs here. The third walked."

Blank look. Then Agent Somers left.

I turned to Stan. "I am gonna *miss* him."

"Damn, Bill." Stan looked nervously out my front door, making sure Somers had moved on. "He's a Feddy."

"Yeah, a Feddy who could have stopped some mercenaries before they actually tried to kill someone but was more interested in avoiding paperwork than a life. As it turned out, my life. Fuck him."

Moe, the first to arrive, came scurrying in carrying his blue tablet. "Okay, please clear."

"The bodies are—" Stan began.

Moe moved past him. "When I need you to tell me shit, I'll hang myself." Then he stopped and said to me, "Having fun yet?"

As a matter of fact, I still felt amazingly relaxed. I shrugged and smiled.

He raised his eyes to the ceiling. "Of course!" And he trudged off to the kitchen.

I winced with each step. "Mind the floor!" Moe wore blue booties over his shoes, but still I fretted for my irreplaceable floor.

A CSI guy holding a red tablet walked through my battered door, without blue booties, and filled the space.

"The coroner's back in the kitchen," Stan offered.

Red tablet gave a heavy sigh. "Yes, Officer, we got it. Please. Clear." He made shooing motions at Maroney.

What the fuck? Maybe Moe could do that shit, but I was somewhat partial to Officer Maroney.

I walked up to the investigator and got in his personal space.

"Citizen, you need to—"

"You fuck up my floors," pause, "and I will be perturbed."

The investigator attempted a bluster. "I am a civil official. Who are you to address—"

"I'm PD Bill Slaughter, mother fucker." I got closer. "I just killed two men, and the only reason I let the third live was because they didn't scratch my floor. Don't. Fuck. With my floor." Sometimes not shouting works so much better.

The investigator looked down. "That is a nice floor."

"And it better stay a nice floor."

Just then a second CSI came walking through the door. The red tablet in front of me barked, "Fuck, Ralph! Be fucking careful on the floor, would you?"

Ralph looked like a scolded dog. "Jesus, okay Mort. I just walked in."

"Fuck that. Be careful! Get me some damn booties and make sure everyone has them on before they come in."

Ralph looked from Mort to me to Maroney and back to me standing in Mort's face and now staring at Ralph. "Uh, suuure. Hello, sir. That's a pretty floor you have."

Satisfied, I walked outside. It was a beautiful spring day.

Stan followed. "You're my new hero."

"Aw, shucks. Anything to help my personal NPD officer."

"Yeah, let's always be friends."

"Sounds good. Now see if you can hurry things up in there." The grocery truck was just rolling up. "I got a date tonight."

CHAPTER 29 – CLARITY CONNECTIONS

The NPD watch commander was the last to go, giving me instructions not to leave town. The handyman had done a passable job on my doorjamb. I'd have to look into something a bit less serviceable-looking and more aesthetically pleasing later. He'd also patched the drywall in my laundry room, no problem. It would need a coat of paint, but I didn't think Julie would be visiting my laundry room. Thankfully, the edge of my granite counter was undamaged.

The locksmith was expensive and worth every penny. Quick, clean, efficient. Had to be ex-military. I liked her immediately.

She put in new siren-enabled locks in front and back. They were physically triggered, so if someone bypassed everything and breached the door without opening the lock, an alarm would sound. A surprisingly loud alarm.

Box spoke through the house speakers. "Marvin calling. Ignore all calls command has expired."

Speak of the devil. "Vid off, connect it. Hello?"

"What, no video? What are you hiding? That scrummy man from The Flame, I hope."

"I'm just not near anything right now. Hold on," I walked through the kitchen and to the living room. The blank video from the call followed me past the fridge and along the walls. I could've taken the call anywhere, but I didn't want Marvin to see me prepping the house.

Once in the living room, I said, "Vid on."

"There you are!"

I could see why Marvin thought video was needed. He wore white pancake makeup with an overabundance of eyeliner. His hair was dyed jet black, and it was ridiculously and erratically teased, floating up in all directions.

Marvin laughed at my reaction. "You like?"

"Uh..."

"I'm going to a costume party as Robert Smith."

"Who?"

"From the Cure."

I had nothing.

"An 80s band."

"Oh." *Julie probably knows all about them.* "I really don't understand this nostalgia for the eighties."

"The eighties was the most fashion forward decade in the last one hundred years! The last decade before the beginning of the Data Generation. Jesus, Bill. You really worry me."

Shee-it.

"Now that you have a reference, you like?" He struck a pose.

"Marvin, why are you calling me?"

"Well, fine, Mr. Small Talk, pleased to see you, hope you're doing well, I'm fine. Thank. You," he said with a pout. "I just thought I should check in, since you weren't calling me."

"I'm busy earning your trust fund. It's been a hectic coupla days."

Marvin got serious. "Really? What have you found?"

"I'm still not sure. Do you know what Frank was doing on the night of his murder?"

"Not specifically. He just said he had a thing."

"Did he ever mention the police chief?"

"No, not once."

"Okay, Marvin. I hadn't thought to call you. Sorry, I should have. But things have been moving along. I can tell you that I'm close to something someone doesn't want me near."

Marvin dropped his clown routine. "Thank you so much. Bill, this means the world to me."

It was weird enough to see Marvin somber, but in his spectral makeup, it was like a visit from the Ghost of Christmas Future.

"It's cool. And if it's any short-term consolation to you…"

Marvin had leaned in so that now his face filled my wall. "Yes?"

"Well, I'm sure you're right. I do think someone else was involved in his death."

Marvin looked relieved and smiled a genuine, nontheatrical smile. "I knew it," he said it to himself and then with conviction to me, "I knew it. People in love don't kill themselves."

I smiled. "They sure don't. I'll be in touch. Discon."

A week ago I'd cynically dismissed Marvin's claim, but now, I saw it as an undeniable truth.

People in love don't kill themselves.

I toured the house, including the dining room, bedrooms, and bathrooms. I was relieved to have the service to do the cleanup. Besides the blood, bowels had released themselves, as they did when you had no working brain telling them not to. The cleanup wasn't a chore for me.

The three-woman cleaning crew had been like a team of ninjas—in and out with the whole place looking spit-shine new.

Aside from the doorjamb, my house looked better than it had in a long time. Everything was shining and it smelled fresh.

I could come to like having a cleaning service.

I'd shit, showered, and shaved. I put on a fresh button-up dress shirt, but I ditched the faux tie and dug out an old-time real tie that still smelled a little like Dad. I wore a smart-looking vest, a pair of dress pants, some calf-skin leather shoes, and a small mist of cologne to finish it off.

It was time. I laughed, nervously. "Box, call Suniti." I walked into the kitchen to get a beer. "Vid on fridge, please."

Suniti's smiling face and grey-streaked hair appeared. "Hello, Mr. Bill."

"Hello, Suniti. I appreciate the service you gave me the day before yesterday. Please send Margot again."

Suniti smiled. "I am so pleased. One moment while I check availability, please."

Yes, Suniti and Julie are definitely on the same page.

She came back after less than a minute. "Margot is quite pleased to date you again in the same way as she did *last* visit. She will be available at 7:30. Is that satisfactory?"

Seven-thirty was in an hour. "That is one slow boat from China I don't mind waiting on. Thanks, Suniti. Oh, please tell her to dress for dinner."

"It is always my pleasure to make happiness, Mr. Bill."

I might have blushed. "Discon."

I began to do some dinner prep. After getting the green beans from the fridge, I dumped them in a colander. While they rinsed, I turned my thoughts to who might have me on their hit list. Someone with the money and know-how to hire out of state mercenaries. Beyond simple dollars, who had the connections to do something this illegal?

I cracked off the bean stems. "Box, forty-five minute timer, please."

Okay, what did I know?

Start simple.

"I know the mayor killed the NuTree. Box, are you keeping a list?"

"Confirmed."

"I know someone killed the mayor. Someone hired people to kill me, but whoever did that didn't know I was enhanced. Which, sadly, rules out the chief, whose house the mayor was at before going to the Fox.

"My trips to The Flame and to church kicked up dust, but

Julie as a NuTree lead is a non-starter. Clyde at The Flame was interesting, but his deployment is only tangentially related to my work."

I cracked beans.

I'm missing something.

I needed a second brain.

"Box. Query a troubleshooting service. I have some random data points I need crunched."

"Is cost an issue?"

"Well, I wouldn't discount it entirely, but I'm willing to spend money if the service is worth it. Give me a breakdown based on services offered, discretion, security, and user rating. And must be non-local, preferably out of state."

Just because you're paranoid doesn't mean they aren't out to kill you.

And in this case, they'd already tried once. But they wouldn't try again. By now, they had to know that there was a Feddy in town. I wouldn't be surprised if the entire operation had gone underground for good.

Chirp.

"Display in spreadsheet format. Top twelve choices based on previous criteria and adding cost and location by city and state."

Chirp.

"Display here." A distorted spreadsheet popped up on my pile of yet-to-be-treated green beans. I cleared a space so I could see the spreadsheet as flat on the counter.

I used my fingers to zero in on a service in a place called Solana Beach, California. They were on the low end price-wise, but had high marks in other categories, including the highest marks for discretion and security. Turned out they had an upfront membership fee on top of their service charges, so not so low-end after all. Still, even with the membership fee, they weren't the most expensive, and that user rating was stellar.

They must be doing something right.

I had Box pay the membership and subscribe me to the Clarity Connections server.

A slick welcome promo began and appeared to float a few

inches above my counter. "Welcome to Clarity Connections. Our queries are fast, deep, and guaranteed private. To begin your service, say 'Begin connecting,' and speak all your data points. The more the better! Once you are done, say 'Commence Clarity Connections!' You may pause, save, and return to your work at any time by simply saying, 'Cloudy weather looms.' You may request a phrase of your choice, but it should not be a common expression. Results will be available immediately; however, the longer you allow me to look, the more thoroughly I can mine the data points and yield what you may feel is a correct result. Typically, users discontinue processing after twelve to fifteen hours. Once you are satisfied with your results, discontinue processing by saying, 'I have Clarity!' Thank you for choosing Clarity Connections. Namaste."

Namaste from a computer? How would that work? "Begin connecting."

"Please continue."

And I dumped it all: from dead NuTrees to out of state, ex-military guns for hire.

Box whistled. "Forty-five minutes has passed."

Excellent. "Commence Clarity Connections. Discon from server." I wasn't interested in anything that might percolate immediately to the top. I'd let the service cook the data for a bit.

I checked the table and made sure it was set. I lit candles.

Julie is coming.

It felt giddy to be nervous like this.

The doorbell rang.

The last time Julie came, she was in a coat and underwear. This time she had on a deep, dark red, eighties dress with a low neckline that showed ample cleavage. Slinky. Mid-thigh. It jumped off her fair skin. Her lipstick was the same vibrant red she'd worn the first time I saw her at the church. Her fingernails and toenails matched her lips. She wore long, yellow-gold bangle earrings. Her black hair was neatly coiffed and off her neck, which seemed to be begging for me to kiss.

She wore open-toed, black stilettos. "You called?" She stepped in and shut the door behind her. I kissed her cheek, then let my lips briefly skim their way down her neck. I hugged her lightly, and discovered that the dress was open in the back.

"You're beautiful."

She beamed. "You look dashing yourself. Suniti told me you'd dressed up. You like the dress?" She put her hands on her hips.

"I like it all. Your nails and hair, and your shoes are the zeit."

She smiled. "Oh, these?" And then she did that turn women have done since they first noticed men: the half-turn that made eyes move naturally up from the shoe, up those shapely stems, over the curve of the ass, past a side glimpse of boob, to rest on green eyes looking over her shoulder.

"Wow."

"Hm?"

"Hm, nothing. You're, uh, wow."

She smiled and lightly patted her hair. "I'm glad you like it. I-I was nervous," she said, then kissed me, lightly to avoid messing her lipstick. "You have something to help a girl relax?"

"As a matter of fact..." I held her hand and walked her over to the humidor. I opened the door, and the smell of Christmas Kush filled the room.

"Oh, Bill. You are a man after my own heart."

I didn't even notice she'd kept her shoes on.

CHAPTER 30 – SMALL GROUP

Julie kept her pumps on as we cooked dinner together. Or I cooked and she drank some wine and nibbled on some cheese and sliced apple. I was beginning to really appreciate a muscular set of calves. I had rolled a petite joint of Christmas Kush for her, and it really loosened her up. She talked and talked. That was fine by me. I loved her voice.

Turns out, she sang professionally. Sometimes she would tour with a local band and sometimes with a theatre group doing musical theatre. That explained the gaps in her church attendance.

"You tour? Isn't that expensive?"

"Of course it is."

"But – what? You just love doing it so you don't care?"

"Well..."

"What?"

"Well, I have a FAACKS trust fund."

FAACKS, the so-called Super Trust Fund. Because of my Dad's PD, I had an above average Federal trust fund. And because I had chosen the military for my service and had performed beyond the minimum service years, any children of mine would be eligible for a Funding with Articulated and Accentuated Capacity and Kinetic Stewardship trust fund. But

I'd never before met one of the fantastically wealthy FAACKS recipients. I bet she wasn't concerned about the cost of touring.

"That's one less worry."

"What do you mean?"

"I guess you're not after me for my money then, huh?"

She laughed the laugh of someone who hasn't been high in a while and who has never been high on Christmas Kush. It was a beautiful sound. "No, silly, I want your floors!"

"Now *that* makes sense!"

"Besides that, I do so love doing it." She took a bite of cheese and a crumb fell down her cleavage.

A snack for later.

"As an added bonus, touring is a very tidy reason to get away from all that is Mitchell."

"I see."

"He wasn't always so completely self-absorbed. Four years ago, he did a missionary trip." She took a cute little puff. "To the Mog," she said around her inhale.

"Wow. Truly? The Mog?"

"Absolutely." She exhaled.

Mogadishu had become a modern day Tortuga, a haven for pirates and terrorists from Africa to Chechnya to Indonesia. With the Oil Crisis in full bloom, pirates stealing oil tankers was more than a pebble in the world's shoe. In a form of cooperation that only a true international crisis could bring about, Mogadishu was sealed off from the rest of the world by sea with a concentric ring of nets, mines, and drone ships and by land with a ring of detonated battlefield sized nukes. Cheaper, by far, than building and manning a fence. Nothing living could cross that irradiated furnace. A sentence to the Mog was death.

It was hard for me to imagine the smooth, polished Mitchell I'd seen volunteering for such a thing. "He must be one of the only living things to ever enter the Mog and come back out."

"I suppose."

"You don't think so?"

"You're probably right. It's just…Mitchell came back, but not the same. It made him very different."

"I can imagine," I said, and I really could.

"The idealist who went to save the least of us came back thinking of nothing but advancing the standing of his church as a business. When I told him I was going to do tours, he couldn't have been happier to have me gone. I'm surprised Pete and Paul didn't immediately rush over to pack my bags. They couldn't wait for me to leave."

"Pete? Mitchell's brother, right?"

"That's him."

"Who's Paul?"

"Paul is the third of the triumvirate. He runs the family counseling business. He's not related to the Slades."

Paul worked in the background at the church. Frank questions came to mind, but there'd be time for that later. First things first. "Dinner is served."

"Finally. I'm starving!"

Julie followed me to the dining room where I uncovered the two thick Alaskan King Crab legs delivered all the way from Chicago. I popped and poured the Chardonnay.

"I haven't had crab in years!"

"Box, display Mount Rainier."

Box projections filled the walls and ceiling turning my hardwood floors into the deck of a cabin. The wall with the kitchen door was the outside of the cabin. The opposite wall was a vista with a river gurgling by the deck. A forest with no NuTrees led to a snow-capped mountain. The Box played gentle forest sounds over the house audio. Above us was a blue sky with puffy white clouds.

She put a hand to her chest. "I wondered why there was nothing on the walls."

"I put this together from dozens of old analog photos. This was the view from the old family cabin. Grampa took Dad, and Dad took us—Mom, me, Sis. So as a family, we'd been in this cabin for decades."

"That's why no NuTrees. It's so peaceful. Is it gone?"

"Oh yeah, completely." I shrugged and cracked our crab legs. "It's good to remember what the world used to be like." The meat from the crab leg came out in a long, reddish-pink shaft.

She dipped hers in the warm, drawn butter before taking a bite. "Mmmm…" She caught herself and looked up to see me noticing her reaction. She finished her mouthful then said, "Leering is impolite. Don't think I don't see you over there. I feel like I should be charging admission."

"I'll pay whatever you want." I'd never gotten an erection over a meal before.

The main course was petite filet mignon steaks and green beans, with a cabernet from a vineyard all the way in Kentucky that the grocer had recommended. The dessert was coffee and carrot cake from my new favorite bakery.

Over dinner, we talked about her last trip away. It had been a tour for a play, a musical of the life of an eighties radical, Chomsky someone. I'd heard of it. I thought it was a farce, but I didn't know anything beyond that. Julie filled the room with laughter and talk of life on the road as an actor.

Play tours were six months and band tours three. But the band tours cost more because they went to more cities, whereas the play tours might stay as long as two weeks in one place.

She went on the way I must have gone on over dinner at her house. I loved listening to her talk. She was sweet, smart, and knew how to tell a story.

I hadn't realized how lonely I'd been without this connection in my life.

When the meal was done, we sat on the couch. We had just shared a piece of carrot cake. She kicked her shoes off, knelt on the couch next to me, and kissed me. "What are you thinking?"

"Basically, how lucky I am to be having this time with you."

She blushed furiously, and I could see her nipples harden under her fragile dress. She kissed my neck. "Don't take advantage of me because I'm a little drinkie and little more smokey."

"I can see other reasons to take advantage of you."

She giggled. "I'm so glad you called." She reached her hands over her head and stretched luxuriously.

I was feeling a little smokey myself.

"It was the perfect night for this."

"In what way?"

"Mitchell is out at his small group all night."

"Small group?"

"Yes." She giggled some more. "You don't think he could actually be bothered to shepherd people, do you?"

"Uh, I guess not." I moved my head and started lightly brushing my lips along her neck. "Mm-hm. What's a small group got to do with it?"

"Mm. Church on Sunday is for big picture stuff. But the real—oooh—work goes on through a network of gatherings at—uh, mm—at people's homes."

"Really?"

She moved to put herself between me and the couch.

"They were a great idea." I slipped a strap of her dress down off her shoulder to reveal a nipple. "Oh yesss, a way of helping people in big churches connect to each other." She slid both arms out of her dress and crossed them behind her head. "Now they're just an excuse." Her breath was shallow.

"Excuse?" I gently kissed her neck and lightly traced my fingernails over her breasts and down her waist.

Distractedly, with her eyes closed, she said, "To shovel work off to enthusiastic volunteers."

I kissed her and brushed her nipple with the palm of my hand. "How lucky you're not invited."

"Mmmm. Mitchell's group is men only." My mouth was halfway to her nipple when she said, "The mayor was a member."

Time slowed.

"Where does Mitchell's group meet?" I asked, but I knew.

"The police chief's house."

CHAPTER 31 – GLOW

The mayor goes to this small group thing and when he leaves, turns off his GPS, goes out of his way, and drives into the Fox River.

"What's wrong?"

I sat on the edge of the couch. "Nothing. My brain is spinning on something else. I, uh, hmmm…"

Julie moved behind me and massaged my neck. "Mitchell told me you were looking into the NuTree thing."

"Sort of." She had really strong hands. "Yeah, right there." She squeezed the base of my neck.

"So you're not?"

"Oh good Lord, that feels good. No. I've actually been hired to look into the mayor's murder."

"Oh. Didn't he kill himself? Besides, who would murder the mayor? He was a sweet, old widower."

"Right. You can go harder…oh, that's perfect. Which is why, initially, I thought it was about the NuTree."

"And now you think you were wrong?"

"Oh, yeah, definitely."

"Is there anything you can do about it tonight?"

What would going to the chief's house look like? PDs had leeway, but they didn't include me busting down the doors of the chief's house without a really good warrant. And I had no proof Frank had even been to his home.

The chief definitely had anti-snooping protections in place. Probably why they held the group at his home. No Fly on the Wall app was going to work there.

"Hello?"

"Sorry." I shook my head free of mayor thoughts. "No, you're right. You're definitely right. There's nothing I can do about it tonight."

Who would—

"The cream on the carrot cake was delicious."

"Yeah, it was good."

—kill the sweet, old mayor?

Julie moved around me and pulled a slice of carrot cake near. "But I need a better utensil to eat it with."

"You want a spoon?"

"Oh no, something harder."

I missed the first innuendo and the second salacious look. Hell, I missed that she was still topless. But I managed to regain appropriate focus when she unzipped my pants and began applying frosting.

She looked me in the eye as she ran her tongue up the shaft of my penis.

She curled up against me, and I luxuriated in the feeling—the warmth of her breath, the sweet smell of sweat on her perfumed breasts, the tickle of her hair on my ear, the frisson of her skin under my fingertips as I stroked her back, arms, and ass.

"Why are you here with me?"

"Why shouldn't I want to be with you?"

"Why would anybody? I don't mean to...I mean."

"What?"

"Nobody in civilian life likes me. I am not what you would call approachable."

She looked at me tenderly.

"I'm not."

"That's not what I saw at dinner."

"What did you see?"

"I saw a man that everyone would like. You're funny, Bill. You're passionate. You're smart. You're handsome. I don't care how the rest of the world sees you. As far as I'm concerned, I'm lucky that they don't see you how I do. If everyone else saw you like I do, you'd never want to be with me."

"You're wrong."

"I know I don't have an opera singer's body, or the kind of body you see in magazines. So, why are you here with me, Bill?"

I gave her my best rakish grin and raised an eyebrow in her direction.

She blushed and pulled some black hair over her face to hide behind, "I'll take that lewd look as a compliment, but no," she dropped the hair and put her cheek on my chest, "I mean, why are you with me?" She paused and asked quietly, "Why do you…feel how you do?" I had no response. There was no logic to it. "Nobody loves me."

"Mitchell?"

"Mitchell only loves himself. He hasn't touched me in over three years. Nobody, until now, has touched me in over three years. As a rule," she shrugged, "people don't even like me. I have a thin waist and big boobs when everyone wants to look like the latest opera diva. I boo NuTrees. I speak my mind, and I don't back down."

I thought of the asparagus NuTree in Moe's photo, "You only don't back down because you're probably right."

She laughed – a free and easy laugh of release and relief that made my cock snap to.

"God, I love to hear you laugh."

She gently but insistently pushed me down to lay flat on the bed. "Bill," she moved to put her hips over mine, "have you ever felt guided by fate?"

"I don't know. Maybe." Why is she talking now?

"Are you thinking of your jam-proof gun?"

"Only a little. There's something about having a woman on top of me that takes priority."

"Oh Bill."

"What?"

"Mm." She put the tip of my penis inside her. "I'll jam your gun," and she thrust herself onto my cock.

Fuckin' A she did.

It was past midnight when she woke me by getting out of bed.

While she showered, I rolled her a Christmas Kush joint for the road. She seemed at ease when she came out. We laughed as she dressed, then we hugged and kissed at the door.

On her way out, I put my hand on her sweet ass and gave a gentle squeeze, which got me a dick-hardening, "Oooh. You nasty, Bill."

I watched her get into her car, then closed the door.

That stupid fucker Mitchell doesn't know what he has.

I shuffled back to the kitchen. It was nearly 1 AM and…

"No fuckin' way I'm doin' those dishes tonight." Why hadn't they come up with a way to automatically collect and wash my dishes?

Two hours later, Box jarred me out of deep sleep with the clarion bell of an emergency call.

"Okay, okay. Answer it!" The alarm stopped.

The call appeared above my night stand.

The vid was off, so all I saw was the Dark Star Countdown. The voice was hushed and strained and unmistakably Julie's. "Bill. I'm sorry. I didn't know this was what he wanted."

In the background, I heard Mitchell's voice. "No, she's here. A call? Is that a land line?"

The line went dead.

"Julie!"

As I pulled on jeans and a t-shirt, I yelled at Box, "GPS locator online. Locator: echo off last call's phone number." I yanked on my wilderness shoes.

On the way to the garage, I stopped in the guest bathroom, pulled the ziplock from the reservoir, and ripped out the dish cloth-covered gun. Out of habit, I dropped the clip again and confirmed in the side slot that it was a full ten-round magazine. I jacked the clip back in, checked the safety, and tucked the pistol into my pants at the small of my back.

I palmed the garage door open. Julie needed me there faster than a volt burner could handle. The helmet clanked to the ground when I pushed it off the Harley and plopped Boxer into the bike's control panel. "Feed destination and directions of call's location into Boxer."

I mounted and sat the bike upright beneath me then thumbed the ignition and fired up the bike. It roared to life with a deep rumble and the deafening snap of air coming from the exhaust. I torqued the throttle to make sure the line was clear. Inside the confines of the garage, the motor sounded like a light machine gun.

The address flashed across Boxer. The nose of the bike was pointing at a sidewall. With the car in the garage, it was tight, and I didn't have time to waddle the bike around. I leaned the bike to the side and peeled back on the throttle as I clamped down on the front brake.

My rear wheel squealed on the concrete and left a black, ninety-degree arc as a rooster tail of billowing white smoke and the stinging smell of burnt rubber filled the garage. But now I was pointed toward the garage door instead of the side wall. I brought the bike back to vertical and let out the clutch.

I shot from my garage in a plume of white smoke and to the sound of thunder and blasts of fire from my pipes.

At the bottom of the drive, I used the gummy rear-wheel from the burnout and my enhanced strength to make a left sharper than should've been possible, and I was off. Screaming down the street and leaving behind a string of neighbor's lights flipping on and befuddled faces peeking around curtains and out of opened doors.

In three blocks I was on 34. As the road straightened out, I really rocked back on the throttle and opened her up. I was going faster than the automated lights could keep up, so I ran them.

When I arrived at the church, there were three cars in the parking lot and a light on upstairs. In a crouched position, standing up on my pegs, I gunned it and pulled the front tire up and over the curb. When I got close to the doors, I leaned into a sidewise skid and let go. The bike smacked into the "Free Coffee" placard and shattered the glass doors.

I slid on my hip like I was trying to steal a base. Just short of the broken entry, I let my lead foot catch, just as if I had hit the bag at second, and pop me up across the broken entrance in a tumble. Once clear of the entry, I slid in a three-point stance—on the balls of my feet and with one hand on the ground—across the shattered glass-covered linoleum before coming to a stop.

The bike had stalled out, but my ears still rang.

The entry area was empty.

"Bill!"

It came from the stairwell, from downstairs. There was no mistaking the voice. I vaulted the railing and was down the flight of stairs in two moves.

As soon as I moved from the stairwell, I had that same feeling I'd had during the church service: a revulsion that pushed me to leave the building.

Julie was at the opposite end of the downstairs foyer, curled up at Mitchell's feet. She was barefoot and dressed in baggy, blue and black flannel pajamas. Flickering, dancing light came from candelabras positioned around the foyer.

Pete stood next to Mitchell by Julie's head, and I assumed that was Paul on Mitchell's left by Julie's feet.

Julie was scared, but there was no blood, nothing appeared broken, and she didn't seem to be in pain. I glanced from her back to Mitchell to find him also looking at Julie.

She was sitting up on her knees now, and her face was pale

but calm. She smiled and looked at me…in an odd way.

Mitchell laughed a deep, guttural laugh, and his eyes glowed red in the candlelight.

"All this over that faggot mayor?" He laughed cruelly. "He thought we loved him. Can you believe that shit? He was as big an idiot as you. I knew you, Mr. Slaughter, were a fool from the moment I saw how my sermon affected you."

I hadn't heard a word of it.

"From the moment you prattled off those pathetic stories about your baseball trips with your loser father."

I hadn't told those stories for his benefit.

"Mercenaries are expensive, but I would've been happy to just kill you. Not now."

I wrinkled my nose. There was acrid bite of cordite and sulfur in the air.

"You still can't see, but you can smell it."

In the candlelight, Julie's black hair hung down framing her pale face, making her look sepulchral.

In my peripheral, a flash of color flickered from Mitchell's eyes. I kept my focus on Julie. Calmly, she said, "Even now, I know God loves me, and I feel His love."

That was what I'd seen on her face: peace. Did she feel she was right where she should be in life?

Mitchell roared, "Love this!" He put his hand over her mouth and nose, and glared intensely into her eyes.

I reached behind me for a gun that wasn't there. It must've spilled out when I laid the bike down. Her body gave a small but definitive jerk then collapsed into a limp heap.

HUCOs. They would have told me my pistol was on the ground. Where is *danger-close*?

Outside the coroner's office I'd slipped into it easily enough, but it hadn't been there during the assassination, or even on the ride over.

She collapsed in a heap, and her head lolled my way; her flat eyes stared at me.

Remotely, I heard another laugh from Mitchell.

Paul moved forward.

He was big and lean, and I could tell he knew how to handle himself. Not that it would help him.

I forced myself to look away from Julie. "You are going—"

In blurred strides, Paul crossed the room to smash a palm strike into my chest that sent me flying back. It would have crushed the sternum of any man without superior reflexes and a steel-like sternum.

He laughed. "What were you saying?"

Mitchell laughed with him. "You haven't met Paul, have you? He has the latest bio-synth processors." His forced jocularity was a sneer. "They're expensive and very high-maintenance, but there's no arguing with the results."

As I got to my feet, I trained my eyes on Paul's chest to better anticipate his moves. If Julie was alive, was going to live, the only way I could help her was to survive. I tried to put myself into *danger-close*. It still wouldn't catch.

The speed he had crossed the floor was at least at near-enhanced levels. Bio-synthetics—a sheathing over the major muscle groups that connected to bone with tendons. Unlike other civilian options, bio-synths were one hundred percent internal. It was on or off tech with no in-between and, so it seemed, recent improvements were impressive. My enhancements were bleeding edge half a decade ago. And now civilian tech was…?

Am I last year's model already?

The military had discontinued bio-synth development. Other than expensive and finicky, like other large-scale efforts to internally combine man and machine, use was accompanied by imbalanced personalities and fits of rage.

"I am going to crush you!" Paul roared.

Other than madness and cost, what could be wrong with bio-synths?

A dry tongue touched my lips. Paul was a problem.

I was out of practice for using *danger-close*, and there were no HUCOs to help. HUCOs were just a tool.

Target in, man the fuck up, and get this shit done.

I tried again to focus and step into *danger-close*. Still, it wouldn't click into place like it had done so easily so many times before. Like it just had done outside of Moe's!

Paul closed fast, feinted high, and came at me with a flurry of jabs to my face and eyes, and knife strikes to my neck. One of the jabs to my face caught my cheek and opened a deep cut. A side kick knocked me momentarily off balance; he used the opening to slip a punch into my floating ribs. My breath whooshed out, but my micro-fractured bones held.

Pete drifted back, bouncing on the balls of his feet. He was shaking his open hands loosely by his chest.

"Aw, look at that, boys," Paul gloated. "Looks like soldier boy is all talked out. He's got nothing to say before I kill him!"

He came at me again, but there was nothing new here.

When he got to the second series of blows, instead of trying to deflect the jab to my face like I had before, I ducked under and pushed the next strike in the sequence high and slapped Paul, hard, across the face. He took a quick step back, shook his head and then came at me a third time—he led with a sweeping, head-high kick. It was sloppy, and his speed no longer caught me off-guard. I blocked it with my forearm and stepped into him to smash an elbow into his jaw. I connected, but only to knick him. His reaction speed saved him from the brunt of it. He took a 1-2 step back, gave a quick shake of his head, then yelled and charged. I grabbed his shirt and used my hips as a lever to body drop him hard to the linoleum.

I stepped away. I didn't need *danger-close* for this fucker.

Pete and Mitchell were silent. Paul got unsteadily to his feet. This time he came at me more slowly, determinedly. While there still was nothing original in these attacks, he gave each strike with maximum effort.

He went for another sloppy kick, telegraphing it all the way from Wyoming.

I dropped beneath it and used a leg sweep to knock his back leg out and up-end him. His legs flew over his head, and Paul came down on the side of his head and neck.

The vertebrae crunched, and his eyes disappeared into the back of his head, leaving only white showing as he lay on the floor, quivering and soiling himself.

Guess enhanced skeletons hadn't made it to the civilian market yet.

Pete looked shaken enough that he might piss himself as well.

Mitchell seemed unfazed. "Paul always did rely too much on the physical."

I stepped away from Paul's corpse. "What happened last week that made Frank drive into the river?"

"My small group is men only." He turned to Pete. "Show him."

Pete, stunned, turned to Mitchel in shock. "Me?"

Mitchell crossed the length of Julie's body to Pete in a blur, faster even than Paul, snatched the front of Pete's shirt in a fist, and lifted him effortlessly off the ground. With Pete's face inches from his own just like Julie's had been, he yelled, "Yes, you!" Mitchell's eyes reflected more of the orange and yellow candle light as he dropped Pete.

Like he'd had his strings cut, Pete fell heavily to his knees, unzipped Mitchell's pants, and removed his erect penis. His motions were stiff, mechanical, as if he moved against a strong wind.

I turned my head away from the sight of Pete's physical and spiritual rape.

When I turned back, Mitchell backhanded Pete away to send him sprawling across the floor hard enough to crack the drywall where he hit and then lay still, unconscious.

Mitchell barked out a maniacal laugh. It was the trumpet sound of sadism triumphant. Mitchell's eyes filled with a roiling orange-yellow glow that I could see now was not a reflection from the light around the room.

"I'm sure Pete did that out of love. Aren't you?"

When he smiled, he looked like a corpse with rictus; it grabbed hold of and peeled the skin off something very primal inside me. This. Was wrong.

A dread panic was filling my chest.

Mitchell frightened me.

"Do you know me now?" he asked.

This time, I saw it all.

Everything above his calves was coated in that glow—a writhing pattern of coruscating orange and yellow. His feet and ankles weren't black, but an absence of color, as if they stood in a void that rejected the life and light of this world.

In a recess of me hidden until now, I knew. I was looking at evil.

Not the bestialities men exercise against men, but a connection to the root, the fountainhead for all of that.

I closed my eyes and heard Julie's words. "Have you ever felt guided by God?" It was easy to deny God in the face of man's cruelties. I opened my eyes. But when confronted with true, unequivocal evil, I couldn't deny the opposite.

In that instant of belief, my world went white.

CHAPTER 32 – SLAIN

Later, William David Slaughter would look back at this moment and realize, it was with this decision that he first knew he was really, truly different. That no one experienced life in the way he was forced to.

But, for now, all Bill Slaughter knew was silence. He didn't hear even his heartbeat or the sound of his own breathing.

Bill saw Mitchell as taller. But then he recognized that he was the one who had gotten smaller. When he held his right hand to his face, he knew it to be a child's hand. His left hand was being held by someone else's hand.

With his child's eyes, Bill followed the arm up.

Without knowing, he had expected to see Dad. But it wasn't Dad. It was his adult self that stood in the church. The cut on his cheek pulsed a steady dribble of blood.

They smiled at each other.

In that look, Bill Slaughter knew love for himself. Pure love, unrestrained by years of soldier's duty and human doubt.

He wasn't certain if he was glowing in a way anyone else could see, or if it only appeared that way to him. However, to Bill, he glowed so brightly white that it shone off the walls making the candles seem dim in comparison.

Though he couldn't hear, it was clear Mitchell was

screaming. His mouth open wide and eyes rolled back as he shook his head savagely from side-to-side.

Bill Slaughter spoke, and it was the only sound he heard. "I…" He paused; it was quick, but filled with penultimate finality.

As he stood holding his own hand, William David Slaughter knew a joy so thorough it could only live for that instant, but the memory of it would echo throughout the rest of his life.

Mitchell Slade was now on his knees still in his orange and yellow shroud howling, spittle flying from the corners of his mouth.

Bill simply said, "You are rejected."

From his knees, Mitchell fell backward. His hands clutched fiercely at nothing, and his spine arched so steeply that the crown of his head pressed the ground. His jaw was now unhinged; his mouth stretched into a frenzied wail of impotent fury.

Then, as his body gave one last spasm, Mitchell's glow snuffed out. His muscles locked in that final, torturously arched position.

Calmly, as if William David Slaughter were settling in for a nap, he lay down then his child self did the same next to him.

As he closed his eyes, he noted that Clyde Somers was coming down the stairs. Behind him was Franco.

CHAPTER 33 – A PLAN COMES TOGETHER

Something stung my cheek, and my head snapped to the left. A second later, the sting came again on the other cheek and my head snapped to the right.

"Wake the fuck up!"

Hot blood ran down my cheek and neck from the cut Paul had given me.

My eyelids fluttered.

"You with me, Billy?"

I looked at Somers. He reached back to slap me again. "That's enough, Somers." It was Franco. "He's awake now."

Somers *tsk*ed in clear disappointed disgust, then he released my shirt.

I got to my feet, and since nobody tried to stop me, I walked to Julie. Her eyes still had a blank look to them. Nervously, I put two fingers to her neck. There was a pulse.

Of course there was a pulse! I knew there'd be a pulse. *Shit, I'm glad there's a fucking pulse.*

"She okay?" Franco called.

I looked over Julie's body at him with Somers standing just behind him. Who in this burg might have traveled enough to establish the kinds of connections needed to put a small town schmuck like Slade in touch with a team of out-of0state, ex-military hit men?

I lifted my fingers from Julie's neck. "That was your hit team?"

"Yes. But I was never worried for you."

"That is a comfort."

"I knew it would not work."

"Why not? I've been shot before."

"Yes. In the Ukraine."

"What the hell? You and Somers get together and exchange notes?"

"No. I just gave him mine."

A shiver ran right down my spine.

Franco shot Somers a look. "Did Agent Somers share details of your military service record?"

I looked at Somers. In our exchange he must have breached some protocol. He still stared at me intently.

Somers turned to Franco. "What?"

Franco put a hand to his chin and walked in front of Somers to the edge of the room and back again, before saying, "It's an interesting choice, Mr. Somers."

I just stood by Julie and watched.

Somers didn't twitch or change expression. "Is the mission a go or not? Sir. And don't start getting all self-righteous. Or has Irving not had a chance to look at that door yet?"

"Interesting, Mr. Somers. Quite interesting."

"Gentlemen, I don't know, and I don't care. I'll just take Julie, and scoot on—"

"We've been watching you a very long time," Franco cut me short. He appeared composed, and at ease in this element.

"That's flattering. But why? What is so interesting about me?"

"It is funny you should ask."

"I don't suppose it's *ha ha* funny, is it?"

He smiled gently, with no trace of irony. "We will know what is so interesting about you soon. Directly after we kill you."

"Yeah, I didn't think so." I had to laugh at that.

Somers and Franco exchanged a look. "What is funny?" Franco asked.

"My weed salesman, the guy I'd just recently shared shit with that I wouldn't have told anyone else," it was Somers's turn to shoot Franco a look, "wants me dead. I think that's officially ironic." I shrugged. "What can I say? Irony makes me laugh."

Franco paused then resumed with a detached, professorial air. "Mankind stands at a precipice. We used to think the universe was too vast to be measured. Now we know its age, and its size and mass. We used to think what we could see in the universe was too vast to be quantified. And now we know that what we see is only one-fifth of the known universe, that dark matter and dark energy make up the other eighty percent. And now, the Dark Star is trying to tap that dark energy. If they do, humans might have found a source of limitless energy. Enough energy to travel even faster than light."

"Franco! What the *fuck* are you talking about? The Dark Star? What does that have to do with me?"

"We have been communicating with the Dark Star crew on the quantum level."

"Okay. A little surprising. But, again, what's it got to do with me?"

"One of the many experiments meant to occupy the crew dealt with quantum entanglement. It was a minor experiment, meant only to confirm quantum entanglement at an incredible and unearthly distance."

"Oh, great. String theory. High school all over again."

"One of the technicians here on Earth was running a routine inspection and noticed a readout indicating the entangled experiment was generating data. Turns out, rather as expected, even incredible distances do not affect entanglement. Our ability to communicate remains very limited. Frustratingly limited. Flipping and reading the particle is…"

"A pain in the ass?" I offered.

Franco smiled. "Exactly so."

"Can't you do Morse code or something with your flipping particle?"

"The particle just flips. It cannot do long then short flips. It was with considerable time, effort, and much patience that we derived the current system that communicates single-digit numbers. Because of the difficulty in communicating anything, messages are kept short."

My head was spinning. "Entangled fuckin' particles?"

"Yes, it works if nobody looks at the entangled particles. We have to measure the effect on the surrounding particles." Franco smiled and spread his French-cuffed hands. "Electro-magnetism is not my field, so I do not know how it works either, but we definitely know that it does."

I shook my head. "C'mon, man. Quit jerkin' me off over here! Where do I fit in all that?"

Franco ignored me. "It is all a question of computing power. And do you know what computers do when they are bored?"

"It isn't sell weed and get high, is it?"

He laughed pleasantly. "That job is spoken for. No." He leaned in and looked at me intently. "They measure."

"They measure."

"Yes."

"What the hell do they measure?"

"Every. Thing."

"Hey, it's not the size, it's how you use it."

"You are precisely right! Which is why your name and serial number pinged on an early version of the military's quantum computer—a computer that it was thought could see all possible outcomes of a variation. But some of your activities, particularly when considered in aggregate, were deviations in the standard that demanded attention."

"I was just lucky. I had a feeling—"

"Is that so? On my first deployment to Indonesia, I went on a routine check with a driver. When I climbed back into the GXV, I looked at the people along the street, and they were all staring at me with this kind of opened-mouthed…I do not know what. I climbed out of the vehicle, and as soon as I did, I saw it. A grenade under my seat. As I was climbing in, someone—probably still in that crowd—must have rolled that grenade in right by my feet."

"Dud?"

"Yes. A dud. A bullet that just missed."

"Every guy who's seen combat has a story like that."

"*A* story. Maybe."

"Even a blind squirrel stumbles across a nut every once in a while. That's how luck works. There's nothing special about it."

"Luck? A happenstance of unconnected and unrepeated results?" Franco waggled a finger at me. "No no. *I* was lucky. Once is luck. Twice is curious. Three times? A dozen times? How many times over your years of service did you have this feeling, did you get this 'lucky'?"

I looked at him blankly. "All the time. Every mission."

"Precisely! The difference in your survival was such a small thing and yet you repeated it over and over. How could a computer not notice? Then, we, or—not to be modest," he put a hand to his chest, "*I* asked the computer to do everything it could to kill you, which culminated in the Ukraine mission."

"Franco? *You* killed Sullivan and Chandler?"

Franco paused to consider the statement. "Technically, yes. I am sorry."

"Are you? Cuz I'm thinkin', not so fucking much."

He looked at me incredulously. "Of course not. But do manners not count for anything? If it helps, I was only trying to kill you. And until yesterday—and, by the way, thank you so much for sharing—I could view the satellite feed, but I couldn't know how you did it. You and that damn bitch cheated!"

"What? Me and…?"

"Clare!"

Somers put a hand out. "Sir!"

"What, Somers? You are going to kill him, right?" Franco

turned back to me and spoke urgently. "You know what the odds were that an unjammable rifle would jam at that exact moment that you were behind the only solid rock in that entire embankment that allowed you to avoid an APM that you could not have known was there?"

I shook my head. "You and this Clare murdered Sullivan and Chandler."

Franco winced. "Bill, please, they were soldiers—"

"Who didn't need to die!"

"*Keep your eye on the big picture!* The odds were non-existent! The fucking computer blew a fucking gasket! Oh God, we would have loved to have kept on trying to kill to you, but," he looked at me suspiciously, "you were shot in the Ukraine. Were you not? You went into that last building, out from under satellite surveillance, and came out shot. You did not mention that yesterday, eh? You know what I think?" He studied me.

After all those years of hanging out with him, I couldn't hide it.

"Oh, you did! You fucking did! You shot yourself. Oh my God, that explains so much." He turned and jabbed a finger at Somers. "I was right to never stop watching!"

If Somers cared about Franco's triumph, he kept it to himself and his eyes stayed on me.

"But for the longest time, nothing. A sloppy divorce followed by years of nothing. Nothing! Then, a break. You used your PD, but I was not ready for it. I waited for it to happen again by itself, but I grew impatient."

"Hold on…"

"Dear Mayor Nelson was so eager to help. I am a man of some international acclaim, after all. Frank was curious about Europe, so I told him stories, and we struck up a camaraderie. He really was quite a sweet, old man."

My stomach fell.

"Yes, that is right, Bill. You would not leave the house," he shrugged noncommittally, "so I had to ask myself, what can I do to *make* you leave the house?"

"Couldn't you just murder me in my sleep?"

"Of course! Poison your fruit. Pump gas into your home. So many options."

"Then why Frank?"

"Because I could only lead you to water! The fight had to be your idea. It is the fight to live we want to watch you fail at."

"You sent Frank to Marvin."

"That is right. And Mitchell played his part as murderer."

"Mitchell wasn't supposed to kill me?"

Franco looked wounded. "Do not get me wrong. It would have been nice. But as I told you, even if you are enhanced," he jerked a thumb at Somers, "he is going to kill you."

"How did you know Mitchell would kill Frank?"

"Please. I did not *know*. This is science. People cannot *know* things. But, you could, if I may be so bold, perhaps say that I am a study of human nature. Do you not think so, Somers?"

Somers had eyes only for me.

"At any rate, I played the odds," he said with a shrug of his eyebrows. "And helped where I could."

"You asked Frank to join Mitchell's church."

"Yes."

"And to start a relationship with Marvin."

"Precisely."

"So that Slade could kill Frank, and Marvin would hire me so that you could watch me fail and die."

He thrust both fists in the air like a touchdown had been scored. "I love it when a plan comes together!"

CHAPTER 34 – OPERATIONAL SECURITY

"But why? Why? Why? Would you just answer *why?*"

"A week ago, a week and one day ago to be exact, the Dark Star crew used a considerable amount of effort to send us a ten-digit number: 2847639272. You know that number."

It was my military serial number. "Jesus, Mary, and Joseph, are you incapable of a straight answer? Why do you want to watch me die?"

"Not die. How pedestrian a thing would that be? It is all about survival! And we want to watch you *fail* to survive."

"Potato, Puh-tah-to. You'll pardon if I don't make the distinction, as both end up with me deceased. What do I have to do with the Dark Star?"

"I have a guess," he said slyly, "but I will *know* the answer to your first question at the conclusion of the experiment, hopefully," he glanced at Somers, "quite soon." Somers remained as he was. "As for your second question, what you have to do with the Dark Star, we do not know."

"Ya don't know. Really?"

Franco shrugged. "Communication is limited."

"Of course you don't know. Just like you don't know why you want to kill me. Until, of course, you kill me! You seem to not know a lot."

Franco clapped his hands delightedly. "Yes! It is exactly so! You articulate what is sublime in science so effortlessly."

"I'm glad you think so. Can I go now?"

Franco looked at the dead Paul and Mitchell and the still forms of Julie and Pete. "Do you have any idea how special your life is?" Franco smiled then said slowly, caringly, "Bill, I am done trying to kill you."

"Careful, you'll spoil me."

Franco laughed again. "I want you to work for us."

"If you can't kill 'em, have 'em join you? That's quite the recruiting slogan. Who is 'us'??"

"We are a simple consortium of private businesses and government agencies with a wide range of interests. It is how I became connected with Pastor Slade."

"No thanks."

"Just like that?"

"I ask you one simple question, and you give me some bureaucratic bullshit."

Franco bent over laughing. "Ah well. Of course, you still would have died."

"Of course."

"But we would have had better control, and maybe even gotten some productivity out of you along the way." He turned to Somers. "You were right. I hate to say it, but you were right."

Somers lowered his chin and gave me a tight-lipped grin full of sinister intent.

Franco continued, "You see, I—and others like me—do not want to kill you. I mean, we do, but we also see value in running the experiment, that is, in you remaining alive. But Somers? Somers here is one of those who really wants to kill you dead."

I looked back to Somers. From the top and bottom of his eyes, clear plastic met seamlessly. There was no mistaking what they were, but I'd never seen retractable HUCOs before.

Franco moved back two steps as Somers stepped toward me. "I should warn you," Franco called, "Somers has the latest military upgrades. He was the first to successfully use nanites to improve power and speed."

"I think you dropped this," Somers said to me. He shot Franco a look then tossed me my pistol from across the room. It hit the linoleum with a clatter and skidded to a stop at my feet.

Franco raised an eyebrow before moving out of the line of fire.

As Somers stood there, I flipped the safety off and put a bullet in his chest.

Fuck! I missed?

He'd moved so fast I couldn't track him. He stood still again, waiting. I shot again. Again. Each time Somers was gone before I could finish squeezing the trigger, and my rounds found only the back wall. I put both hands on the gun and missed on three more shots.

Six shots. Four left.

When I stopped shooting, he stopped. Somers had crossed just over half the floor. In fact, I would've said he'd crossed exactly six-tenths of the distance between us.

He's playing a game. He's showing he can kill me anytime.

He must be reading my arm's movement and moving before, or as, I pulled the trigger.

Even enhanced, I wasn't fast enough. Without *danger-close* I had no chance. I couldn't react quickly enough.

I looked at the space between us.

I brought the gun up and fired at where Somers stood. Then, as quickly as I could pull the trigger, I expended the last three bullets in a chest-high pattern where I thought he would stop to take his eighth step.

Somers laughed. He genuinely laughed. "You sneaky bitch!" He touched his shirt. "You put holes in my shirt." One of my bullets had gone just to the side of him and perforated the right armpit of his shirt.

He reached up and pulled his shirt off as if it was tissue. Underneath, the muscles on Somers's slim body popped, as if they were already taut from exertion. With each fluid step, his torso rippled with muscles like hammers striking inside a piano.

I tossed the empty gun aside and dropped into my fighting form: hands up to the side of my face, on the balls of my feet, knees bent. The man could dodge my bullets. What good could my fists be?

So what was I going to do? Give up? Ship it in and just die? *Fuck that!*

He closed the last few feet so quickly all I could do was brace for impact. I took the first kick off my left arm and shoulder, and it sent me tumbling.

He was too fast. Too strong. I hadn't even seen that kick.

I got to my feet and back into a stance. My left arm was throbbing and useless.

"I would've killed you after the mercs blew it, but," he glanced at Franco, "I wasn't given proper notice."

"Let it go," Franco said.

Somers turned back to me. "And that cop got to your house too fast."

The next kick was a front snap kick that I jerked back from just in time to avoid having my chest staved in. I sensed more than saw the punch that followed the kick and managed to dodge the full brunt of the blow. I tasted blood in the corner of my mouth.

"Bill the Mighty." Somers had a feral look to his eyes. "The mighty quantum computer crasher!" Somers mocked. "Nobody can put Bill's ass in a casket. Nobody? *Nobody?*"

Somers is losing his shit.

He came at me with a barrage of punches, a maelstrom of sledgehammer blows. He could've killed me with any one of them if that was his intent. Even with my skeletal system, I was pretty sure something had broken in my left arm.

A slap to my head spun me around and set my ears to ringing. A knife strike slipped easily past my left elbow and under my ribs to impale my guts. It felt like being shot again. I coughed and a batch of blood shot out.

I staggered back and fell to a knee.

"Somers," Franco said, "stand down."

Reluctance etched in his movements, Somers backed up. His steady breathing was a stark contrast to my painful rasping for air. In addition to my left arm, my left eye was swollen nearly shut, and I had a couple of broken ribs on the right.

Franco stepped between Somers and me, wincing when he saw the damage up close. "This is so, so unnecessary. Is death better than working with us? Better than helping your country? Bill, join us."

I turned my head and spat a mouthful of blood then struggled painfully to my feet. "Franco?"

"Bill."

Every breath brought multiple stabbing pains. "You remember this moment."

Franco's shoulders slumped, and he shook his head.

"Life won't always be this happy."

"Oh, Bill." He spread his arms out apologetically. "This is not the outcome I chose."

"Namaste."

Franco sighed. "I suppose I will finally be able to cut off this damn ponytail." He moved back behind Somers.

Somers stepped forward. I couldn't touch Somers, let alone fight him.

This was where I was going to die. *God, glad we got know each other here at the end. I've had a good run at it.*

"Of course," Franco went on, "Somers will finish off what is left of the Slade family when you are done."

"Franco. No."

"It has to be. You know that. OPSEC. We cannot leave these loose ends."

Somers stepped toward me with that wicked grin on his lips.

They were going to kill Julie.

I was hurt, but I couldn't give in.

I won't give in.

Somers closed in.

CHAPTER 35 – ONE AND THE SAME

Where was it? *Danger-close* had been so easy with the chief.

I'm going to die? The thought made me angry. *I am not* fucking *dying here!*

And like that. Easy as holding a pen. The world congealed. This wasn't the *danger-close* I'd had with the chief. This was the *danger-close* from the Ukraine.

HUCOs really are just a tool.

In this condition, Somers moved at simple enhanced speeds. But my wounds slowed me considerably, and my left arm still hung by my side.

Somers was now dashing toward me at a speed I couldn't have seen outside of *danger-close*.

I'd have one shot, one chance to catch him unprepared with a *danger-close*-timed attacked.

His mouth open in a scream, fingers like the point of a spear, he aimed for my heart.

Just as he closed to within arm's reach, I used my right hand to swat his arm away. I let my left arm swing behind me naturally, as if trying to protect it.

Surprised rippled across Somers's face.

Ignoring the pain, and with every bit of enhanced strength left, I swung my left fist toward his face.

Dammit!

Somers was still fast enough to pull his head back. I was going to miss!

Instead of a blow directly to the occipital lobe of Somers skull, my fist smashed into Somers's mouth. I felt his teeth crumple and then there was a brilliant explosion.

My ring and index finger were still attached to my hand but bent in angles no fingers should go. The skin on my knuckles was gone; bone and sinew were clearly visible. I grimaced at the site and mentally clamped down on the pain.

My blow and the blast had snapped Somers's neck back, his mouth a smoking, gaping hole. Not only were his top teeth missing, but a portion of his upper jaw was also gone. He toppled over backward, in exactly the position he was in when the explosion happened, and it seemed he fell at half speed. I blinked to clear my vision as Somers clattered to the ground like a board and lay unmoving.

I recognized that explosion. That was a THZ Toob. Franco said Somers had nanites. Had the EMF from the Toob shut down the nanites?

I'd think on it later. This was my chance to live.

I straddled Somers's chest. It was like sitting on a steel I-beam. I couldn't just pummel him.

I pinched my fingers together and forced my right hand into his mouth. I reached into the back of his neck, at the base of his jaw, between his impossibly hard and corded neck muscles, curled my finger around anything that would squish, and squeezed until my fingers touched my palm through the soft tissue.

The cartilage of his windpipe crackled in my palm like thin strips of crab shell. With his jugular vein and carotid artery in my grasp, warm blood pulsed against both edges of my hand.

From an arm's distance away, I looked into his eyes. They didn't move, but through the HUCOs, I could see in his wildly contracting and dilating pupils that he felt my hand around his throat.

Somers was fully aware.

I leaned in close to his face. I gripped even tighter and my nails furrowed into, then through, the soft blood vessel walls.

My bruised and bloodied face was reflected in his HUCOs.

My breath fluttered his eyelashes.

An animal yell erupted from deep inside me, and I jerked back with everything I had left.

Blood geysered from his mouth. I tried to raise my left hand to shield my face, but it didn't respond, and his warm blood splattered onto my battered face and once white t-shirt.

Somers's body went limp. His jaw lay open, impossibly wide. I must've broken it on the way out, and, with nothing inside his throat, it was a crater spilling over with blood.

Panting, I got to one foot then the other, clutching Agent Somers's throat in a death grip. His blood ran over the open wound on my palm.

Franco stared, open-mouthed. When he spoke, it was with a quiet reverence. "When I see this…I touch something science cannot know."

With the combination of my wounds and Somers's blood on me and pooling around my feet, I must've been a sight to see. Adrenaline alone kept me upright.

He put a hand to his forehead as if to hold himself up. "What-what just happened?"

"I just…" I cleared my throat. "I just killed Somers."

"But how?"

I growled and held my right hand out and shook my trophy for Franco to see. "*I ripped his fucking throat out!*"

"But he—he could have killed you at any moment, *any* moment. What was he thinking? Why did he decide to not just kill you?" Franco caught himself and then spoke rapid-fire, "Quick, while there is no network, you must know this: I am your friend."

I laughed, loudly. Even to me, it sounded unhinged. "With friends like you—" I felt myself wobble but corrected it to keep on my feet. For now.

"You continually beat odds so vast they—in the most literal sense—defy logic!"

"You haven't seen me play poker."

"You are special. You are beyond unique. My work—"

"Where you try to kill me?"

"—is the one and only thing that will keep you alive and non-vivisected! I will see to it you remain as free as you have been, but they will never stop watching you."

"What a hobby."

"If not for Mitchell's misguided efforts to kill you, Somers would have killed you, and I would not have been here to see this. I'm saying, you should know that Mitchell's delay saved you."

"Saved *me*, or your experiment?"

Franco smiled broadly, as if he was giving me a big hug. "But they are one and the same!" He said it fondly, paternally. "Go someplace where everyone knows everyone and then do not trust anyone, and never any new person."

"You'll still find me."

"Undoubtedly so, but you will have limited our direct action options."

"Why are you telling me?"

"Despite all this," he gestured broadly to include everything in and out of the room, "I. Am your friend. I have sacrificed much to protect your life."

Franco walked over to Mitchell in his anguished pose. "Will you tell me something?" He pointed at Mitchell. "Did you see him in his enhanced state?"

"I s'pose."

"Good God. Both of them…" He looked unbelievingly at Mitchell. "Will you tell me how that happened?"

Everything was beginning to hurt. I couldn't block it out anymore. There was an intense pain from my left arm that made me gasp. I looked down at my disfigured left hand and remembered the white, the joy of my child hand holding my adult hand.

"Did I die?"

Franco cocked his head. "Did you what?"

My knees went weak. I had lost too much blood. Still

standing over Somers's body, I dropped to my knees into the splay of blood on either side of him.

I glared at Franco. "I'm going to find you and kill you."

"That would be wonderful!" he shouted with such spontaneous glee I wasn't sure who liked the idea better. "Find! Clare!"

It hurt to breathe. I winced at the piercing pain in my back below my ribs. Internal bleeding. The coppery tang of blood welled into the back of my throat.

My head fell to my chest and blackness began closing in on the edges of my vision.

I heard Franco say, "Here. Alive. Somers is down." Quick pause. "Yes, *down*." Then a longer pause. "That is not my job."

Franco waved congenially and mouthed, "Bye," before disappearing through an exit.

Noise made me turn my head.

Julie looked from one section of the room to the next. From the still, candle-lit forms of Pete, and then Paul, then Mitchell, locked in that impossibly elongated and arched position. Her face recoiled into greater and deeper shock with each body. Then, abject terror as she turned to the grisly scene of a man beaten near to death sitting on a mangled corpse in a pool of blood. And, finally, revulsion when she recognized that the man was me.

In delirium, I looked to my right fist and back.

Julie, you're safe.

I held out the token of my affection: a bouquet of red blood vessels, white trachea, and pink tongue. It was quiet. The only sound was the blood splatting from my bouquet into the larger collection of blood around me.

See.

As my wounds overtook me, I collapsed to splash face first into the blood pooled in Somers's throatless neck. I was just awake enough to hear Julie's beautiful voice scream before darkness.

CHAPTER 36 – CIVIL RIGHTS

I drifted through cool blackness. Nobody glowed here. There were no entangled particles. No nano-enhanced agents. I dreamed of Julie.

But only her voice. I swam in the vast, warm ocean of her voice. There were no words, but Julie clearly could be felt behind the sounds flowing around me, washing up against me. Occasionally, there was the thought, *It's ok to be tired, to stop, and to sink into the still and the darkness.*

Every time I tried to leave swimming behind, Julie's voice buoyed me and drowned out that thought.

I wished I knew what she was saying.

When I woke, I was in a hospital bed.

Dim daylight came through the curtains. A noninvasive patch similar to my home's med unit was attached to my left arm, delivering fluids and keeping tabs on my vitals. A yellow light on the patch was flashing, and a nurse came striding in. "How was your nap?"

I started to talk, but the words couldn't make it past the back of my parched throat.

The nurse picked up a cup with a straw from my bedside table. I worked the first sip around my mouth with my tongue, so it would stop feeling like a stick. The next sip was longer and felt fantastic on my parched throat.

Slowly, I asked, "How long was I asleep?"

"Just for a bit, don't you worry." She patted my chest lightly. "I'll let the doctor know you're awake." My stomach growled. "And hungry!" She smiled, checked my patch, and left.

Hospitals. Waste of fucking time.

My left hand and arm tingled. My arm was in a NuCast from the shoulder down.

A short time later, the doctor came in. He was a young man with an easy air about him and short brown, neatly parted hair. The name tag on his white coat said Stuart. ""I wasn't sure if that was a last or first name.

He smiled warmly. "I'm glad you're awake." He came into the room and stood by my right arm away from the door. "But you should sleep, or at least move very little. You had several traumas but, of particular concern, was the punctured kidney we replaced."

"The one on my left?"

"Yes. The serial number on it says it was military issue."

"You don't say."

He laughed congenially. "I do say, *and* you're healing quite well. Rather incredibly, you're both alive and very much ahead of initial prognosis. Given the trauma from your wounds, we were surprised it was the fever that had us most concerned."

"Fever?"

"Yes."

I looked at him blankly.

"Your fever. The fever you had when we brought you in."

I used the straw to finish the last of my water, slurping the last bit, before saying, "Oh, that fever."

"In fact, you were especially lucky."

"Really?"

"Yes'. We happened to have some training scheduled for a hyper-hydration system. If we hadn't had access to that machine, I doubt we could have kept your body from, literally, sucking itself dry."

"That's quite a coincidence. Did you just schedule that training?"

"Oh no, not at all. The hyper-hydration system is new and production hasn't ramped up. There are only a few of them in the country, and we've been on the training schedule for months. Anyway, your fever finally, quite simply, broke and went away. We never found the source." He patted me on my right arm. "And don't worry if recent memories seem fuzzy. They'll return after some rest."

He stood by my bed. Smiling. He cleared his throat.

"Is there something else?"

"I don't mean to," he put his hand to his mouth and rubbed his jaw, "overstate things; however, I should say that your survival odds when you arrived were...not high. We're rerunning the calculations now. But we do see these things from time to time."

"See what things?"

"I don't mean to imply that you're recovery was not phenomenal—"

"Oh Christ. Just say it, doc."

"Bill... May we call you Bill?"

"I'd prefer it."

He smiled. "Noted." He reached over and rolled a stool with a hip-high seat next to my bed and sat down. "Medical computers don't misdiagnose. Just not something that happens. Cows don't fly and MedComs don't make mistakes. However! It does happen."

"The thing that can't happen?"

"That's right. Cancer goes into remission, someone wakes up from a coma—healings we can't quantify. It's the first time I've ever witnessed it. That any of us on staff here have ever seen it, outside of journals."

"Well. Aren't I irreplaceable?"

"It would seem so." He smiled. "Per your civil rights, during your treatment, we did collect and still do retain any and all parts of your body including all fluid samples obtained during your treatment. These, of course, remain your property.

224

Often patients appreciate the hospital's disposal service from which we sometimes retain samples. Would you like us to take care of these for you?"

"Take care of?"

"Your recovery represents a unique chance to study—""

"Destroy them."

He blanched. The color literally left his face. "Bill, please. If I may, these samples are an incredible learning opportunity for the—"

"Doctor."

"Call me Stuart."

"Stuart, I'm doing you a favor. Destroy all of it. You might not think so, but—"

"It's okay, Mr. Slaughter." He held a hand up to stop me. "It is disappointing, but I see you feel strongly about this, and that's perfectly fine." His smile was forced this time. "That is your right."

"Thank you."

Stuart touched my shoulder then smiled stiffly as he tapped instructions into his white tablet.

"I'm going to give you something to help you sleep."

Ah, the one thing hospitals *were* good for: drugs.

When I woke up again, I was still hungry, but I just lay there in my bed. No flashing yellow lights sent a nurse scurrying to my bedside. One light blinked green—it read "MED." I lay back and tried to relax. The hand and arm in the NuCast itched.

I had time to note that the ceilings in hospitals looked a lot like the ceilings in a coroner's building before the meds washed up in my blood and things went goofy. Cogent thinking went first, but came with a pleasant hallucination: my body was sheathed in a very thin layer of light blue. I could see my finger go through the light, but I couldn't feel the light. I laughed. Why should I be able to feel light?

Silly blue skin.

When I held up my hand and pulled on the blue, it felt like peeling dried glue off, but when I let go, the blue snapped back.

I knew I was trippin' balls, but I didn't care.

I held my hand close. The blue was filled with a frenetic zig-zag of white contrails.

I laughed at my hallucination, and the sound of my laughter came out of my mouth in three large "HA" balloon letters that looked like they were made of orange, incandescent bubbles.

Yeah, this is why I like weed.

When I next opened my eyes, I was staring at the ass of a nurse bent at the waist and fiddling with something at the foot of my bed.

The nurse turned and rolled his eyes into a smile. "Some men, even on their death beds, pumped full of meds, still think with only their smallest parts."

"You wound me."

"I don't think it was me who did this."

"True. What time is it?" His badge said Justin.

"You were brought in almost two days ago. It's 2 AM on a Friday."

I lay back down and stared up at the ceiling.

"By the way…"

"Yes?"

"I know who you are."

I raised an eyebrow. "You should. You have my chart."

"Mm-hm. And I saw you at The Flame with Marvin."

"Oh."

"Some government men came by. They insisted they had the right to unsupervised time with you."

"Okay. Well, did they?"

"You know one thing all gay men know?"

"Uh…how to play charades?"

"How clever. Yes, but also our civil rights. You bet your ass they did *not!*"

I lay back with a smile. "I knew this country still had a copy of the Constitution somewhere."

"Damn straight. Me and the girls made sure nothing and no one touched you without one of us in the room. Go ahead and try that national security bullshit on us. *Fernandez v. Federal Government*, bitches! 'A nurse has the need to know about the care of their patient.'" Justin tucked the bed sheet in around my arm pits. "Any friend of Marvin's is a friend of mine." He smiled and left.

The memory of Somers's eyes and the hollow popping of his trachea snapping in the palm of my hand seized me, and something between a thrill and a shiver ran through me.

Much later, during mid-morning business hours, a Detective Virgil Larcher came for my statement. As he sat in the visitor's chair, he had that distinct, new car "smell" to his bright blue eyes and his fresh-cut hair and his unvarnished face—as if he'd just come off the Detective production line.

I started simply and explained about the phone call from Julie, my arrival at the church, and the fight with Paul.

"What happened to Pete Slade?"

"Mitchell did that to him."

"Why would he hit his brother?"

"I didn't say he hit him, but you'd have to ask Mitchell why he did what he did."

"You do know Mitchell Slade is dead, right?"

"Oh, really?" How far could I get with playing at not knowing?

"You didn't know that?"

Right. I was the only surviving witness still around who had been conscious for the fight. "After Somers came down the stairs—"

"Somers?"

"Federal Agent Clyde Somers. The guy."

Sweat began to bead along Larcher's upper lip. "The guy?"

Did I really have to say it? "Yeah, *the* guy."

Larcher had nothing.

"The guy whose throat I ripped out? He was in town earlier this week. Didn't you know he was here?" I was getting confused. "I did rip out a guy's throat, right?" I held up my hand. "It would've been in this hand when you found me."

"Right, right." Larcher shot a nervous glance toward the closed door. "Sooo…Somers?"

"Yeah. Somers. The last thing I can remember was passing out over his dead, throat-less body."

The detective looked uncomfortably down at his Box. "We, uh…we knew there was another body—"

"You knew? You didn't see?"

"Oh, some of us saw it."

"I sense a 'but.'"

"But, uh, right. But, just after CSI began processing the scene, Federal authorities showed up, and, uh, scooped up the carcass. And, uh, the, uh," he ran a nervous finger under his shirt collar, "unattached body parts. They even vacuumed up all his blood and confiscated any pictures or video from the church, or that NPD had taken."

"Where was I?"

"In transit to here."

"Fuck." What would've happened if EMS hadn't gotten me out of there before they arrived?

"Yeah. In fact, it, uh, seems my Box failed to continue recording just now. I didn't get anything after I told you Mitchell Slade was dead."

I raised an eyebrow at the detective. "Really?"

Larcher was now sweating freely. He wiped his brow and scooted his chair closer to my bed. In a lowered voice he said, "Nobody is interested in pursuing anything here."

"Do tell."

"What with the death of the NuTree, the mayor's sudden passing, and now this…incident in the church—" He glanced at me purposefully.

"The Feddys got NPD a bit freaked out?"

Larcher whispered urgently, "Fuckin' A they do!"

I understood what was going on here. The new guy had drawn the short straw to go and interview the pain-in-the-ass PD who was the cause of all kinds of closed door, hush-hush meetings and a sudden outbreak of nervous crotch sweat from the chief of police and his ilk.

I couldn't help but feel for the kid. He'd been handed a shit sandwich and told to eat up with a smile.

"Detective, if I may, Virgil. It looks to me like I'm in the clear here."

Virgil opened then closed his mouth.

"So, why don't we just back this up and give it some thought?"

"I'm not—I don't want to do anything—"

I held up a hand, palm out. "Nobody, and I do mean nobody, in this burg is interested in pursuing a murder prosecution where the Feddys have swooped in and confiscated a big chunk of the evidence and then classified what they couldn't confiscate, right?"

His relief was palpable. "Did you have something in mind?"

"You got Julie's phone call on record? There was no reason for that to be confiscated."

"Yeah, yeah, we got that."

"I came to help Julie."

"Yeah."

"Paul assaulted me."

"Yeah." Hope dawned on Larcher's face.

"Mitchell hit Pete for reasons unknown."

"Yeeeaah, okay. Yeah, sure why not."

"Dead men tell no tales."

"Absolutely!"

"Somers…"

Virgil winced.

"How 'bout, parties unknown?"

Virgil's eyes lit up. "Parties unknown, oh *that's* fucking brilliant!"

"Killed Mitchell."

Virgil punched his left palm. "And now we don't have to

come up with a cause of death. Brilliant!" Virgil leaned back in his chair and looked at me with new eyes. "Maroney was right about you."

I smiled. "Now, why don't you hit the delete, and I'll see you for the first time in my life when you come into my room."

"Okay." Then to himself, "Okay." He stood and started toward the door but turned back before crossing the threshold. "Thank you."

"Think of me fondly, and we'll call it even."

Yeah, it wasn't the truth, but what the hell. It was close enough for government work.

CHAPTER 37 – MESSAGES

They sent me home after just one more night's observation to keep an eye on my new kidney. I had strict instructions to leave the disposable, bio-powered hospital bracelet on. It would remotely observe my vitals and, through Box, keep hospital staff up-to-date on my condition. If all was well, in twenty-four hours it would deactivate and fall off.

My face was still mottled with bruises, but the lacerations had all healed. I had a thin scar on my cheek. With a little more surgery, they could get rid of it, but because the surgery was cosmetic, it was a different HMO billable and required far more forms than I cared to deal with.

My ribs and arm were mended, and overall I thought the rest had done me good. I had a decided spring to my step.

I had Box send for the car, and on the ride home, I rolled down the windows. It was a beautiful old-fashioned Spring day. The hospital had laundered my jeans and shirt for me.

I'd just gotten home and was still standing in my garage when a patrol cruiser rolled to the curb. Officer Maroney stepped out. "Up and about, Citizen?"

"It would seem so, Officer. Detective Larcher says to say hello."

"He told me he'd made your acquaintance. You're making

all kinds of new friends."

"Oh yeah?"

"I saw the pastor's wife while you were in the hospital."

My mouth went dry. "You did?"

"She came by the hospital to see you while I was standing outside your room." Stan stubbed the ground with his boot. "Of course, not being family, they wouldn't let her in. Hospital administrators are heartless that way. Anyway, according to her statement, Mitchell lost his shit when she told him about you two and that she was going to sue for divorce."

"Okay." Had Julie and I been part of Franco's plan? Was my dream?

"Seems Mitchell was using his wife's FAACKS to fund some business dealings."

"Okay."

"You care to tell me what really happened?"

I smiled. "There must be a report around with those details."

"Off the record?"

I shook my head. "The less you know about what's not in the report, the better."

He thought for a moment before saying, "Don't worry about it. You good now?"

"Right as rain."

"Okay, well, do me a favor. If the chief asks, you didn't see me. He wants me to watch you, but that doesn't seem like a good use of my time. But, now I can say you've been officially watched, and I can enjoy some Spring." Stan started down the driveway. "I think I'll go fishing."

"Okay, and thanks. Y'know, for your help."

He smiled back. "To serve and protect, Citizen. But seriously, watch yer ass around the chief. He's got a real hard-on for you."

"Yeah." *I bet.*

I palmed the garage door closed and walked into my house.

"Box, any messages?"

"You have six new messages."

"From?"

"Five from Marvin. One from Julie."

Did I want to hear that message? Was I afraid to hear that message? I answered yes and no, but I wasn't sure which reply went to which question.

"Also, your Clarity Connections account indicates further processing is not likely to yield deeper results."

"Hm. That should be interesting. Show top five Clarity Connections results."

The first result felt that the police and the church were connected, though not officially, and that the chief's home and the church were related. Something I'd found out later that night. There were a lot of hit-or-miss speculative details to support the results. But, all-in-all, the top results were impressive.

"Next five."

The next results were speculative variations of the first. The mayor knew Slade but the police weren't involved, or the police had information about the church that wasn't connected to the mayor. Nothing substantive.

The tenth result read, "I miss you, too. Clare."

My entire body went cold.

Were these results tampered with? "Box, connect to Clarity Connections customer service."

Chirp.

"Hello —"

"Yes, I have—"

"—this is Clarity Connections. If you have a question about the results of your query, please understand that this is the result of your data points. Clarity Connection had no input and guarantees, one hundred percent, that there was no outside influence. Do you wish to continue your call to customer service?"

"Discon."

Franco's words came back to me: "*Find! Clare!*"

"Box, discard all results but the tenth. Save that to my permanent, secure storage."

"Confirmed."

Julie's message? "Call Marvin. Vid on."

Chirp.

"Oh my God, Bill!"

"Hey, Marv."

Marvin appeared on the wall topless, with a ridiculous pink-sequined bandana and cowboy hat with a sequined purple band.

"Going to the rodeo?"

"Screw that!" He whipped the hat off. "Oh my God, your face! When did you get out of the hospital?"

"About thirty minutes ago, I guess."

Marvin looked upward. "Dammit, Box, you worthless whore! I told you to tell me when he was discharged!"

Marvin's Box replied in a lispy drawl, "Hospital protocol does not share release records with non-immediate family."

"Whatever!"

Poor Marvin. "I'm glad you weren't so worried that you were going to miss the next costume party."

"I was at the hospital, but I'm not immediate fucking family, so they wouldn't let me in. What was I supposed to do? Sit around and mope? I had to get out of there."

"It's okay. I was only kidding. I'm glad you didn't sit around worrying."

"You might have been in that deep sleep, or whatever they call it, for days, or weeks even." As he started to tear up, Marvin used both hands to fan his face.

"Hey, Marv, I'm solid."

"Really?"

"Swear to God."

"Because, oh my *God*, you look like shit!" He touched his own face where mine was scarred or still discolored. Amazing that they could transplant a kidney and mend broken bones in days, but they couldn't make bruising go away. The wonders of science.

"Give me a day to get things in order and then let's meet for lunch."

"About Frank?"

"Yeah," I said, but I was not at all sure what to tell him.

"Okay, tomorrow then." Just then the guy with the mustache from the counter at The Flame walked behind Marvin dressed as the queerest looking Indian maiden imaginable. "Dammit, Eugene! I'm on the phone!"

I laughed. "Discon."

Stiffly, I sat on the couch. My hands shook. "Play Julie's message."

Julie sprang to life on the wall beside my fireplace. "Hello." She looked pale, and her eyes were red with dark rings under them. "I don't know where to start. I…"

She closed her eyes tight then quickly opened them.

"I can't get that sight out of my head. I'm not…I care for you. I do. But all those dead bodies and that man with his, his throat in your hand, and your face, and the blood. Oh my God, the blood on you and all around you."

She put her face into her hands before marshalling resolve and looking up to continue.

"I know you saved me. I know you came there because I called you. Part of me wishes I hadn't called. I know you love me, or you wouldn't have done…all *that*. But I can't look at you the same way." A sob came out. She looked away and put a fist to her mouth before turning back with a blank face to continue. "I'm sorry, Bill. Thank you, thank you, and I love you, and I'm sorry."

The wall went back to being a wall.

My poker sim lay on the ground next to my recliner. It felt like forever since I'd booted it up.

I stood and walked into my bedroom. It smelled like Julie.

CHAPTER 38 – WALK ABOUT

When I got in the car, GPS let out a squeal. "You're back, and you've lost weight. Sexy! I've been so bored." I knew it was just silicon and wires, but the processing in these personalities was really something.

"Tint windows. Direct route to Marvin's."

"Aaand we're off! Would you like me to display the Dark Star Countdown?"

It was a quick ride to Marvin's place—a nice, upscale condo. Inside, it was all so anally neat it looked more like a showroom than a place an actual person lived. Marvin made me what he considered to be coffee and what I considered to be coffee-flavored steamed milk. We sat outside on his padded rattan patio furniture.

I'd given some thought on what to, or not to, tell Marvin. I told him everything. I started with meeting Maroney at the river's edge, then me at the mayor's door, at church, at dinner, with Julie, the mercenaries, the glow, the white, everything.

Everything except my conversations with Moe, Detective Larcher, and, of course, any interactions with Franco and Somers. Marvin didn't have a need to know about enhanced or augmented.

I explained that Mitchell was evil, had used that evil to

create a hedonistic cell that included his brother, Paul, the police chief, the mayor, and who knew who else. When Frank had confused sex acts with love acts, Mitchell was incensed. He couldn't tolerate the mayor in his group, but he also couldn't just kick him out and risk discovery. The latter was all supposition on my part, but it felt right.

Julie must have told Mitchell that I was interested only in Frank, and that I knew he had left the chief's house. Mitchell must have felt he had to do something about me.

I told Marvin how I didn't absolutely know, but I was certain what had happened to Frank at the river must've been like what Mitchell had done to Pete.

It had been Mitchell's bad luck that the mayor killed a NuTree and that my investigation led to his anti-NuTree wife.

I told Marvin I'd killed Paul. Then I explained, to the best of my imagination, how I'd killed Mitchell. "And now I'm here," I finished.

His jaw hung open and his face was pale. He snapped his mouth shut. "You did all that?"

I picked up my cup, but the coffee had gone cold. I put it back down.

"So, are you, like, religious now?"

"Undoubtedly."

"Seriously?"

"Hundred percent." I'd never seen Marvin bewildered. I smiled and went on, "Someone told me that they couldn't save me. That I'd have to live my own religion." I hadn't actually spoken these thoughts. But, like it always is, saying the truth was easy. "My truth is that God is always there for all of us, just a decision away. But no matter how many people tell us God's there, we can't believe them because we can't know their truth, we can only know our own God. Once you do…once you *know* there is a God, there is no going back. Am I religious now? Yes, but my religion won't be your religion."

Marvin grinned from ear-to-ear in genuine delight. "Cousin. I've never heard you talk like that. What's your religion?"

"I don't know. I'm figuring it out, but…" I looked at my

now augmented hand. "I am fearfully and wonderfully made."

"Oh shit. I give that a two-snap salute." Which he did.

"What?"

"I feel sorry for the bastard that's on the end of that look!"

"Maybe so. I gotta give it more thought."

"And Julie…"

"Suniti says she's on the road, touring with her band."

We sat in silence for a bit.

Then Marvin said. "Funny."

"What is?"

"How it all fell together. Like maybe God really was involved."

God, or a mad scientist with a flair for the study of human nature.

"Fell together? I don't think I'll be seeing Julie again."

"I guess I meant together except for that. I suppose that isn't helpful, is it?"

"It seems that, maybe, sometimes…some things may happen for a reason. Just not sure this was one of those things." I looked out at the squirrels doing their high-wire act, jumping from tree limb to tree limb.

Marvin touched my knee. "Thank you. I didn't know, how could I know that this would happen to you?"

"Marvin—"

"Shut up and take a thank you, would you please."

"Y'see. *This* is why I hate leaving the house." Marvin gave a confused frown. "I end up having to kill evil fuckers."

Marvin looked at me, evidently unsure how to take that, and then I smiled, and then tentatively and then uninhibitedly, we laughed.

"Remember that time we played cowboys and Indians on that hill, and you yelled at Jim Balis and Craig…" Marvin snapped his fingers trying to recall.

"McCullogh."

"McCullogh! He threw that corn cob at you, and you got so angry! You stood there at the top of that hill and yelled, *I will fuck your nuts up*!" He laughed some more. "Be oh-so glad you never said that in front of anyone else."

"Yeah, that might've slipped out one or two other times when I was in the Army."

Marvin crossed his arms. "You know what I think?"

"How could I ever?"

"I think you should take a vacation."

"A what?"

"You've got all that money now, or you will. I'll drop the chit off in a few days. Go clear your head. Oooh, the aborigines in Australia call it a walkabout. Sassy!"

Yes, let's call it an extended vacation.

Out to Solana Beach. To the headquarters of Clarity Connections.

EPILOGUE – MARVIN

Marvin Jacob Thomas hated having three names, and he was nervous about going to Bill's house.

Marvin was no fool, but he was often foolish. For instance, as he was on the way over to Bill's house, he thought maybe driving manually would relax him.

"GPS, manual."

Marvin's GPS responded with an incredulous, "Are you kidding?"

"Fucking GPS! Don't give me shit. Manual!"

"Okay, you asked for it. Initiating previous directive, bitch. Audio playback."

Marvin's own voice came from the speakers. "You dumb bitch! Do not drive manual! Last time you almost hit an oncoming bus. I don't care what you want to distract yourself from, *do not drive manual!* I can't even believe I have to record this. BZZZT!"

GPS's voice came back. "N-M-F-Y! No Manual For You, oh, suh-nap!" And behind his crisp, British lisp, Marvin could hear the finger snap.

Marvin did not take not getting his way well, even when it was himself telling him no. He crossed his arms, slumped back into his seat, and pouted all the way to Bill's. As Marvin's car glided to the curb, a tow truck was just pulling away. Bill stood in his garage with one of his prized possessions, what Marvin could only think of as "that smelly, Gawd-awful loud gas burner his father had bought him."

"Hey, Bill!" Marvin yelled and gave him the two-handed wave he knew Bill hated.

Bill ignored Marvin's gay-wave and just smiled back.

"What's with the motorcycle? It looks scratched." In fact, the handlebar was tweaked and the gas tank clearly dented.

This time Marvin was delighted to elicit an eye roll from Bill. "Ya think?"

But Marvin found it distasteful that he had to say something stupid to get a reaction.

"Come on in. Want some coffee?"

"Sounds good!" It didn't really, but when Marvin considered the amount of money he was about to hand Bill, he felt due a little something, even if only a cup of bitter coffee.

Bill slapped the garage door control on his way in and slipped off his shoes in the mud room as he entered. Marvin followed suit; he knew how Bill felt about his floor.

The first thing Marvin noticed was that the house had been cleaned. "Oh, Bill," Marvin teased, "You've been entertaining, haven't you?"

"Why do you ask?"

"Because I could actually sit on your couch and not feel like I was injecting myself with the plague."

"The place had a smell to it, so I had it cleaned."

"Well it looks *faaaa*bulous!" Marvin began giving a two snap and a fling salute then realized he still had on elbow-high white gloves. They matched his skintight white, skinny-legged pants. Just the other night he'd seen the Irish opera star Candace McGivens wearing the same thing.

Bill stopped. "Marvin," he said it gently. "There's something I didn't tell you the other day. I hope that you would know this, but just in case. You should know, no matter what his motivations where for doing it, what happened to Frank wouldn't have happened if his love wasn't real. If Frank said he loved you, I'm sure he meant it."

Marvin had known it, had always known it, but hearing Bill confirm it was something else. Marvin began to tear-up. He looked away because he knew Bill was squeamish about human things like emotions and *I really could go for him not being mean or patronizing right now.*

When Bill put a hand on Marvin's shoulder, Marvin jumped. When he looked from Bill's hand to his eyes, Marvin could see that they were red. And then, so beautifully, like a slow-motion wave crashing on the shore of new found land, a tear welled up and rolled down his cheek.

"You were right, Marv. He was in love with you, and he would never have killed himself."

Bill hugged Marvin, and Marvin hugged Bill until he spilled tears on his shirt. And it was like they were kids again, they were inseparable again, and they would do anything for each other.

Marvin used a gloved hands to wipe his eyes, smearing mascara in the process.

Bill cleared his throat. "I'd like to talk to you about the money you owe me."

Marvin laughed lightly. More sensitive, but still Mr. Small Talk. "Of course. I have it with me."

"That's okay. Y'see, I've come into a bit of money. Yesterday I won a pretty big, actually, a very big poker tournament."

"How exciting!"

"Yeah."

"It wasn't exciting?"

"Not as much as it used to be. Anyway, I was thinking maybe you could do me a service instead of paying me."

Marvin, always looking for an opportunity to annoy for attention, gave Bill what he was sure was his most coy look. "Why, not even I, as stunning as the experience would be for you, charge that much."

Bill smiled.

It took Marvin back. *Holy Christ, a smile! And not a scary smile.*

A real fucking smile. And look at him.

Marvin stepped back and looked at Cousin Bill with fresh eyes. He seemed somehow lighter, like the air around him had deflated somehow.

Bill, of course, got the wrong idea. "Yeah, not the service I had in mind."

Marvin didn't mind and gave Bill his best pout. "Your loss."

"I'm sure."

"What then? And have you lost weight?"

"I weigh about the same; I'm just a little trimmer these days. Anyway, I was thinking about your vacation idea, and maybe an extended road trip is a good idea."

Ohmygodohmygod. Oh. My. God! "You! Me? Watch your house?" Marvin was unaware that he was prancing, but he wouldn't have cared if he had known. "Oh my God! Bill! Really?"

Smiled and lit a joint. "Really."

Marvin had lusted for Bill's home and his beautiful floors for decades! Of course, Marvin had never bought a home; it was too much effort.

In Marvin's estimation, *Renting was the gay way.*

Bill cleared his throat. "A few rules."

"Absolutely! What are they?"

Visions of dinners and parties already filled Marvin's head. *And that huge bed of his will fit three easily…*

"No more than four people in this home at any one time."

"Whaaat!"

"You gonna watch my house?"

"Okay, okay. No more than four." Marvin was sure that what Bill didn't know wouldn't hurt him.

"Box, confirm."

Bill's Box chirped.

"What? What was that?"

"My Box has just confirmed that item in the contract."

"Contract?"

"If my Box gets more than four heartbeats in this home,

he's going to call my own personal NPD officer. Clear?"

"Your Box has a heartbeat sensor?"

"Am I clear?"

"I'm wounded that you don't trust me, Bill! Wounded!"

"If you hurt my floors," his eyes got what Marvan called the "ninja look" in them, "I will be upset."

"Okay." Marvin swore to himself, *no way is that clumsy buffoon Eugene coming over.*

"Clear?"

"Yes, of course." And Marvin, at least in this moment, really, really meant it.

Box chirped again.

Marvin *tsk*ed and swatted at the ceiling. "Does it have to do that?"

"I know you could never do it, so I've arranged for a yard service."

"Damn straight. Nails like these were not made for getting dirt under them."

"I'm sure."

Marvin ignored Bill. "Is that it?"

Bill walked over to his humidor; as soon as he opened the door, the room flooded with the sweet, heady smell of the finest green. Marvin always got horny when high.

Okay, maybe one *visit from Eugene,* Marvin thought.

"You can smoke anything that's in here, except the bundle in this box." He pulled out a separate, cigar-box-sized mini-humidor. "This is my stash of Christmas Kush."

He said it as if Marvin should know what it was.

"Don't smoke it. Clear?"

"Of course!" Marvin said and simultaneously couldn't wait to try it. "Ummm…how can I say this without appearing eager?"

"When do I leave? Shit, Marv, you a greedy bitch." But he laughed.

"Can't blame a fellow for being eager."

"It'll take a day or three to fix up my bike, then I'll be off."

"Your bike? The fuel burner?"

"Yeah. Why?"

"Why? Bill, who uses a fuel burner?"

"People who never have to worry about working again?"

"That must've been some tournament!"

"Yeah, and I've been on a winning streak of late."

Then Bill asked, what was to Marvin, a very curious thing.

"You ever feel like your life had a purpose? Like you were being guided?"

"Guided?"

"Recently, I've been feeling that I'm exactly where I should be in life."

Marvin hugged Bill again and wondered who this Bill was. He appraised Bill and decided he looked undeniably youthful; there was now a palpable sense of energy to Bill.

Marvin was delighted that his cousin could again, in some part, be the boy he once was. "Have you decided where to go for your vacation?"

"I'm thinking I'll ride on down to the Baja peninsula and take in some baseball games. Stop off in a little beach town up the coast called Solana Beach while I'm on my way."

Marvin clapped excitedly. "Like when you were a kid with your dad!"

"Somethin' like that."

"All the way to Baja on a motorcycle? You badass!"

"Fuckin' A, cousin."

FINI – R.I.P.

It was only a couple of workouts before the nanites kicked in. What was it Detective Larcher had said? They hadn't just carted Somers away; they'd also vacuumed up all his blood. I thought of the wounds on my hand, the gash on my cheek, and my split lip, and the fount of blood from his mouth. Not to mention the final gruesome face-plant into the puddle of Somers's blood.

I only realized how much Somers had been playing with me after my first nanite workout. Being enhanced really was last-generation tech.

Arrangements for the trip ran longer than expected, mostly due to delays at the machinist's shop in repairing my motorcycle.

In those weeks, I didn't dream of Sullivan and Chandler once, and I ate at Cheng's regularly.

I missed Julie, but some things weren't meant to be. If there was one thing I absolutely could empathize with, it was having unwanted images in your brain.

I thought of the church, of being white, of being slain.

And I wondered about Franco.

"…you could maybe say that I am a study of human nature."

His wide-eyed look of disappointed astonishment as I stood

up with Somers's throat in my fist.

His delighted cry, *"That would be wonderful!"*

This whole thing, even before Marvin rang my doorbell, had been a manipulation to give Somers the chance to kill me. What about the NuTree, and Julie? Had that been part of it? Did he know about the Clarity Connections note?

When everything for the trip was good-to-go, I left the next day before the sun was up.

As I headed west into the plains, the dark ground became mottled with grey and then morphed into color as the sun, after a long night, rose over the world.

What was it Marvin had said? *Can you imagine how free Frank must have felt?* And I had thought, *Is it okay if I don't?*

Damn, Frank, sorry. We're all a work in progress.

"On behalf of a grateful nation, thank you for your service, and rest in peace."

As I rode, I saluted the memory of Frank Nelson. My first salute in a long, long time.

It was crazy how being on a bike, on the open road, felt like freedom. After being inside, or in a city, for so long, seeing the wide expanses stretching in every direction was like a new discovery.

I didn't know what waited for me along the road to California, but I knew it would be violent. I knew I was once again putting my life in harm's way. And I knew for the first time that it was my choice, my mission. Not an order, not a PD investigation.

Be careful what you wish for, Franco, cuz here I come, mother fucker.

I peeled back on the throttle, took off like a bat outta hell, and laughed like a child, thrown in the air by a loving parent.

www.ingramcontent.com/pod-product-compliance
Lightning Source LLC
Chambersburg PA
CBHW060923120626
46557CB00003B/858